Praise for

The *Love, California* Series

"A captivating world of glamour, romance, an(
— Melissa Foster, *NYT* & *USA Today* Bestselli

"Jan Moran is the new queen of the epic romance."
— Rebecca Forster, *USA Today* Bestselling Author

"Jan rivals Danielle Steel at her romantic best."
— Allegra Jordan, author of *The End of Innocence*.

The Winemakers (St. Martin's Griffin)

"Beautifully layered and utterly compelling." — Jane Porter,
New York Times & *USA Today* Bestselling Author

"Readers will devour this page-turner as the mystery and
passions spin out." – *The Library Journal*

"Moran weaves knowledge of wine and winemaking into
this intense family drama." – *Booklist*

"Spellbound by the thread of deception."
– *The Mercury News*

Scent of Triumph (St. Martin's Griffin)

"A gripping story of poignant love. Perfumes are so
beautifully described."
— Gill Paul, Author of *The Secret Wife*

"A sweeping saga of one woman's journey through WWII.
A heartbreaking, evocative read!"
— Anita Hughes, Author of *Lake Como*

.

ESSENCE

A Love, California Novel 💋

Book Number 4

by

Jan Moran

SUNNY PALMS

PRESS

Library of Congress Cataloging-in-Publication Data
Moran, Jan.
/ by Jan Moran
ISBN 978-1-942073-14-7 (softcover)
ISBN 978-1-942073-31-4 (epub ebooks)

Printed in the U.S.A.
Cover design by Silver Starlight Designs
Cover images copyright 123RF
For Inquiries Contact:
Sunny Palms Press
9663 Santa Monica Blvd, STE 1158, Beverly Hills, CA, USA
www.SunnyPalmsPress.com, www.JanMoran.com

Books by Jan Moran

Contemporary Fiction
The Love, California Series
Flawless

Beauty Mark

Runway

Essence

Style

Sparkle

20ᵗʰ Century Historical Fiction
The Winemakers: A Novel of Wine and Secrets

Scent of Triumph: A Novel of Perfume and Passion

Life is a Cabernet: A Companion Wine Novella to The Winemakers

Nonfiction
Vintage Perfumes

Browse her entire collection at www.JanMoran.com.
Get a free read when you join Jan's VIP list.

1

"I KNOW IT was sudden, but I wanted to attend the film festival." Dahlia sat at an outdoor table at a café overlooking yachts in the Vieux Port harbor of Cannes, hoping her grandmother wouldn't detect her studied nonchalance over the phone—or the undercurrent of nervousness she felt. "Several actresses are wearing Fianna's gowns," she added, proud of her friend's work.

"And I hope they're wearing our perfume." Camille's imperious voice crackled across the Atlantic. "Just as important, while you're there you should meet our Formula 1 driver. Alain Delamare has a home in Cannes and he's quite charming. He just won the Grand Prix in Spain. He's from a fine family originally from Normandy, though they live in California now." She paused to take a breath. "You should have dinner together, ma chére. I've known his family since before you were born. His aunt was a friend of your—"

Camille broke off and Dahlia knew she'd started to say

"your mother," but caught herself. Still, she recognized the conspiratorial pitch of Camille's voice. "I appreciate the thought, but I don't need your matchmaking."

At that, a man at the table near hers glanced up with interest, and Dahlia found herself staring into his blazing blue eyes, which crinkled at the corners in a bemused expression. She couldn't help but smile. With the Cannes Film Festival underway, the area was teaming with filmmakers, actors, and press. She wondered who he was.

Camille continued. "I think you do need my help, as evidenced by Kevin." She sniffed in disdain. "Alain has such lovely manners. We had dinner together in New York—"

"I don't want to hear any more about Alain Delamare." Dahlia glanced away from the man, breaking his captivating gaze.

Another pause. "Kevin is with you, isn't he?" Camille's tone was flat. "Tell him it's business, which technically it is. What's one evening?"

"That would be awfully rude. Besides, I'm no longer part of your company. I have my own business now."

Her grandmother was relentless, but Camille's inexorable drive was how she'd made her fortune and continued to expand it. Today, Parfums Dubois ranked in the lofty upper echelons of luxury perfume beside Guerlain and Chanel. The purchase of the Formula 1 team and the rebranding of it to Team Dubois had catapulted the company to front pages and magazine covers around the globe, increasing sales and the value of the company even more.

"My offer still stands, dear. Both offers, but we can start with Alain."

Camille had been angling for Dahlia to return to work for the family business, but Dahlia had plans of her own. "And I appreciate it, but the answer is still no. On both counts, Grand-mère." She was pleasant but firm. Nothing was going to spoil this special trip.

A fragrant café au lait steamed before her, chasing away the fresh morning chill. The early sun warmed her bare shoulders and clear skies formed a canopy over the turquoise water of the Mediterranean Sea. Chirping birds flitted through gracefully arched palm fronds and bracelets of vivid magenta bougainvillea tumbled across ancient stone walls. Lovers strolled hand in hand, pausing to admire sleek harbor boats and artful boutique windows.

Dahlia glanced at the time on her phone. Kevin should have been here more than half an hour ago.

The man at the nearby table had returned to reading his book, but she wondered if he were still eavesdropping. Her interest piqued, she studied him surreptitiously through half-lidded eyes. He was undeniably attractive; he wore a dark blue T-shirt that was stretched across his trim muscular frame, along with white cotton pants and deck shoes. Slight morning stubble matched his short, sun-bleached chestnut hair. Probably belongs to one of the boats, she surmised.

Her grandmother continued talking about the success of

the Parfums Dubois Formula 1 team. Camille had been a fan of the sport since she'd been a child in France and her father had raced a Bugatti in an early French Grand Prix. Parfums Dubois had long been a sponsor next to Red Bull and Rolex, Chandon and CNN, but ownership now elevated the brand to a rarified level. Team Dubois was the newest owner in a sport in which few in the world could compete.

Camille read part of an article to her over the phone from Fashion News Daily, the industry trade paper, which hailed the new ownership as "'a bold move timed with the launch of a new masculine fragrance line from Parfums Dubois,'" Camille said. "The editor included photos of Alain and the racing team, too. Alain is quite handsome. He'll be an excellent spokesman for the new line."

As Camille spoke, Dahlia let out a breath of relief. Her grandmother had no idea of the real reason of her trip. After hanging up, Dahlia lifted her coffee to her lips. Once again, she met the steady gaze of her neighbor.

"I couldn't help but overhear your conversation." He sounded American and his baritone voice had a gravelly quality that was intriguing. "Matchmaking? I haven't heard that term in a long time."

She laughed. "That was my grandmother."

"Ah, I see. I hear that from mine, too." A friendly grin creased his tanned face. "Are you here for the film festival?"

"We've seen a few films." Kevin fancied himself a producer, but he had yet to make a film.

"I heard you say you have a business. What do you do?"

"I'm a perfumer." She drained her coffee cup, half-wishing she could stay and talk with him. Kevin should have been here by now. He was probably still on his business call in the hotel room. He'd told her he had a quick call to make, but then, he usually ran late.

"Sounds interesting." The man inclined his head. "I'd like to hear more about your work. Perfume is a new passion of mine."

Unlike most men, he truly sounded interested in what she did.

The man shifted toward her in his chair, his movements demonstrating quiet confidence. "Would you like to join me for a walk on the Croisette? I'd really like to learn more about what you do."

His magnetic gaze drew her in, and she caught herself imagining strolling the wide boardwalk promenade by the sea with him. Everything about him stirred her emotions, and she grew uncomfortable by her fascination with him. "I can't today. But thank you."

"Tomorrow, perhaps?" He held his hand out to her in a gesture of hope.

"Actually, I'm here with someone. And I really must go." As she got up to leave, the strange tug on her emotions was almost palpable, but she swiftly swept her feelings away. She was nearly a married woman. She hoped to have a family of her own soon, and she would never, ever leave her children as her mother had done.

Dahlia hurried along the Boulevard de la Croisette, a light breeze cooling her heated chest and rippling the long skirt of her azure print sundress. As she walked, she breathed in the fresh sea air and the sweet scent of dewy morning jasmine to clear her mind of the man she'd met. With her senses on overload, an idea for a romantic perfume emerged and danced in her mind.

Soon she neared the grand Hôtel Martinez, where Kevin had booked a palatial suite that resembled a film set from Downton Abbey. Inside the hotel lobby, she threaded her way through guests in fashionable summer resort attire on her way to the elevator.

"Dahlia, I was just on my way to meet you." A robust, barrel-chested man strode toward her. "Had a long business call that kept me in the room." Kevin's breathing was labored. He brushed her cheek with a hurried kiss.

"Relax. I had a long call with Camille." She leaned in, detecting a familiar fragrance that clung to his clothing. Bulgarian rose, to be precise. With a touch of bergamot. Was it on his thin windbreaker jacket?

"And how is the dragon lady?"

At his curt tone, she shot him a reprimanding look. "Kevin, that's my grandmother."

"Hey, I'm only kidding," he said, laughing a little too loud.

She shrugged off his comment, though it was partly true.

Camille was known to be demanding, but she was also highly creative and fiercely protective of those she loved. Still, she wished he'd show more respect toward Camille, even if they didn't get along. "What was so important that your client called from Los Angeles after midnight?"

Kevin coughed and cleared his throat. "Well, he's not really in L.A."

"Where is he?"

Kevin ran a hand over his hair, which looked windblown. "He has homes all over the world." He sounded stressed, too.

"So where is he?" she repeated. Kevin had been acting odd ever since they'd arrived in France. He had booked the trip months ago for the festival. When he had invited her and proposed, it had been wildly romantic to imagine eloping. Now that they were here, she had to admit she was tense, too, but she imagined that was how every bride felt.

"Where is he? Oh, somewhere in Asia, I imagine. Hong Kong, I believe." He removed his jacket and swept his arm around her. "I'm hungry. Let's have breakfast in the café here. After that, we can go shopping." He winked. "There's a wedding dress in your future."

There it is again, that scent. Dahlia wrinkled her nose. It wasn't on the jacket; it was on his skin. "Where'd you get that fragrance you're wearing?"

"Fragrance? I'm not wearing anything."

She tapped his neck. "Yes, you are. I have an excellent

nose."

Kevin sniffed his shirt collar. "Oh yeah, some cheap cologne I picked up somewhere. It was in my bag. Forgot all about it."

"Doesn't smell cheap to me. In fact, that's one of ours."

"Our what?"

He sounded like a parrot, repeating everything she said. "Parfums Dubois."

"How can you tell?" He sniffed again. "Maybe it was something you wore that didn't wash out from the fabric."

She'd never worn that perfume. "You must have been fairly close to someone who had it on."

He shrugged with exasperation. "Who knows? Maybe the maid had it on, Dahlia."

She arched an eyebrow. Unless he'd been hugging the maid, he shouldn't be reeking of perfume. "I have a sensitive nose, that's all." She'd been trained since childhood to identify scents. Still, she let it go. She didn't want to argue with him, not now, not on the romantic trip that would be the beginning of their new life together. Turning to one side, she inhaled to clear her nose. Maybe he'd stood close to a woman in the elevator. Very close. "Let's get a table by the window."

Dahlia tossed her dark hair over her shoulder. They were both having a case of nerves, but wasn't that normal for a couple who were about to exchange vows?

2

STANDING BEHIND THE woman he'd met at the café, he listened to the conversation she was having with a man he presumed to be her boyfriend. He wondered why the man had just emerged from a taxi in front of the hotel, why he'd kissed the blond in the backseat, and why he said he'd been on the telephone in the room. The burly man had nearly mowed him down in his hurry to get into the hotel and flag down the woman from the café. Stepping closer, he listened intently. They called each other Kevin and Dahlia.

Dahlia. A rare flower.

He hadn't meant to follow her after he'd spoken to her at the café, but here she was at the hotel where he was meeting his publicist. That man, Kevin, was a type he saw all too often in the hotels he stayed at around the world, but this petite, dark-haired woman certainly didn't deserve such poor treatment. He could tell from her speech and mannerisms that she was a fine woman. His chest tightened in response to his thoughts. A beautiful woman, too.

Who just happened to have an enormous solitaire ring on her left hand. *They're engaged.* The thought hit him like a bucket of ice.

Furrowing his brow, he wondered who was planning on matchmaking the two of them. Her grandmother, she'd told him, but who was the grandmother? Probably a friend of his own grandmother. Wouldn't be the first time he'd had to entertain one of her young friends.

He shook his head. The women were usually nice enough, but they were never his kind. Besides, he wasn't made for the white-picket-fence life they seemed more suited to. Dahlia was sure easy on the eyes, but she clearly had a big problem. A six-foot-four problem, judging from the size of Kevin. Nope, that wouldn't work.

At least Dahlia hadn't recognized him. He loved his fans, but that wasn't why he did what he did. When he was younger, he'd had his share of groupies, but he'd soon found himself feeling more alone than ever. Few people would understand that he found more enjoyment with stimulating conversation or a good book than a vapid groupie who simply wanted to wear him out and brag to her friends.

He'd grown tired of the game of conquest. Where was the love like his parents shared? Six boys and two girls later, and they were still madly in love.

Despite his better judgment, as he watched Dahlia walk away he found himself hoping he'd see her again soon.

3

STANDING AT THE entrance to the lounge, Dahlia blinked against sepia lights illuminating the dark edges of two silhouetted strangers. The pair were seated on a damask sofa in the lobby lounge, entwined in an intimate midnight conspiracy, brandy snifters beside them. With every mild sea breeze, shadows of palm fronds swayed across the high ceiling and walls of the hotel, a private seaside enclave. As Dahlia peered through tall doors that stood ajar, the scent of white lilies and salty air wafted to her nose.

Where is he?

She'd woken after midnight alone in the spacious suite and found she couldn't sleep until he returned. It wasn't like Kevin to disappear, and she was worried. She turned back to the lounge.

The woman's silky blond hair grazed the man's cheek as he trailed a finger down the woman's bare arm, lingering on her hand, their fingers twining in seduction. The woman arched her neck, and her lover drew his lips along her skin.

Such a romantic scene, she thought idly, like something out of an artistic French perfume commercial. Even now, in her half-groggy state, her creative mind was always at play. She blinked, straining to see the lovers while she eavesdropped on their murmured conversation.

The couple's soft laughter rippled through the sultry midnight air.

Dahlia's breath caught in her throat, and she clutched her cotton sweater. Had she heard correctly? She glanced behind her but saw no one else.

Deep laughter rang out again. *His laughter.*

Oxygen whooshed from her lungs. Disbelief and confusion roared through her mind. *No, it couldn't be.* Suddenly light-headed, she touched a wall for support.

Sleep had eluded her for the last two hours. Missing Kevin, she'd pulled on dark jeans and a French blue-and-white striped sweater and searched the hotel and gardens looking for him. Since they'd been in Cannes the past few days, he had occasionally left their suite to make a business phone call or have a nightcap, claiming insomnia. But *this?*

Never would she have imagined he was seeing another woman.

She must have cried out when her knees buckled, because the two figures quickly parted, and she slammed against the wall, rocking a potted ficus tree in a Chinese urn as she did. Gasping for air, her breath came in short fits.

"Dahlia, what are you doing here?" Kevin leapt to his

feet and strode to her, his face masked with annoyance. "You should be sleeping."

She pushed herself from the wall. Kevin was a head taller than her, but Dahlia raised herself to her full height, refusing to be intimidated. "And miss seeing the man I'd planned to marry with another woman?"

"Don't be ridiculous." Kevin furrowed his brow in irritation. "Nothing has happened."

"Only because I interrupted you. Is she the *business call* you've been making?"

The woman on the sofa shot a look of victory toward Dahlia. Her pale, precision-cut hair skimmed her shoulders, and her skirt hiked high on shapely thighs. She crossed her arms in petulance and stared at Kevin. As much as Dahlia would've liked to have given her a piece of her mind, she turned back to Kevin.

"This isn't what it seems. Trust me." Kevin's face relaxed and his brown eyes melted into hers, reassuring her. As his charm re-emerged, his easy smile revealed perfect white teeth. It was the same charm that had made her fall hard for him only a few months ago. "She's an old friend of the family. She needed some advice tonight."

The bartender behind the gleaming cherry wood bar pursed her lips and slid her gaze toward Dahlia. As Dahlia met her eyes, the woman arched a fine eyebrow. In an instant, she had unequivocal confirmation.

"Is that the way you treat all your *friends?*" Anger burned through her and she jerked her arm from Kevin's grasp. Her heart was shattering, but she wouldn't give him the satisfaction of tears. Only a few hours ago, they'd lingered over a romantic dinner with a view of the calm, azure waters of the Mediterranean Sea. They'd laughed and kissed and spent the evening planning their life together, sharing a rare vintage wine Kevin had chosen to celebrate their elopement. It had been a perfect, intimate dinner, just the two of them.

Dahlia had no need for an extravagant wedding such as her grandmother Camille, who'd raised her from a toddler, would have surely insisted upon. That is, if she'd approved of Kevin. Camille had called him ambitious, but not in a good way. "He's not marriage material, Dahlia." And she'd grown icy when Dahlia told her they'd become engaged. Which was why Kevin had wanted to elope.

Yes, this had been his idea. What was he up to?

Dahlia pressed a hand to her forehead as the shimmering future she'd imagined with Kevin dissolved like a mirage. She'd always been attracted to exciting, charismatic men, but they seldom lived up to her expectations. In her heart, she shared the traditional values that Camille had instilled in her from childhood after her mother had abandoned her.

"Dahlia, you can't possibly think she means anything to me." Kevin's voice dropped a notch, reverberating in his chest, where Dahlia had rested her head just hours ago as they'd danced. She shook her head, casting out the memory.

"And you can't possibly think I'd fall for that," she

snapped. "Don't you dare come back to the room." Dahlia spun furiously from him and charged through the lobby.

After her grandmother had vehemently opposed their decision to marry, Kevin had immediately booked flights for them to Europe. They'd be married in France, he assured her, as Dahlia had told him she'd always dreamed.

Had she been blind to his transgressions? Kevin was the picture of power, success, and extravagance. He'd clearly been relishing this dual role, but for how long? Who was this woman? Were there others?

She flung open the door to their—her—suite and slammed the door behind her. What did any of it matter now? She marched to the telephone by the rumpled bed where they'd made love earlier that evening. Speaking quickly in French, she requested a bellboy.

When the uniformed bellboy arrived, she pointed to Kevin's bespoke suits, Gucci loafers, and Armani shirts. "Mr. Blackstone is moving to another room. Please remove all of his belongings." She turned away and stepped onto the balcony. Moonlight illuminated the placid sea, shadowing yachts in the harbor nearby. This was to have been the setting for the beginning of a magical new life. She closed her eyes, feeling sick to her stomach.

"Will there be anything else?"

Dahlia turned back to the young bellboy, who had loaded all of Kevin's clothes and toiletries onto a rolling cart.

"Yes, please inform him. He's in the lobby bar. With a

blond."

"*Oui*, mademoiselle." The bellboy lowered his eyes and executed a crisp half bow, showing no sign of judgment.

After he was gone, she lifted her face to the cool ocean air. Her grandmother had taught her to take decisive action in all that she did, but that didn't mean she wasn't devastated. Soon, she'd have to tell Camille that she'd been right about Kevin all along. The thought of that made her shudder.

Camille Dubois was a force to be reckoned with. She still ran the global empire that was Parfums Dubois, and she still rose every morning and energetically embraced the day, just as she had six decades before when she was introducing her first perfume in Paris. Though Dahlia tried, it was difficult living up to the lofty standards of a legend.

She ran her fingers across the smooth stone balustrade as Camille's words of warning echoing through her mind. "He's overly enthusiastic with regard to our business," Camille had commented after Kevin had angled for a business deal with Parfums Dubois. "He has nothing to offer you. By his age, he should have accomplished something of note in his life." She'd narrowed her eyes. "And do you know where his money comes from?" Dahlia had to admit that she didn't. That was embarrassing enough.

Kevin was older and it was true that he had nothing to show for his years of globetrotting and partying, yet he still spent money like a prince. He was charming—too charming, she realized, bitterness welling in her throat. Camille had certainly seen through Kevin. Why hadn't she? But then, she'd always been lousy at choosing boyfriends.

Dahlia loved being swept up in the thrill of romance. All her friends at home were coupling up, so when Kevin came along it seemed like a natural time for her as well. She desperately wanted to have a family, a place where she felt she belonged. She'd never had that, except with her grandmother.

She brushed angry tears from her cheeks. She wasn't crying over him, she told herself, pushing her hair from her face. Intellectually, she knew he wasn't worth it. Still, she was hurt, but more than that, she was furious with him and angry with herself that she hadn't spied what Camille had so easily deduced.

Oh, but what fun Kevin had been at first. Skiing, sailing, traveling, shopping. He had catered to her and acted as if he adored her.

Acted.

She blew out a breath. It had all been an act to ensnare her. No, not her. *Her money.* Dahlia wrapped her arms around her slender frame. Not that she had millions, and what she did have was from saving and investing. Yet everyone thought she had access to Camille's fortune, although Dahlia never asked her grandmother for anything.

Camille was a firm believer in self-reliance and insisted that everyone around her earn their own way—her granddaughter included. Dahlia couldn't count the number of calls and emails she'd received from anxious stock brokers and venture capitalists who were sure that she was worth millions, or would be soon. In actuality, Camille's plans were much more complicated than people knew. Her grandmother had made sure that the fortune she'd built would never be squandered. A significant portion would be channeled toward charity. Whatever Dahlia stood to inherit, she would have to earn, just as Camille had.

Dahlia was proud of her independence and wouldn't have it any other way. Most people assumed that Parfums Dubois would pass to Dahlia upon Camille's death. She clenched her jaw. Kevin was probably among them. Or was he merely incapable of committing? The reason didn't matter anymore.

It was over.

Sometimes Dahlia envied her girlfriends of modest financial means, like Scarlett and Fianna, although both were working their way up the financial ladder with diligence, hard work, and calculated risks. They could be sure that the men who loved them were truly interested in them, not in their money. They knew who their friends were.

Not Dahlia. People often befriended her only to pitch ideas for investment. And when she told them she wasn't interested—because they wouldn't believe she didn't have *squillions* at her disposal—they dropped her and moved on to wealthier prey. This didn't hurt her as much as it once had, but it still disappointed her.

The only true friends Dahlia had were those at home in Los Angeles that she'd known for years. Verena, Scarlett, Fianna, and Penelope. Camille had also been quite interested in Fianna and her fashion line, because Parfums Dubois often licensed designer and celebrity names for fragrance lines.

Dahlia lifted her face to a soft breeze as she thought about Fianna, who'd nearly lost her business when her runway show had been sabotaged in Dublin, injuring several models. The fashion press had skewered her, but Fianna had risen to the challenge and created a new fashion line that soared in popularity until the press could no longer ignore her success. Dahlia had created a perfume especially for the new line, and it was selling so well Fianna could hardly keep it in stock.

Fianna's fragrance was Dahlia's first independent foray into the perfume business, besides her family business. And she had done it all on her own, from the investment capital to the packaging, perfume, and promotion. Admittedly, it was a small success but a success nevertheless. What she really wanted was to continue building her own branded line, Dahlia D. She didn't use her last name because she had no desire to invite comparison to Parfums Dubois and her grandmother.

Though in truth, Camille had been grooming Dahlia to step into a leadership position at Parfums Dubois for years. To placate her grandmother, she had dutifully gone to Harvard Business School and earned an MBA. On Camille's insistence she'd even served as interim president while the board was head-hunting another more seasoned president. Camille had gained board approval on the basis that having Dahlia at the helm would be good for publicity.

After that experience, Dahlia wasn't entirely sure she wanted to run the company. Parfums Dubois was far different from the creative, entrepreneurial business Camille had founded. The firm had become a corporate machine that ran on spreadsheets and numbers.

Being the founder's granddaughter was challenging, too. Dahlia was held to a far higher standard with intense scrutiny from within the company, as well as by investors and the media. Co-workers envied her, or worse, tried to ingratiate themselves with her. She often wished she could just be normal-no-one-from-nowhere. Just as her grandmother had been when she'd stepped off the ship from France so many years ago with nothing but a few perfume formulas and the fervent desire to succeed.

Behind her in the room, her phone emitted a soft signal she instantly recognized. Thankfully, it wasn't Kevin. She hurried inside and answered the phone. As soon as she heard her friend's subdued greeting, she knew something was wrong.

"Verena, is everything okay?" It was one of her friends from Beverly Hills. Their grandmothers had known each other for years. Mia Valent, Verena's grandmother, had even known Dahlia's mother, which was more than she could say.

Essence

"I'm so sorry to have to call you," Verena said. "Camille is resting now, but she had a stroke. You have to come home right away."

4

DAHLIA FELT HERSELF reeling from the news. She touched the bedside table and sank onto the bed. "Verena, how is my grandmother? How bad was the stroke?" Kevin quickly receded from her mind. She could hear a commotion in the background through the transatlantic phone line.

"It's affected her entire right side," Verena replied. "She was admitted to Cedars Sinai. I'm here at the hospital with Mia and Pierre. Camille is having tests now."

"I'll catch the next flight I can." Dahlia forced the words from her constricted throat. Camille was the only family she had, or rather, the only family that cared anything about her. "Will you call me when she's back in the room? I want to talk to her before I get on the plane."

There was a long hesitation. Verena began to speak, but her voice caught. Finally she choked out her words. "Dahlia, I'm so sorry, but she's having trouble speaking. She's alert, though. She knows what's going on."

A chill of disbelief coursed through Dahlia. *No, this*

can't be. Camille was a survivor. She'd joined the French Resistance when she was but a girl, survived the Nazi occupation of Paris and near starvation, and later paid her way to America. Camille started over in a country where she didn't even know the language. Already intent on packing, Dahlia clutched the phone in one hand, scooping her jewelry from the nightstand with the other. "Please call me if her condition changes. I'm on my way."

Dahlia rang the bellboy again. She flung her clothes into her suitcase, leaving behind the white silk dress Kevin had bought her for their sunset wedding on the Mediterranean.

Once downstairs, the doorman called for a cab for her.

"How soon will it arrive?" Dahlia was pacing the entry in front of the grand hotel. She was so upset she could hardly think. She'd tried calling the airport for a flight, but she was having trouble getting a call through.

The doorman shrugged. "This time of night, with the film festival? You should wait until morning."

Her face grew heated as frustration and anger welled within her, threatening her tenuous control. She didn't care if she had to spend the rest of the night at the airport. She couldn't stand to spend another minute at the hotel when she could be trying to find a flight home.

Her attention was drawn to a black Mercedes that pulled to the curb. The driver opened the rear door, and a glamorous couple emerged. They were a little older than Dahlia. In their early thirties, she guessed. The man was lean but well-built and wore an expertly fitted tuxedo that exuded sophistication. The beautiful willowy woman beside him wore a slinky alabaster evening gown with ropes of pearls. They both stood a head taller next to her.

Dahlia addressed the doorman again. "I have got to go to the airport right away." She stifled a sudden sob with her hand and swallowed hard to maintain her composure. As she choked back a small strangled sound, the tuxedoed man glanced her way. "Doesn't the hotel have a car?"

"I'm sorry, but all our cars are in service tonight, mademoiselle."

Her stomach coiled in on itself, but she continued her efforts. "I *must* get on the next flight to Los Angeles that I can." With any luck, she could get a direct flight from Nice, or make a connection through Paris. *Whichever is the fastest route.*

"Why the hurry?"

"What?" Dahlia whirled around. "What business is it of *yours?*" she snapped, her patience thin.

"Maybe I can help."

Dahlia blinked, recognizing his voice. "Wait, I know you. From the café."

At her memory, a flicker of pleasure crossed his face. He nodded toward the sleek car. "My car is available. Take it."

"You mean it?" When he nodded, Dahlia blew out a breath of relief. "Thank you," she cried. "You have no idea how much this means to me."

"Whatever it is, it must be important." The man motioned to the driver, who swept Dahlia's suitcases away.

"It is." She raked her teeth across her lower lip. "It's my grandmother. She just had a stroke and I'm trying to get back to Los Angeles."

"To the matchmaking grandmother?"

Dahlia could only give a wan smile and nod at his recollection before she had to swallow a lump in her throat. "I really appreciate this." She wasn't used to accepting such favors from strangers, especially those who affected her the way he did.

The man turned to the woman and touched his face to her cheek. "Go on, Tiffany, get some rest. I'll see you in the morning."

The woman glided inside as the man turned and said to Dahlia, "Let's go."

Dahlia was already sliding into the back seat. The car was pristine and smelled factory new, and the black leather seats were smooth and cool under her touch. "You don't need to come with me. Go on with... with her." Wife, girlfriend, whatever she was.

"She understands." As he climbed in beside her, he gave instructions to the driver.

Dahlia doubted that the woman understood. They'd clearly been to a fancy affair. What woman wanted her husband or boyfriend to drop her at the door and race off into the night with another woman? *Another woman.* That thought, unfortunately, brought Kevin to mind. Was this man like her ex-fiancé? She curled her upper lip with disgust. "Well, thanks anyway."

Glancing down, she became aware of the jeans she'd hastily pulled on, and now she noticed how wrinkled they were from the day before. She didn't care though, all she wanted was to see Camille as quickly as she could before her grandmother's condition worsened. Her throat tightened. Though her grandmother still had amazing energy, she was far past the usual age of retirement. And Camille had been pushing herself too hard lately.

The man removed his tie and slipped open the top button of his white shirt. "Glad to help. I know what it's like to be alone in a foreign country and have an emergency."

She started to correct him, but stopped herself. France felt like home to her. Camille kept an apartment in Paris, a chalet in Chamonix, and a seaside home in St. Tropez. Dahlia had been coming here since she was a little girl, but she didn't feel like explaining.

The man interrupted her thoughts. "What time is your flight?"

There was that gravelly voice again that probably had most women at hello. "I don't have a reservation, but I'll find a flight."

"You'll have a hard time getting a flight out of Nice with the film festival in full swing." He took his phone from his jacket and tapped a message.

As the engine purred to life, Dahlia fixed a blank gaze on the darkened window, struggling to tamp down the turmoil she felt inside. She usually prided herself on being calm and organized, but between Kevin and Camille, tonight had stretched her to her emotional edge.

They rode in silence. A few minutes later, the man's phone vibrated in his hands. "No flights from Nice, but you can fly direct from Paris." He looked up at the driver. "Change of plans. Let's take this lady to the Cannes-Mandelieu airport."

Mere hours ago, she and Kevin had been sipping champagne over a romantic dinner, talking about where they would spend their honeymoon, while she wondered how she would break the news of their elopement to Camille. Watching the harbor and village slide silently past, she touched the cool window. Her engagement ring sparkled in the low light, mocking her.

Dahlia jerked her hand back as if the glass had burned her fingertips. She twisted off the platinum and diamond ring Kevin had just bought for her. She felt like flinging it into the Mediterranean. Instead, she dug into her purse and crumpled the ring into a tissue. She'd stuff it into her luggage and send it back to Kevin the first chance she had.

From the corner of her eye, she noticed the man watching her. However, she offered no explanation. She closed her eyes to ride in silence.

The man's phone buzzed. "Yes, thanks, do that," he said,

his voice carrying an air of authority. He slipped the phone back into his jacket. "You have a private flight to Paris. When you arrive there, you'll find a seat on an Air France flight to Los Angeles being held for you at Charles de Gaulle airport."

"What?" Dahlia bolted upright in the seat. "I didn't ask you to do that." How dare this stranger interfere in her life? "I can take care of myself."

One corner of his mouth lifted in a half smile. "I'm sure you can. But I don't mind helping ease your burden."

Dahlia's thoughts were swirling in a tangled mess. She knew she should thank him, but what did he expect in return? "Look, whatever it cost, I'll reimburse you."

"Don't worry about it. It's on the company."

"What company?"

He paused before he spoke, and in that moment Dahlia felt his vivid blue eyes drawing her in again.

"The company I work for. It's a corporate plane. Look, if it makes you feel any better, I'm putting this on my expense account. I'm way under budget for the quarter."

"I shouldn't let you do that. Really, I can cover this." She dragged her gaze away.

"It's done. When you arrive in Paris, show your passport at the Air France counter and board your plane."

Dahlia sat back in amazement. Total strangers just didn't do this. But then, she usually didn't get into cars with men she didn't know in the middle of the night either. "You're really too kind."

He waved her words away with his hand. "Call it karma. What goes around comes around."

Karma. That's the word Camille's friend Mia often used. And *kismet.* Fate, destiny. She touched her bare ring finger, wondering why fate had been so cruel to her. Pressing her lips together in a resolute line, she decided that if karma were real, Kevin would surely get what he deserved someday.

They fell silent again, Dahlia idly thinking about what it would be like to have such a thoughtful man like this in her life. A wistful smile crossed her lips. That woman in pearls was lucky indeed. Like her friends. A moment later she sniffed, chastising herself. Just because others had formed blissful relationships didn't mean she had to race into one. Or have a relationship at all.

Her grandmother had been independent most of her life, except for a brief period when she'd married and had Dahlia's mother Laurel. Maybe being on her own was best for her, too. She sat up straighter, pushed her shoulders back, and folded her arms.

Before long, the car's headlights shone onto a runway as they approached. The driver pulled into the parking area of the private airstrip.

"I've got this," the man said to the driver.

He took Dahlia's hand and it was unexpectedly warm against hers. His grip was firm and she matched it, sliding from the back seat to emerge into the pre-dawn stillness. Strangely enough, his hand was rough with calluses. That didn't fit with the tuxedo, the car, or the plane.

"You'll have to hurry to make your connection in Paris." Resting his hands on her shoulders, he stared into her face as if to memorize it.

His touch felt so reassuring. Her heart pounding, Dahlia met his magnetic eyes again. "How can I ever thank you enough?" Mia would say he was an angel, or at least sent by one, though Camille would scoff at the thought. "You make your own way in this world," her grandmother always insisted.

"This smile is enough." He touched her lips with his finger for a brief moment. "Now, go, your grandmother is waiting."

His expression was so caring and genuine that he restored her faith in men a tiny bit. The driver passed her bags to another man who carried them onto the jet. She climbed the stairs and turned around, lifting her hand in farewell.

The man was leaning against the car watching her, one long leg angled across the other one, his white shirt gleaming against his tanned skin in the moonlight. He raised his hand in response.

Once on board, she sank into a buttery beige leather seat and buckled her seatbelt. The interior of the plane was outfitted in burl wood and chrome. Behind her, two leather couches stretched beneath a row of windows on either side of the cabin. Groupings of tables and leather seats were arranged for dining or entertaining. She was alone on the aircraft, except for the crew of two. The engine roared to life. She gazed from the window and saw that the man was still there, waiting, and she found that strangely reassuring.

Only then did she realize she didn't even know his name.

5

ALAIN WATCHED HIS sleek Bombardier Challenger 605 climb into the clouds. The moment he'd heard Dahlia's smooth, cultured voice that morning at the café, he'd been mesmerized. *And those eyes.* Large, expressive green eyes framed with finely arched dark brows. Even tonight, with her face devoid of makeup, she was lovely. Just thinking of her bow-shaped lips, his abdomen twitched with desire. Most women would have cried on his shoulder—not that he would have minded—but not her. She hadn't asked his name and frankly, he was relieved.

He'd already stretched the truth as far as he was comfortable doing. Tonight was about helping her, not talking about himself, which is what usually happened once people discovered him or learned his name.

Yet he couldn't get her—or the scent that surrounded her like an aura—out of his mind. He'd ached to pull her close and lose himself in her thick mane of shiny black hair. He closed his eyes and ran his hand over the leather where she had sat next to him. The car still carried the faint whiff of her perfume.

Intoxicating. Just like her.

Where was the guy he'd seen her with at the hotel? And why had she jerked off the ring she wore on her left hand? Not that it was any of his business. Besides, he'd probably never see her again.

The chauffeur cleared his throat. "Going home now, Mr. Delamare?"

Clouds enveloped the silver sliver in the sky. "Yes, thanks." A strange feeling of loneliness washed over him. He had seldom been alone; he had always had his choice of eager companions until the novelty had worn off. Women desired him for his public persona, not for his true self. Still, that knowledge hadn't stopped him from enjoying whatever the lovely creatures offered him. Since he never spent more than two or three weeks in the same location, there had been little danger of complicated relationships. That's the way he liked it. He took enough risks in his line of work. Although lately he'd grown tired of these short-term relationships.

He eased into the car. One thought nagged him. When he'd been at breakfast and overheard Dahlia talking on the phone, whomever she'd been talking to was obviously intent on introducing them. Who was trying to set them up? he wondered. Not that he'd ever had any luck with blind dates or set ups. Those dates were generally doomed to misfire from the beginning. He didn't know what he was looking for in a woman, so how could anyone else? No, he'd probably averted disaster this evening. Though he'd done what he could to help her.

Feeling good about his helpful deed, Alain rested his head against the seat cushion and closed his eyes, exhaustion taking over. *That's all it was*, he decided, as her voice echoed in his mind. Lack of sleep had made him vulnerable to her.

"Alain, please don't tell me you took advantage of that poor girl last night." His publicist shot him a withering look over the table on his terrace.

"I don't take advantage of women, Tiffany. Truth is, it's more likely the other way around." Alain pressed his hands against the stone railing supported by balustrades, staring at the placid sea stretching beneath their perch. The old cottage on the hillside was his refuge. He'd bought it after his first big win and restored it to his taste. It was just large enough for him, his library, and a hot tub. He kept a vintage Mustang car he'd restored in the garage, along with whatever other car caught his interest at the moment. What more did a man need?

Tiffany laughed. "If that's your story, keep it quiet. It won't work with the strong, sexy hero persona who conquers all in his path that I've created for you in the press."

"I should keep the conquests to the track." He narrowed his eyes. "Is that why reporters keep asking me about my personal life?"

"That's called creating an image and keeping your profile high."

"Won't winning races do that?"

"Yes, but being a sexy superhero helps sell your image. And that's what makes sports endorsements more valuable."

"I have enough money now, Tiffany. I only want to focus on winning. I'd really like to scale back on deals where I have to take time to pose for ads. I'm a driver, not a model." He was more accustomed to racetracks, though he'd done his fair share of ad shoots.

"You have a lot of responsibilities, Alain. That's why you hired me in the first place. And now you've become a brand."

"That will crash and burn if I don't stay on top."

"I hope you have a long career, but you're like every other athlete. Right now you're building a retirement for you and your family."

She was right, of course. Racing had been good to him. He'd augmented his parents' income for a long time, paid his brothers' and sisters' college tuitions, and helped them all start businesses. Yet his career—and his life—could end with one slight twist of a wheel. Alain scrubbed his hands over his face as if to erase the thought. That kind of thinking was exactly what could get you killed. "I have to focus, Tiffany. I mean it. Until after the Monaco Grand Prix anyway."

"I hear you. I'll handle the media and put off any additional interview requests until then. But you're already committed for the photo shoot with Camille Dubois for the

Legends campaign. This is vital for the market launch."

Alain banged his hands against the terrace railing. "Can you change it?"

"Her schedule is as impacted as yours. Parfums Dubois really needs this for your fragrance launch."

He lifted his palms skyward. "How did I ever get involved with this?" His brothers had been teasing him mercilessly.

Tiffany glared at him. "Look, a successful fragrance endorsement can last years, decades even. What's one more day of photos?"

6

AS THE AIR FRANCE jet approached Los Angeles, Dahlia considered what awaited her. She knew Camille needed her now, and it frightened her a little. Her grandmother had never needed anyone before. Camille was entirely self-made.

Dahlia thought about how Camille must be feeling right now, trapped in an ailing body and stripped of her seemingly endless energy. Camille, who was always in charge, was a founder accustomed to directing people and resources exactly where and when they were needed. She was the force behind the company and the visionary who'd propelled Parfums Dubois into the upper echelons of the perfume industry through a brilliant combination of unparalleled creativity and savvy business skills. Camille was the woman who'd conceived the world's most iconic perfumes, the woman who'd pioneered the designer fragrance industry, the woman who'd built it all one brick at a time, as she'd often said.

Now silenced.

How cruel, Dahlia thought, dabbing the corners of her

reddened eyes. She had to compose herself before she got off the plane. She'd called Verena from the airport in Paris, and her friend promised she'd meet her at the airport and take her straight to the hospital.

Amid soft French murmurs around her, she leaned her head against the cushy business class seat that the angel of a man she'd met in front of the hotel had reserved for her. He was probably an executive with a multinational company, and the woman he'd been with was probably his wife or girlfriend. She'd been so distraught over Camille and Kevin that she hadn't even thought to ask his name.

Once on board the corporate jet that had whisked her to Paris, she'd asked the flight attendant and the pilot who her benefactor was, but both of them were substituting on short notice for the regular crew and didn't know his name. Only the company: ADR, Inc. After boarding the Air France flight, she'd searched the Internet on her phone and discovered a medical transportation company with those initials. That made sense, she decided.

As the plane approached the airport, Dahlia watched the landscape of the Los Angeles basin materialize between the clouds. Instead of the blue skies outside, she was drawn to the memory of his brilliant blue eyes and the way his steady gaze had met and held hers. There was no denying her mystery man was handsome, but he had something more. The French would say he had a certain *je ne sais quoi,* an indefinable, distinctive, highly appealing quality. He had the air of a champion.

Why hadn't he introduced himself? She'd been so consumed with worry about her grandmother that she hadn't thought to ask. Furrowing her brow, she pondered this. Perhaps the woman wasn't his wife, but his girlfriend. If he had a wife at home looking after the children, the dogs, and the house while he was gone, that would explain it. Maybe he was just like Kevin. Her heart sank with disappointment. Why did men have such a thirst for conquest that even on the eve of their wedding they'd stray?

She smoothed the crease between her eyebrows, feeling sadly disillusioned over her mysterious acquaintance, even though he'd come to her rescue. Not that she couldn't have handled the situation on her own—she'd traveled by herself for years on company business. But it was nice to have someone show concern for her, even if that person was a stranger on loan to her, a man she'd certainly never see again. Her chest tightened with wistfulness.

Shortly after the airbus touched down on the runway, her phone vibrated. She'd called Verena from Paris before boarding. "Hi Verena, the flight just arrived and it's still on the runway. Any news from the hospital?"

"The same. At least she's no worse."

Dahlia suddenly felt claustrophobic on the plane. All she wanted to do was to see Camille and talk to the doctor about her prognosis. At once, the magnitude of Camille's predicament hit her. Her grandmother had a full, busy life.

She still chaired the board of her company and steered the company with the help of her executive leadership team. Surely they would step in and cover her absence.

Then a terrible thought occurred to her. At her grandmother's age, this might not be a temporary situation, but a permanent medical condition. She shuddered at the thought, imagining how dreadful it would be for Camille to be trapped inside a body that refused to yield to her extraordinary will.

"Dahlia, are you still there?"

Verena's voice swept her from her thoughts. "This is so hard. I'm awfully glad you and Mia were with her when it happened." Verena told her they had been at the Polo Lounge in the Beverly Hills Hotel having lunch. She and Mia had noticed that Camille's words were beginning to slur—and it wasn't due to the champagne they were drinking. One side of her face had drooped, and she couldn't hold the silverware. "Thanks for taking care of her."

"You would've done the same for Mia," Verena answered softly. "That's what friends are for. You were there when I needed you, too."

Verena's grandmother had suffered a heart attack not long ago. Dahlia and Camille did everything they could for Mia and Verena. They often looked after Verena's younger twin sisters, Anika and Bella, while Verena went at the hospital. Camille arranged for hot meals to be sent to the house for weeks. The two families, both headed by strong-willed matriarchs, were so close they might as well have been related.

Dahlia spoke with Verena while the plane taxied to the gate. "I'll call as soon as I've cleared customs."

Dahlia stood in a seemingly interminable line at customs. She had been waiting weeks for an appointment to apply for special clearance from Homeland Security. Once approved, she could use a machine to recognize her pre-approved status and she could sail past the customs line.

The last time she'd reentered the United States, she'd spent four hours in line next to a poor woman with a baby and a toddler. The woman had been incredibly patient—Dahlia admired her for that—but disgruntled passengers in line around them took out their frustration on the young woman every time one of the children cried. How could people be so rude? Dahlia had helped entertain the little boy, letting him look at photos on her phone and teaching him patty-cake and itsy bitsy spider hand games, even though they didn't share the same language.

Today it took only an hour and a half to go through customs. When her turn came, Dahlia stepped up to the customs officer and answered a few questions. She wondered, again, when her appointment at LAX—Los Angeles International Airport—for security clearance would be scheduled. She'd registered weeks ago. After a couple of minutes and a "Welcome home," greeting, Dahlia took her passport and wheeled her luggage from the line.

A black car was waiting for her at the curb. Camille's personal chauffeur, Thomas, greeted her with an anguished expression. He tried to say a few words to her, but choked up. Dahlia hugged him.

Thomas had always been there for Camille. He'd been driving her grandmother for years and the two of them had tremendous respect for each other. Camille was often on her phone in the backseat of the car, so Thomas had been privy to many private conversations, but he'd always been loyal to her, and she to him. She'd made sure his four daughters had all gone to the universities of their choice and the eldest one was now a practicing physician.

Thomas opened the rear door for Dahlia, then scooped up her luggage and deposited her bags in the trunk.

Dahlia slid in next to her friend, a slender blond with glowing ivory skin. Verena's hair was wispy and her expression weary. "It's good to see you, Verena."

Verena put her arms around her and drew her close. At once, Dahlia broke down in the safety of her friend's embrace. As the pent up fear and sorrow seized her, tears wet her cheeks. Her friend held her until she regained control of herself.

"Scarlett stopped by the hospital earlier." Verena said. "She wants you to call her if there is anything she can do for you."

Scarlett was her attorney for her indie perfume business, but first and foremost, she was her friend. They'd met years ago through Verena, when she and Mia still had the skincare salon in Beverly Hills. Now Scarlett had her own law practice catering to beauty clients, and Verena was selling a new organic skincare line she'd created from vintage formulas through television infomercials—and supporting her grandmother and younger sisters with her efforts.

Verena and Scarlett had always been grounded and now they had gorgeous boyfriends who were running a hot new restaurant, Bow-Tie, together. They were all like family, and like most families, they also had their share of differences. But they came together when tragedy struck, such as when Verena's parents died and Mia had her heart attack.

Now it was her turn for a tragedy. Dahlia pressed her fingers to her eyes. Could Camille overcome this? Her grandmother was her life, the woman who'd taught her everything. She couldn't imagine the profound loneliness of being without her.

Dahlia swept tears from her face with quivering fingers. "I'm so glad you were with her when it happened."

"Me, too. The doctor said it should help that she got to the hospital so quickly."

"I hope so." Dahlia rummaged through the center console until she found a tissue. After wiping her eyes, she shrugged out of the lightweight jacket she'd hastily grabbed to wear on the plane. She felt grubby. The jeans and striped cotton sweater she'd pulled on to look for Kevin were even more wrinkled after the flight. After brushing her thick black hair, she clasped it at the nape of her neck with a clip. Camille had always insisted she look presentable before she went anywhere, but this was the best she could do under the circumstances.

As they drove, Verena asked, "Do you need to stop at home for anything?"

"No, I want to see Camille first." Her grandmother, demanding as she was, had been her rock throughout her childhood. Dahlia didn't know who her father was, and her mother had disappeared when Dahlia was just two years old. Camille had been devastated when her only child had vanished, leaving behind a toddler.

Verena nodded with understanding and took her hand, twining her fingers with hers. Dahlia rested her head against her friend's shoulder, thankful that she had such good friends. In the black recesses of her mind, she'd always known that someday she'd have to face a health crisis—or worse— with Camille, but she wasn't ready. She closed her eyes and rested as the car snaked through dense Los Angeles traffic, summoning the courage she'd soon need.

Upon arrival, the hospital's sharp, antiseptic odors assaulted Dahlia's highly sensitive sense of smell as she hurried through the corridors with Verena, whose high heels tapped a staccato rhythm that echoed through the stark halls.

"Here it is." Verena stopped in front of a partly open door.

Trembling, Dahlia hesitated, dreading what she was about to see.

"Are you okay?" Verena wrapped her arms around her.

"No," Dahlia murmured and hugged her friend, drawing strength from her until she could face the situation. Finally, she turned and pushed the door open.

Her powerful, imposing grandmother looked oddly small beneath the starched white sheet. Medical monitors blinked and beeped beside the bed, measuring her pulse and respiration. Camille was motionless and her eyes were closed.

Mia sat in a chair beside her, her hand resting on Camille's, and Dahlia was instantly struck by their friendship and love. This was agonizing for all of them, she realized, blinking back the tears she'd sworn a moment ago she'd shed no more.

When Mia saw Dahlia, she rose and held her arms out to her. "My dear girl," she murmured. "She's a fighter, you know."

"Like you." Dahlia gratefully succumbed to Mia's embrace. The older woman wore a robin's egg blue silk dress, and her silvery blond hair was twisted into sleek coiffure. The two women were known in Beverly Hills as the doyennes of beauty, Camille for perfumery and Mia for skincare. Together they'd started their respective businesses—at a time when they were considered mavericks for doing so—and stepped in to care for their granddaughters when fate had intervened. Mia had lost her son and daughter-in-law in an auto accident not long after Verena had turned eighteen.

With their similar histories, Dahlia and Verena had become as close as sisters, and Mia was like a favorite aunt.

"She's been sleeping off and on." Mia took Dahlia's hands in hers and spoke softly. "We'll wait outside. The staff doesn't want too many people in the room at one time as it can be tiring for her. Pierre will soon be here, too. He's bringing food from Bow-Tie for everyone." Pierre was Mia's close gentleman friend. Verena touched Mia's shoulder, and the two of them left the room.

Dahlia eased into an upholstered chair next to the hospital bed. A chill of fear ran up her spine, followed by overwhelming empathy. She leaned over, touching her grandmother's forearm and watching her face, which was remarkably smooth for her years.

Even now, a subtle perfume surrounded her like an aura—it was one of Camille's own creations, of course, and one of the most perennially popular perfumes on the market today. Dahlia drank in the familiar aroma and felt comforted, as she always did. Camille's boudoir and wardrobe emitted this scent, too. The perfume had been embedded in Dahlia's memory since she'd been a little girl, barely old enough to talk.

The monitors beeped and Dahlia glanced at the digital dials. Turning her attention back to Camille, she wondered if she should she speak or let her rest. She'd hardly had a minute to think about it when she felt Camille's fingers twitch, and her eyelids fluttered open.

"I'm here," Dahlia said, inserting strength she didn't feel into her voice. She kissed her grandmother's forehead, and saw her lips curve on one side and part slightly as if to speak. "It's okay, I understand." Dahlia swept her hand across Camille's cheek. "You're one tough lady, and I'm sure you'll be giving your medical team orders in no time."

Camille's expressive blue eyes sought hers, and she seemed to speak to Dahlia through them. Dahlia knew she was pleased and relieved that she was here, but there was concern in her eyes. Dahlia blinked hard, willing herself to be strong for her.

Struggling to speak, Camille managed a few mangled words, which Dahlia could scarcely understand. The right side of her grandmother's face drooped and failed to respond to efforts.

Dahlia drew a ragged breath. Anticipating her grandmother's questions, she began to speak for both of them. "You'll be glad to know that I returned from France alone. You were right about Kevin."

Camille's eyes turned heavenward, and she sighed with relief. She raised her brow in question and tried to speak again.

"Let's just say that I discovered his true nature. It couldn't have been clearer. I'd already thrown him out when Verena called me about you. I'm so sorry I wasn't here for you."

Camille's eyes darted to one side, dismissing Dahlia's concern. A moment later, her left hand gripped her granddaughter's sweater, urgently pulling her toward her.

"What is it? What's wrong?" Dahlia searched her face.

Camille touched Dahlia's heart and inclined her head.

"Yes, I'm fine. I—I love you so much, Grand-mère." She'd meant to say more, but her words lodged in her throat. She managed a smile for Camille and smoothed her grandmother's coiffured hair, which had held up surprisingly well considering her ordeal.

Camille responded by pressing her hand against Dahlia's heart, and then caressing her cheek. Dahlia caught her hand and kissed it.

Her grandmother motioned toward her mouth, shot a glance toward her right leg under the sheet, and sighed with exasperation.

"We'll work on it together. I'll help you." The thought of Camille losing her ability to walk and speak struck terror in Dahlia's heart. What a cruel sentence for such a vibrant woman. "You have the best team here at the hospital." Which was true. Camille had been a major donor to the hospital for decades. Verena had told her the chief of staff was personally overseeing her treatment team.

Camille seemed to accept her words and closed her eyes. She rested like that for a few minutes while Dahlia continued to reassure her with words of encouragement. She ached for her grandmother and prayed with all her might that Camille would recover her abilities.

While Dahlia spoke confidently, her mind whirred with the incessant ticking of the large round clock on the wall. She had to talk with the doctor, bring items from home to make her grandmother more comfortable, call the office, and so much more.

As if on the same wavelength, Camille's eyes flew open. Her eyes widened with intensity and she gripped Dahlia's hand.

"Don't worry, I'll let everyone know at the office and keep them informed. They can manage without you." That was only partly true. Camille was the visionary, the creative control, and the one who knew what stirred the imagination. She had an innate sense for perfumery. In the laboratory, she was a mercurial savant. Camille created perfumes that had the fire to ignite hearts, the magic to capture time, and the power to enchant generations. Though Camille had taught her everything she knew, Dahlia could only hope to follow in her footsteps. She had yet to prove herself.

"Nnnn…" Camille struggled to speak, but emitted only a slight fervent noise brought forth by sheer fortitude. She became even more agitated and jabbed her forefinger repeatedly at Dahlia's chest.

Dahlia sat back, shocked. *No.* She knew exactly what Camille wanted, but she didn't want to acknowledge it. She *couldn't* acknowledge it. To do so would be to recognize the full extent of her grandmother's affliction. More than that, the permanence of it. "I don't understand..." she began, stalling the inevitable, willing it away. There was a chance—*wasn't there?*—that Camille would recover. She glanced nervously away.

Camille gripped Dahlia's hand with a force that surprised her, demanding her attention. Demanding *more* from her, as always. Camille demanded more from everyone, including herself. She believed that everyone was capable of achieving more than they could imagine, as she had. The difference was that her grandmother had come to believe that nothing was out of reach if the will was strong enough. She expected that of her granddaughter, too. *Especially* her granddaughter. Could Dahlia ever live up to her expectations?

With reluctance, she dragged her gaze back to Camille. "Can't we wait a while? See how you do?" But from her grandmother's stoic expression, she knew she'd wasted her breath. This was no surprise, as Camille had previously informed her of her plans. In her grandmother's logical, orderly manner, it was merely time to act on her plan. "I'd rather spend time here with you."

That triggered a softening of her grandmother's features—she was human, after all, and Dahlia knew she loved her deeply, but Camille was pragmatic. With what life had served her, she'd had to be. A slight movement of one shoulder accepted this request, but Camille tilted her head forward and widened her eyes, indicating she still meant business.

Dahlia moistened her lips. "All right. I will." It was her responsibility, at the very least, to put Camille's mind at ease.

Her grandmother was insisting that Dahlia take her place at the company, if not in position, then in action and deed. The thought of it panicked her.

Camille's lips curved up on one side and she closed her eyes, clearly relieved. Dahlia couldn't deny her grandmother a measure of comfort. She kissed her forehead again. "I'll send Mia in. I'm going to find the doctor."

Camille gave a satisfied sigh in response.

Dahlia rose on unsteady legs and stood for a moment, gazing at her grandmother.

When Dahlia emerged from the room, Verena and Mia were waiting in the corridor. "Mia, I think she'd like you to be with her now." Mia hugged her and disappeared through the doorway.

Verena turned to her. "How're you doing?"

Dahlia pressed her fingers against her throbbing temples. "Seeing her like that is a shock."

"I felt that way when I saw my grandmother in the hospital, too. But look at Mia now, she's doing really well. Strokes are serious, but if anyone can rally from one, it's Camille."

Dahlia shook her head. "Two days ago I was shopping for a wedding dress with Kevin, dreaming of honeymoons and making babies. Now, forty-eight hours later, I've sworn off men, Camille's had a stroke, and she's insisting that I take her place at the company. What a nightmare."

"I'm so sorry to hear about Kevin."

"Camille never liked him." The mysterious man who'd come to her aid flashed through her mind. She wished she could thank him for his kindness, which meant a great deal to her. More than he would ever know. She shook her head with regret. She couldn't imagine that Kevin would have ever done such a thing without expecting something from a woman in return. "How come she saw through him, but I couldn't?"

"Because you wanted to be loved." Verena hugged her. "We all do."

"I should swear off men."

"No, just proceed with caution. Ask the tough questions, even if you're afraid to hear the answers. The truth always comes out."

"Good advice." Verena sounded a lot like Camille.

"Did you try to talk to her?"

"We were able to communicate." Seeing how difficult it was for her grandmother to speak had nearly crushed Dahlia. "She wants me to step into her place at the company. I told her I'd do what I can. That's what she needed to hear." After Dahlia's brief tenure as president, she'd been more than happy to relinquish the reins to the new president. Her mind swam with memories of financial spreadsheets and legal documents. She far preferred the creative arts, though she was trained in and capable of the necessary left-brain analytics to run a company.

"That's an awfully big job." Verena, who'd also had a go at running her grandmother's company at one time, was clearly impressed. "There are others at the company who can help, too, aren't there?"

"It's a matter of trust. She wants someone who shares her vision, who cares about the quality of the products and the integrity of the company." And yet, even as she uttered those words, Dahlia's chest tightened with the anguish of even having to consider such a decision. Could she really handle it this time, especially now, without Camille's daily guidance?

On the other hand, how could she renege on the promise she'd just made to Camille?

7

A WEEK LATER as Dahlia entered Camille's office suite, her grandmother's assistant, Sue McGregory, greeted her. "How is Camille doing? We've all been so worried about her."

Dahlia had hardly left her grandmother's side, silently urging her on as she slept, and keeping her spirits up when she was awake. "Her doctor says she's fairly stable now, which is why she insisted I come into the office." The sound of Dahlia's high heels were muffled on the fine Persian rugs Camille favored. She touched her fingertips to the gleaming cherry wood surface of Sue's desk. "She's regained her speech and most of the use of her right side, although she will need physical therapy. Her gait was impacted."

Dahlia was grateful that Sue had managed Camille's business affairs for the past week. "She's made such remarkable progress since the stroke. She owes that in part to Mia and Verena, who were with her and made sure she received immediate medical help. That's key in a stroke situation."

"I'm glad she was with someone." Sue opened the door to Camille's office for Dahlia.

"So am I." Dahlia followed her in.

Sue motioned to a large glass desk situated in front of two panoramic windows. "You'll find a note on her desk from George, who wants to meet with you this morning." The older woman brushed lint from the sleeve of her stylish navy dress. "I took the liberty of telling him that you would review your schedule with me when you arrived."

"Sue, you're a treasure." George Wilstead had been hired by the board of directors as a high-level management consultant, but the rumor mill pegged him as Camille's successor, which Camille staunchly denied. Her grandmother was still holding out hope that Dahlia would ascend to the helm of the company someday. "You've always taken such good care of my grandmother. How long has it been?"

"Forty years," Sue said with pride. "This was my first job."

Dahlia took Sue's hand and noticed it was trembling. "Why, you're shaking. Do you feel well?" When Sue didn't answer, Dahlia peered at her. Sue's eyes were rimmed with red behind her smart navy glasses. "Let's sit down."

Sue removed her glasses and drew a handkerchief from her pocket to dab her eyes. "Your grandmother has been more than a mentor to me, Dahlia. She means the world to me. I've hardly slept since she was admitted to the hospital.

And we were in the midst of planning an important new launch." She ran a hand over sleek silver hair that curved around her narrow face. "I'm so glad you returned. There's a lot for you to do."

Dahlia poured a glass of water from the carafe that stood on an antique, marble-topped bombe chest. The executive office suite was situated on the top floor of a high-rise building the company owned on Wilshire Boulevard. Through a broad window, Dahlia looked down on an important entertainment talent agency across the street. To the west, beyond Century City, West Los Angeles, and Santa Monica, the Pacific Ocean stretched to silvery blue infinity.

Dahlia handed Sue the water and sat beside her on the French-styled settee. As Sue composed herself, Dahlia glanced around. Everything in the room reflected Camille's taste, from the Impressionist paintings to the fresh lilies, from the modern ergonomic chair to the photo gallery that illustrated the company's successes.

The executive suite consisted of an outer reception area, Sue's office and several smaller ones for other assistants, Camille's spacious office, a boardroom, a creative workspace, and a kitchen. It even had a private bedroom and a bath for Camille to take a nap and freshen up when she worked all night. It was a veritable compound. Camille had run the empire she'd built for decades from this lofty perch in Beverly Hills. She had also established smaller offices in other important locations, including New York, Paris, London, and Hong Kong.

Dahlia touched Sue's shoulder in empathy. "This has been a strain on all of us," she said gently.

"You have no idea." Sue drank again and cleared her throat. "Things have changed around here," she began, but before she could continue, the door burst open.

A trim, athletic man with a Malibu tan, a bespoke suit, and salt-and-pepper hair strode through the door. "Dahlia, I heard you were here. Shouldn't you be at the hospital?"

Dahlia and Sue traded a quick, subtle glance. George was as oily as they came; nothing stuck to him. Dahlia had taken an instant dislike to him from the moment she'd met him last year. "My grandmother is in stable condition now. She insisted I come into the office."

He leaned against the doorjamb. "Why? You don't have an official position here. Anything in this office is highly confidential."

Dahlia bristled at his rudeness, but before she could respond, Sue interjected. "Madame Dubois asked for the material."

George lowered his eyelids and glared at Sue. He had been hired as a management security expert to stem the intellectual property leaks the company had been experiencing. Other companies had copied bottle designs and artwork Parfums Dubois had created in-house prior to public unveiling. It had happened too often to be a coincidence, and they'd had to scramble to change designs. Based on George's findings, two offending employees had been terminated for selling corporate secrets.

George jerked his square chin toward the files Dahlia held in her hands. "You'll need board approval before those files can be released. Not to insult Camille, but I'm sure she hasn't thought of the danger of having sensitive data files open for anyone in the hospital to see. Those files won't be safe in her hospital room. Camille's probably not in her right mind, but then, she's often careless."

"That just sounded like an insult to me," Dahlia said, but kept her anger in check. The word careless could hardly be applied to Camille. "I suggest you take this up with the board. After all, they approved this action at an emergency board meeting this morning." Why the board kept him on as a consultant was beyond her. Was he this rude to her grandmother?

George's thin upper lip twitched involuntarily. "I will confirm that, Dahlia. You're not to leave until I do. I'll call security to escort you out." He pushed off from the doorway and turned on his heel.

"Good day, George." Dahlia rolled her eyes and turned back to Sue. "What else will I need to take with me today?"

George slammed the door and Sue made a face, muttering under her breath.

"Does he act like that with Camille?" Dahlia shook her head in disbelief. This was the most flagrant display of rudeness she'd ever seen in the executive offices.

"He's always challenging her, but Camille puts him in his place." Sue dropped her voice, even though they were alone. "It's been so stressful with him around. I thought his work was over, but the board renewed his consulting contract, which gives him carte blanche access throughout the company."

This wasn't the kind of atmosphere Camille had meant to create. When Dahlia had worked here before, her grandmother had a steady hand on the company and its culture. Inappropriate behavior and language was not tolerated. Parfums Dubois had been named one of the best workplaces in America for years, and Camille fought to keep it that way.

Sue stood and moved to a nearby computer. "Going back to business, I do have questions about the Monaco trip. Would you rather leave Friday or Saturday?" She tapped the keyboard.

"I have no idea what you're talking about. Monaco?"

"For the Formula 1 race." Sue removed her glasses. "You do know that you're taking Camille's place, don't you?"

"Camille was having tests when I stopped by the hospital this morning. Was this discussed at the emergency board meeting?" As Camille's assistant, Sue took notes at all board meetings and conference calls. Dahlia knew the call had been hastily arranged, but she didn't know what had been discussed.

"That's right. The board approved you as a marketing

consultant. The advertising campaign is centered on the themes of legends and excellence. Advertising and Marketing had planned a campaign around images of Camille, as a legend in perfumery, posing with the Formula 1 race car driver. Since women buy the majority of fragrances for men, the concept tested well. It's seen as smart and sexy, and empowering to women. And naturally, it appeals to men."

"So I'm to help come up with a new campaign? But there are plenty of marketing aces on the team here."

"You misunderstand, Dahlia. They want you to be *in* the campaign. As the face of the new generation of Parfums Dubois."

"Oh, no, no, no." Dahlia pushed herself from the settee and paced the room. "Did anyone think to consult me?"

"It was Camille's suggestion."

Dahlia stared from the window. She'd promised her grandmother she'd help, but this was highly irregular. Turning, she said, "Sue, I have to think about this first. And I don't want to leave my grandmother." That much was the truth.

"I assure you, she will not be deterred on this. And you're rescuing the advertising and marketing teams, who've been scrambling in desperation to find a new angle on short notice. If you think about it, this new twist in the campaign makes sense. It's even better, in fact. Much more modern."

Even Dahlia had to admit that.

"There wasn't time to consult you, dear." Camille motioned to a hospital attendant to help her adjust the lunch tray she'd brought in.

Dahlia watched her grandmother closely. She was improving every day. Her speech had returned, though she had a slight impediment she would need to work on with a speech therapist upon her release. "Maybe the race car driver could come here for the photo shoot. Is the trip to Monaco really necessary?"

"I wouldn't ask you otherwise." Camille peered at her lunch. "We need on-site photography, especially for social media. You know how important that is these days."

Dahlia nodded in resignation.

"Now, I have another serious problem. Look at this meal. Applesauce? And these limp green strips can't possibly be haricots verts. What happened to them? And there's no butter, no cheese, no wine. What kind of a meal is this?"

"You're clearly feeling better." Dahlia would've laughed, but a hospital dietician had drawn up a strict diet. "It can't be that bad. It's far healthier than the traditional French food you were raised on."

"If a croissant hasn't killed me by now, it's not going to. And so what if it does? I'd rather die by butter than by choking on this." Camille held a slimy green bean aloft, inspecting it with suspicion. "I don't trust this, do you?"

"You'd better take it away," Dahlia said to the attendant. She turned to Camille. "I'll call Bow-Tie and have Lance make something healthy and delicious."

"Thank you, dear. He'll know what proper green beans are." Camille waved the tray away and adjusted herself in the bed. She did look better. Her hair was coiffed and she wore light lipstick and blush, along with a fresh verbena and honeysuckle perfume. An aqua silk bed jacket covered her regal shoulders and pearl studs graced her earlobes. "Now, I assume you've heard about the emergency board meeting."

"Sue filled me in." Dahlia placed the files she'd brought with her from Camille's office onto the bed where her grandmother could reach them. "George threatened to call security unless I'd had proper clearance for these." She delivered this information in a light, pleasant tone. Although Camille looked better, she knew her grandmother was still in recovery and needed rest. Stress had probably played a large factor in why Camille was here, so Dahlia didn't want to exacerbate her condition. "But don't worry, Sue set him straight."

"George Wilstead. What a character. The way he courts certain board members is a travesty. That egotistical man wouldn't have the slightest idea of how to start a company— or run one. Ignore him, dear."

"I do, but evidently the board supports him."

"That's true," Camille grudgingly admitted. "Some people believe I'm too old to think logically anymore. Imagine that. They've forgotten who created the positions they hold. They're the doddering old fools, not me. Now, how soon can you fly out?"

"Sue is booking the flight now." Dahlia met and held Camille's gaze. "I still wish you'd spoken with me first."

Camille waved a manicured hand. "There wasn't time. Decisions had to be made."

"Did you stop to think about how appearing in ads for Parfums Dubois might impact my business?" Dahlia's indie perfume line was gaining traction with customers and retailers. She'd worked hard to build her own Dahlia D. line independently of her grandmother and Parfums Dubois.

Picking at a loose thread on her bed jacket, Camille was quiet for a moment.

"I can't appear in ads for Parfums Dubois. Technically, our companies are competitors, Camille."

"Yes, yes, I thought about that. But this campaign will raise your profile."

"I don't want my profile raised. My perfume line, yes, but not me personally. And I'm definitely not a print model." At least her grandmother had acknowledged her business. "Surely the board had concerns. Why don't they just get a tall, slim model and shoot the campaign. Your creative team will think of another angle—that's what they're paid to do, after all."

Camille nodded slowly. "All of what you say is true. However, this path will require the least amount of revision for the campaign. And it's our most important launch in years. This represents a new men's master brand for us. Alain

Delamare Lifestyle. We plan to co-brand with fashion and automobile companies, too. It's quite extensive."

Dahlia inclined her head. "Alain Delamare? Isn't that the race car driver you wanted me to have dinner with in Cannes?"

A smile played on Camille's lips.

"I won't do it." Dahlia rose from her chair and placed her palms on the windowsill, looking out over the Los Angeles traffic snaking through the city. "Please get me out of this, Camille."

"I will not," Camille declared. "It's an excellent opportunity for you, and the company will make it worth your while. You don't stand to inherit much, and as you know I have my reasons for this. But you have started a business and the lifeblood of any business is cash flow. This will give your business a large injection of capital. Look at it that way. When this campaign is over and you've gone back to your company, we'll plan a campaign announcing Dahlia D." A smile brightened her face. "Or perhaps you'll decide to stay on."

"No campaign. This is an indie line and I use social media, not glossy ads. The brand heritage is about artistry and personal discovery." Beyond the traffic, Dahlia watched brown-and-white-winged doves darting in pairs outside the window, flitting from one tree to the next as if playing a game. In the grand scheme of things, is that what this was? She cast a glance over her shoulder. "So how much is this consulting contract worth to me?"

When Camille gave her a generous six-figure number, Dahlia felt her head swim. The truth was, she'd always thought there was nothing she wouldn't do for her grandmother. She loved her as if she were her own mother.

But Camille had built her business, and now it was time for Dahlia to do the same. Creating and running her business was an experience that Dahlia wouldn't trade for the world.

"I'll need to think about this," Dahlia said.

"Of course." Camille had a pleasant expression on her face, which belied her tough interior. "You can have until tomorrow."

8

"HEY BOSS, I'VE got some news for you." A lanky, sandy-haired man strolled across the terrace at Alain's home.

Alain rolled out of his meditation position and stretched. Meditation helped him calm his thoughts and gain focus before racing. "I'm not your boss, I'm your brother. What's up, Jack?"

Jacques, or Jack, as most people called him, had managed his career since they were teenagers practicing on the track. Alain grabbed two bottles of water from a side table and tossed one to his brother.

"Thanks, bro." Jack caught the bottle and unscrewed the cap to take a swig. "Couple of things. Here's the long-term weather forecast." He tossed a print-out on a teak wood table top. "Track conditions look good, no rain, mild temperatures, light wind. We'll have a fine day for winning."

"Don't jinx it, mate." Alain swung his arms from one side to another around his trim physique, loosening his muscular upper body. Few people realized the physical toll racing took. He had to stay in prime condition and maintain a lean weight for racing. He hitched up his dark blue running shorts, the only garment he wore. He liked to get sun on his chest and back when he could. "What else have you got?"

"Mattie rang from the States. There's been a change in the Dubois campaign you're shooting soon."

"Yeah? What kind of change?"

"Seems the old lady—"

"Hey, show some respect," Alain said. "She built one hell of a company. I had dinner with her in New York not long ago. Pretty impressive woman. Even worked for the French Resistance when she was still practically a kid."

"Sorry. I'll start over. Camille Dubois is in the hospital."

Alain stopped in mid-movement. "What happened?"

"She had a stroke. She's in stable condition now, and I'm told the doctors expect a full recovery, but she's been grounded. No air travel for her."

Alain rested his hands on his knees. "Poor woman, I'm really sorry to hear that. Please send flowers and let me know when I can talk to her."

"Will do." Jack tapped a note on his phone and then shoved it back into his pocket.

"So has the campaign been pushed back?" Jack meticulously planned his schedule for him to allow for business commitments and travel time between racing venues, as well as time to relax and stay in optimum health. Photos shoots could easily eat up a day or more. He only had a couple of weeks between the races in Spain and Monaco, and he had to visit the engineering team in Silverstone, England. Any delay could spell disaster.

"No, the Parfums Dubois team has arranged a replacement."

"That's good. Another model?" He couldn't recall how many endorsement campaigns he'd appeared in. Having sponsorships paid for the team overhead, and every sponsor wanted something in return. But this was an important long-term partnership with Parfums Dubois. He had to hand it to Camille. Even at her age, she was a true visionary. No wonder she'd been so successful.

"Sort of."

"Look, I really don't care what model they get. Things happen, but they're all pros." Alain picked up a small, hard lacrosse ball and dropped to the mat where'd he'd been meditating. He began to roll out his gluts and quads, focusing on the major muscle groups as his physical therapist and trainer had instructed him. "I'm sure the shoot will be fine. You'll handle the details, won't you?"

"Tiffany is on it." Jack picked up a free weight and pumped it a few times. "I think the ad campaign will be better with the granddaughter anyway."

"Granddaughter? Oh geez. Is she a kid?" Alain switched sides and continued rolling on the ball to release his tight muscles.

"No, she's an adult. Twenties, I'd say. Pretty hot, too."

Jack waggled his eyebrows.

Alain shook his head. "No. No way. I don't have time for entanglements right now."

"I love getting your leftovers."

"As if you ever had any problem on that score. You were the one who got all the girls in school." Alain swiped his brother's leg with a free hand.

"But you're the famous race car driver now." Jack laughed and snatched the ball from him, mimicking a basketball throw.

"Hey, give that back." Alain grabbed Jack's leg and brought him down to the mat with a thud. They were wrestling when a slim blond appeared at the doorway.

"So this is what you guys really do when you're alone." Tiffany picked up a hand towel, marched over to them and swatted them on the shoulders. "Get back to work, you two. You're more than thirty years old, but you're acting like you're five. I don't know how your sainted mother dealt with the lot of you."

The two men rolled apart, laughing. Alain swiped the ball back from Jack, while Jack cuffed him on the head.

In response, Alain jabbed him in the side and then scuttled away. "Jack says you're handling the Dubois photo shoot."

"Yes, and you're not to take advantage of the granddaughter."

Alain was disappointed in her assessment of him. "Come

on, Tiffany. You know me better than that now."

"Yeah, yeah, that's the man you used to be. I hear that all the time." She laughed. "But you *have* changed, thank goodness. I got so tired of doing damage control when I was working for you-know-who." She tossed her straight hair over her shoulder.

Alain picked up a black exercise band. "Let's keep the ad shoot to one day. The schedule is too tight before this next race and I don't have time to coddle inexperienced young girls."

"Oh, I don't think she's inexperienced. She was president of the company for a while. Just stepped back in, as I understand. She earned an MBA from Harvard, too."

"Really?" Alain liked smart women. Not that he had much time for them, though. Someday, after his career began to wind down, he'd think about finding a partner and starting a family. But that was a long time away. Racing was his sole focus now.

"If you'd like, I can set up lunch or coffee so you can meet the day before the shoot. It would have to be day after tomorrow. There isn't much time. They were rushing to get her out on the next flight they could."

Alain stretched the band and began to knot it for an exercise. "Sure, why not? Make it coffee. I'd like to give her my personal regards for her grandmother anyway. What's the girl's name?"

Tiffany checked her phone. "Here it is. Dahlia Dubois.

Ever heard of her?"

"Dahlia?" Alain jerked his head up and as he did, the exercise band snapped from his hands and sailed over the rail to the hillside below. "Damn it. Are you sure?"

Tiffany tucked a strand of hair behind her ear. "That's what it says."

"Do you have a photo of her?"

"Hang on, I'll look her up," Tiffany said. A moment later, she held out her phone. "Looks like she has a perfume line of her own, too."

Alain took the phone and studied the photo of Dahlia. She was wearing an evening gown and standing in front of a Hollywood-style step-and-repeat banner at a charity gala in Beverly Hills. Her glossy black hair, pulled sleekly back, revealed a long, slim neck. A strapless black gown showed off her toned arms and fine cleavage. He tapped the photo to enlarge it and then touched her face. She was so beautiful.

He felt his heart rate increase, just as it had when he'd first seen her that morning at the café, and again on the way to the airport. It had been so loud he was sure she'd heard it in the car that day, but she'd been so upset over her grandmother. He smacked his head. *So that's why she needed to go to Los Angeles.* She'd said her grandmother had had a stroke. Everything fell into place. Then he wondered about the guy she'd been with. *What was his name? Keith? No, Kevin.* Alain made a face. He hoped that—

"Is he going deaf from the roar of the engines?" Tiffany

asked Jack. "Alain, I asked you a question."

"What?" Alain raised his eyes from Tiffany's phone and handed it back to her.

"I asked if ten o'clock Monday morning would work for the shoot."

Alain released the breath he'd been holding. "Circle back and see if they're really serious about this. It's not like she's a professional model."

Jack punched him on the arm. "Neither was Camille Dubois, but that didn't seem to bother you before. What's wrong with you?"

"Look, I just can't commit to that right now. I've got to be ready for the race." Before Tiffany or Jack could comment again, he snatched a white hand towel from a woven basket and walked inside his hillside home. Scrubbing his face with the towel, he wondered what the hell he was going to do.

9

DAHLIA SAT AT her desk in her neoclassical Louis XVI study, which was connected to her bedroom and suite of rooms in the large, stately home she shared with Camille in Holmby Hills, adjacent to Beverly Hills. The scent of snowy white lilies, fresh from their cutting garden, wafted from a crystal vase on the fireplace mantle. A violin concerto on the built-in music system filled the air as she sorted through mail and answered social invitations and letters of well wishes for Camille, whose friends still wrote letters rather than sent email.

The world knew Beverly Hills and Rodeo Drive, which entrepreneurial retailers Fred and Gale Hayman of Giorgio and Jerry Magnin of I. Magnin's department store had put on the map, but Holmby Hills was hardly a household word. Long ago, Camille had moved from Beverly Hills just for that reason. Residents of the elite enclave tucked into the west side of Los Angeles preferred the anonymity of their address. Few tour buses rumbled through the neighborhood as they did in

Beverly Hills.

At 20,000 square feet, Camille's elegant, historical estate had far more space than she and Dahlia needed, but there were others who lived on the property, too. Dahlia had also transformed the old horse stables into a creative lab for her perfumery.

Camille had bought the grand French chateau when her daughter Laurel had moved home after she'd had Dahlia. Camille had immediately arranged a live-in nurse for the baby. Camille's personal lady's maid, butler, and chauffeur also lived on the property in separate quarters. The cook, head housekeeper, groundskeeper, other maids, pool attendants, and staff lived off-site but reported to work daily through the security gated entrance. Camille had created a private retreat from the world in Holmby Hills for herself and her granddaughter.

Dahlia opened an invitation for Verena's younger twin sisters' birthday party. She smiled, realizing that Anika and Bella were becoming teenagers now. Dahlia often dreamed of her friends' cozy homes. Scarlett had a stylish townhouse near the village of Beverly Hills, while Verena lived with younger twin sisters and her grandmother in a quaint Spanish-styled bungalow south of Santa Monica Boulevard and north of Wilshire Boulevard. Although Verena's parents had both died in an automobile accident when she was eighteen, she'd grown up in a normal family with siblings, parents, and grandparents.

Dahlia had only Camille. She'd always longed for a large, close-knit family. Her friends had become the sisters she'd never had, but as they began spending more time with their boyfriends, Dahlia had again started to feel like an outsider. Verena and Lance, Scarlett and Johnny, Fianna and Niall. When would she find someone to love and start a family with?

A tap sounded at the doorway. "Come in."

Camille's house manager, Winifred Douglas, was a mature, pearls-and-twin-set dressed woman who had started work years before as Camille's social secretary. She entered with the morning's mail in her hands.

Dahlia groaned. "More mail, Winnie?"

She handed Dahlia two letters. "I thought you'd want to see these right away."

"Thank you, this is what I've been waiting for." Dahlia tore open the first letter. "I have my appointment at LAX for security clearance. No more four-hour lines to go through customs." She opened the next letter. "Perfect timing. It's my birth certificate." After Camille had misplaced Dahlia's original birth certificate, Dahlia had contacted their family attorney, who promised he'd get a copy for her. It had also taken weeks to receive the registered copy she needed for the security clearance. "You know, I've never seen this before."

"Really? What about when you got your passport?"

"Camille arranged my first one and I simply renew it every time it's due." Holding her breath in anticipation, her eyes skipped over the document, searching for a name. Finding nothing, she sighed in resignation and tossed it on the desk.

Winnie sat in a carved chair next to the desk. "What's wrong, Dahlia?"

"See for yourself." She gave Winnie the certificate.

"I see your mother's name, Laurel, and your father..." Winnie's voice trailed off. "Unknown." She put her hand on Dahlia's forearm. "I'm so sorry. You'd hoped to find something more here, hadn't you?"

Dahlia nodded. "After all these years, you'd think it wouldn't matter. But I'd still like to know who my father is."

"There's still no word about your mother?"

"No. Camille resigned herself to the situation long ago, she says, but I see the sorrow in her eyes." Dahlia hesitated. She'd confided in Winnie many times over the years; the older woman was more like an aunt to her than an employee. Camille had created a family-like atmosphere of long-term employees around them. Though they all cared deeply for each other, Dahlia still wished she'd known her parents.

Dahlia raised her eyes to Winnie. "I didn't go to Cannes to see the film festival."

"No? Why did you go then?"

"Kevin and I eloped." She made a face and leaned into Winnie, who put her arm around her. "That is, until I discovered him having an intimate moment with another woman after midnight. And then Verena called about

Camille, so I rushed home right away."

"What a shame, my dear. I'm sorry you had to go through that. But perhaps it's for the better."

"I know, but it still hurts. Oh, Winnie, when will it be my turn? I don't want to climb the corporate ladder and run a billion-dollar business, I just want to create my own work on my own terms and start a family with a man who truly loves me. Why is that so hard to find?"

"You'll find it, Dahlia. Maybe not tomorrow, but you will. Don't settle on a man who won't treat you well. Marriage is forever." Winnie sighed, stroking Dahlia's hair. "Well, not always, but it's pretty to think so. And often it is."

After Winnie had returned to her work, Dahlia slid open the top drawer of her desk and fished out a small leather photo book. She'd gathered the few photos she could find of her and her mother. Dahlia suspected her grandmother had disposed of, or packed away, the rest of them—perhaps they were unbearable to have on display in the house.

In the first photo, her slender, dark-haired mother held her in her arms. She stared into the camera, a tight smile on her face.

She wished she could remember that day—any day, in fact—or the sound of her mother's voice, the touch of her skin, the smell of her hair. Her mother was a ghost in Dahlia's life, lurking in the waves of her own black hair, the tilt of her chin, the cut of her cheekbones.

Camille recognized these physical similarities, too. Her

grandmother had remarked on it once—only once—one New Year's when she'd had a little too much champagne. Never before had she seen her grandmother weep with such a sense of loss. That night was imprinted in her memory forever.

Dahlia glanced at an ornate, gold framed mirror on the wall. There were also mysteries in her face that could only be attributed to her father. Her vivid green eyes, narrow nose, and bow-shaped lips with a full lower lip. What was her true heritage?

She traced her mother's face, trying to decipher what was in her eyes, but she never had. On Camille's insistence, she'd gone to a therapist when she was younger. Over the years these sessions helped ease the sharp stab of rejection to a dull ache, but none had provided the one answer she desired.

Which was simply: *Why?*

Not even Camille could answer that.

What would make a mother abandon her child? Why hadn't Laurel confided in Camille?

Or had she?

Dahlia picked up the birth certificate, deeply disappointed. Only then did she actually read it. It was a record of birth from Monaco. She lowered the document, perplexed. She'd always thought she'd been born in Los Angeles. She made a mental note to ask Camille about that.

Her grandmother had always maintained that her mother had refused to divulge the identity of Dahlia's father.

Then, two years later, she'd simply vanished.

Were it not for Camille, Dahlia would have been adrift in life. Camille was her only anchor. When Dahlia was young, Camille had spoiled her, anxious to make up for her mother's disappearance, but as she grew older, Camille had become a stern taskmaster. It was as though she was trying to prepare Dahlia for a world without her in it. Camille's current state of health only reinforced that feeling.

Dahlia turned to another photo taken at the swimming pool, one of her mother in a white bikini with Dahlia splashing at her feet. She knew every detail of every photo by heart, but it was never enough. As she studied the photo, looking for a clue, the word *Unknown* mocked her. What had happened? Did her mother not know the father? Had she been raped or drugged? Had she been with more than one man? Or had she decided to conceal the father's identity for some reason?

Her head aching with questions, Dahlia closed the photo book. She had no more answers now than she ever had. She tucked the birth certificate into her purse. Glancing through the window to the expansive lawn below and beyond to the tennis courts, the Olympic-sized pool, and the Bentley in the motor court, Dahlia felt a twinge of guilt for feeling as she did. Having been raised in a wealthy household, the outside world thought her lucky.

But Dahlia knew that wealth was a cold playmate for a lonely child. All the possessions in the world were no replacement for the love of a devoted family.

Dahlia blinked, forestalling the tears that lingered so closely these days. Someday Camille would be gone and she would be alone. Not long ago, Camille had told her she had fewer years ahead than behind. The thought of it terrified Dahlia. She wasn't as strong as Camille, who ran her business and her estates like a benevolent general.

In contrast, Dahlia was an artist at heart. She saw the world in a brilliant symphony of scents and accords, textures and hues, rhythm and light. She'd gravitated toward the artistic pursuits as a child—ballet, painting, and perfumery. Always perfumery, her first love. She still recalled running through fields of French lavender when she was a little girl visiting Provence with Camille.

However, what truly mattered to her in life—love, family, and children—still seemed beyond her reach. She'd never been a part of a traditional family, had never watched a mother and father interact over the dinner table. She didn't know the true role of a wife and mother, nor did she know what a man's role was in the family beyond the external surface view. Sure, she'd seen her share of television and movie families and she'd been around the families of her friends. Was this lack of first-hand knowledge why she always chose the wrong men?

Stop it. Chastising herself, Dahlia shook her head sharply and pushed herself away from the desk. She would *not* feel sorry for herself. She had work to do, and if Camille had imprinted any attributes on her, it was that work awaited, people depended on them, and she must act.

"People at the shop are clamoring for Runway," Fianna said, her mismatched eyes—one marine blue, one hazel-brown—blazing with excitement. She had her own fashion boutique on Robertson Boulevard. "My customers love the perfume. I have to order more, and I'd better double—no, triple—the number of bottles in that last order."

"I'll have more delivered right away." Excited at the prospect, Dahlia leaned forward and folded her arms on their table at Bow-Tie, a popular restaurant in a charming cottage in the middle of Beverly Hills. Two of their friends, Johnny and Lance, who had once worked at The Beverly Hills Hotel on Sunset Boulevard, had started the casual restaurant, which had become a popular spot for celebrities to meet. They sat outside on the sunny terrace, surrounded by a fashionable crowd in sunglasses and summer clothes.

Dahlia had blended a custom, private-labeled perfume for her friend. Runway by Fianna Fitzgerald had launched to enormous success at a time when Fianna was on the brink of professional disaster. Initially, Camille had been interested in creating a designer line for her, but she'd had to pass because Fianna wasn't well known enough for their company's broad distribution. Dahlia had agreed to create a perfume for her— the first in her new artisan venture separate from Parfums Dubois. She lifted her nose to the air. "You wear Runway so well, Fianna."

"It reminds me of Hawaii. Sweet orange blossoms and seashores." Fianna fluffed her wild red mane. "I spray it lightly in my hair, too. Niall loves it."

"I could also make a light oil-based version of Runway without the alcohol. We could package it as a conditioning hair perfume." Dahlia loved creating new products. "Women who have dry or colored hair could safely use it."

Fianna's eyes lit up. "My customers would love that. We've had a lot of requests for candles, too. Can you do that?"

"I can have them made for you. I know someone in L.A. who can pour the wax. All you need to decide on is a container and packaging." Dahlia gazed across the crowd. "Something unique that would appeal to your clients like these." She drummed her fingers on the table. "You should come by the lab soon. I'd like to share a new idea with you. I've been working with pikake and ginger and I think you'll like it. I also received the most incredible pure lavender oil from the south of France."

"I'd love to have an entire perfume line." Fianna tapped a heel on the tiled patio and twirled a curl around her finger, thinking. "Did you get any other ideas in Cannes?"

"I wasn't there long enough to do much shopping, although Kevin insisted on buying a dress for me." Dahlia lowered her eyes and sipped her lemonade.

"No! I'd been working feverishly on your dress to have

it in time for your wedding. That traitor." Fianna narrowed her eyes. "Would you mind if I told you exactly what I thought of Kevin, or is it too soon? I know he hurt you."

Dahlia pushed her sunglasses up over her head. "He did. But I hurt myself more."

"No way, don't you dare take the blame, girlfriend."

"Oh, I'm not. He's definitely the one at fault. Although I was furious with him, I'm so relieved I found out before we married. But I'm still at fault for choosing the wrong man." She cupped her chin in her hand as she spoke. "Kevin wasn't perfect, but I really thought we could become a family. I love Camille dearly, but some day, I'll have no one else."

Fianna slid her hand across the table and grasped Dahlia's hand in an empathetic clasp. "I understand. Family is important. I have a large extended family in Ireland, so I don't know what's like to feel alone in the world. But you always have us, you know. No matter what happens." She grinned. "We've made our own family here in LaLa Land."

Dahlia nodded, her thoughts still on Camille. "If anything happened to my grandmother, I couldn't imagine staying in that enormous house by myself. I wouldn't, of course, not for long. That's Camille's life, not mine."

Two blond women in brightly printed summer dresses approached the table. Dahlia rose to greet them. "Scarlett, Verena, I'm glad you could make it." Her friends embraced her and sat down.

"Those look like my mother's empanadas," Scarlett said,

eyeing an appetizer platter on the table.

Fianna slid the platter toward Scarlett and Verena. "That's right, your mom's in the kitchen. Johnny brought them as soon as we sat down."

Scarlett touched Dahlia's shoulder. "How is Camille doing?"

"She's remarkably improved. But she tires easily." Dahlia steepled her fingers in front of her, thinking about her grandmother's request. "Which is why she wants me to step in and spearhead the new campaign in Europe."

"That's timely," Verena said, brushing her pale blond hair from her smooth ivory face. "Our masculine skincare line is one of our fastest growing segments. It should do well. Do you have a spokesperson?"

"Alain Delamare. And that's the problem."

Scarlett leaned in, her eyes widening. "The race car driver?" As Dahlia nodded, Scarlett grinned and went on. "He's a handsome problem to have. You could do worse."

"Not him, exactly." This is why she'd invited her friends to lunch. "Camille asked me to step back into the company and oversee the ad campaign with Alain, among other things in marketing."

"Isn't that part of what you used to do when you worked at the company before?" Scarlett asked.

"Yes, but this time Camille wants me to be *in* the shots with him." She knew her displeasure resonated in her words. She wasn't looking forward to the task. Why did she need to be in the photos? Alain was the face of the campaign.

"Wow. If you don't want to do it, I'll volunteer," Fianna said, laughing.

"You already have a hunky guy," Scarlett shot back. She swung her attention back to Dahlia. "The exposure would be good for your fragrance business. But what about your line? Can you manage both businesses? And has the board executed an employment or consulting agreement for you? If so, I can review it for you."

"Always the questions, counselor." Dahlia appreciated her friends' assistance, especially now. "I'll email the proposed consulting contract to you." Even though Parfums Dubois had started as a family business, it had long since surpassed that stage. Camille was the majority shareholder and chaired the board of directors, which managed Parfums Dubois. "I wanted to let you all know that I'm leaving for Monaco soon. We'll shoot before the Monaco Grand Prix."

"What an exciting race," Fianna exclaimed. "My aunt Davina took me once. Besides being a thrilling race, it's quite the social scene. Penelope was there, too. A lot of the models are invited onto the yachts in the harbor, so we all watched from one of the largest yachts, which was amazing. And what a race it was! The Circuit de Monaco is really prestigious, and it's one of the most demanding courses for Formula 1 racing."

"It's Camille's favorite, too, but she hasn't gone in forever." Dahlia thought it sounded fun. Now that Parfums

Dubois owned a team, she was sure they'd go more often. "In fact, I've never been to Monaco. She did ask me to go to Austin with her for the inauguration of the Circuit of the Americas Formula 1 track, but I had The Children's Hospital fundraiser I was chairing. So what makes racing in Monaco so difficult?"

Fianna brushed a strand of wavy auburn hair from her face. "The Monaco Grand Prix is run on the streets of Monte Carlo, which has tight, hairpin turns and steep changes in elevation. Driving there is treacherous enough, but racing is especially tricky. And there's a tunnel drivers must pass through—the dramatic change in light is really hazardous. It's tough to reach speeds of 100 miles per hour on those roads, while on other tracks the cars are clocked at well over 200 miles per hour."

"Sounds fascinating." Dahlia hadn't realized Fianna knew so much about the sport. "But I don't think I'll stay for the race. I don't want to be away from Camille that long."

Fianna's eyes widened. "You can't travel all that way and meet one of the top drivers in history without staying for the race."

"Even if I did, I couldn't enjoy it, not with Camille in the hospital. No, I'd never do that to her. She needs me now and I won't let her down."

Verena caught her gaze. "I can imagine how you must feel. When Mia had her heart attack, I felt so helpless."

"I'm glad she's doing so well now," Dahlia said,

touching Verena's arm. "Camille has always been self-sufficient. She's not the needy type—far from it. So now it's my chance to be there for her."

"I understand," Verena said. "Still, Camille's health outlook is very positive, so if she's determined that you stay for the race, you should. It would be good for business."

Fianna's face lit with excitement. "I should come with you. Even though you'll have a stylist, I could help. I could design a special outfit for the shoot." Her freckled face flushed. "It would be a great credit. I'd love to have a shot for the boutique."

Scarlett interjected. "Why would you work for free, Fianna? Excuse me if I'm speaking out of turn, Dahlia, but Fianna should be paid fairly for her work. Parfums Dubois can afford it."

"Exactly, and I'd insist that she would be." Dahlia's spirits lifted with the prospect of Fianna going with her, and she beamed at her friends. "I think it's a great idea, Fianna, and I'd love to have you there. I'll talk to the team. I know they're all under stress with the change of date, so that could actually be a huge help. Would you have enough time?"

"Are you kidding? I'll make the time. Some of my employees at the boutique are out sick, but if they return in time, I'm there. But I can always send outfits with you. And maybe Penelope will be there again."

"Then come back to the office with me. I'll introduce you right away. If we're going to do this, we haven't much time." Dahlia glanced Scarlett. "Can you come, too? That way we can expedite everything that needs to be done today." Camille had taught her expediency, and now it was part of her nature.

"Attorney on call, that's me." Scarlett checked her schedule on her phone. "I have a meeting I can probably shift."

Verena chimed in. "Don't worry about Camille. I'll have Lance make something light and healthy for lunch for her. I'll take it back to her at the hospital. Mia was planning to spend the afternoon with her anyway."

"Well, I'm starving," Fianna said, picking up the menu. "Do you know if Lance is making anything special today?"

"He can make whatever you want, as long as he has the ingredients." Verena's eyes shimmered with delight. "I have a surprise to share, too. Lance has been invited to compete in an Iron Chef competition."

"That's wonderful," Dahlia said. She looked around the table at her closest friends, each one of them uniquely talented in their areas of specialty, from intellectual property and business law, to skincare and fashion design. They thrived on creativity and when they gathered, the synergy often pushed them farther than they would have dreamed on their own. Dahlia cherished this talented group of friends, but talent aside, they were like the sisters she'd never had.

While the others talked about what they were going to order for lunch, Dahlia's thoughts drifted back to her birth certificate. Her place of birth had been listed as Monaco. She wondered if she could discover any information about who her father might be while she was there. And what would Camille have to say about this new information? Was it an oversight on her grandmother's part, or had she purposefully lied to conceal some aspect of the truth?

Whatever the case might be, Dahlia had a feeling this trip could change her life.

10

Silverstone, England

ALAIN STOOD OVER the engineer's shoulder at the new Team Dubois racing headquarters. The lingering smell of engine oil, grease, and tire rubber crowded his nostrils. He glanced around, taking in the surroundings. The cleanliness of the engineering bays nearly rivaled that of surgical theaters. Every gadget around him was the latest in technology, while award-filled glass enclosures and photos of past wins lined the walls.

He leaned in, inspecting the race and mechanical data on the large screen before them. Silverstone was also home to seven other Formula 1 teams, including McLaren, Red Bull, Williams, Mercedes, Lotus, Force India, and Marussia. A team's engineers and mechanics were vital to its success. Though Alain was one of two drivers for Team Dubois, just as much of the winning effort could be attributed to those responsible for engineering, race and track data analysis, and racing strategy. They had been working all day formulating strategies for practice, qualifying, and race days for Monaco. Alain tapped the screen. "According to this data, our strategy should be sound."

"You would think, given the mechanical changes we've made, but look at this column," the head engineer said, as he ran his finger down the screen and consulted with another engineer for clarification of a detail. Russ had been in charge of the team for the past couple of years.

Alain had known Russ for years before signing a contract to drive for Dubois. As a driver, Alain trusted him with his life and career.

"Hey guys." Tiffany hurried to Alain's side. "How's it going?"

Alain shook his head. "We need to make more adjustments, but we're getting there. Let's hope the good weather holds out." So many variables affected the performance of the car and races were clocked—and sometimes won—by 1/100th of a second. Weather, track conditions, tire, wind—the battle for supremacy raged on the track and was won not only by sheer speed, but also by a team's strategy and the driver's skill in overcoming obstacles. Even minor obstacles were magnified at speeds as high as 230 miles per hour. Alain turned to Tiffany. "Any news of Charlie?"

Every member of the racing team present paused at the question, listening. Often, obstacles were fellow drivers.

Charlie Saber was a talented, well-respected driver and the second driver on Team Dubois. Less than two weeks ago in the Spanish Grand Prix held at the Circuit de Barcelona-Catalunya in Barcelona, Charlie had narrowly averted a minor collision. Subsequently, he lost control and collided with an emergency vehicle on the track. Charlie had been dragged from the wreckage barely alive. He'd been in a coma ever since. Doctors doubted if he'd ever race again, so the team had replaced him with another young driver.

"No, I'm sorry. No change today." Tiffany sighed. "I'll let his folks know you've been asking about him."

"Thanks." Alain prided himself on being in control, but in situations like this he was helpless. Though drivers fought aggressively on the track, most of them didn't wish others harm. Alain had a special friendship with Charlie. At just twenty-two years old, Charlie had been like a kid brother to him. He'd mentored Charlie in the junior Formula 1 motorsports events on the circuit. The two had become close friends. Alain turned away from Tiffany, overcome with emotion as he thought of his young friend. He strolled around the car under the auspices of checking the screen above the steering wheel on the new Turbo 6.

Younger drivers had less fear, but as drivers approached thirty years old—and older—they often retired. They'd seen too much. A split second of fear or hesitation could cost them the race—or their life and the lives of others.

Tiffany trailed him. "We have to change the date of the

photo shoot with Parfums Dubois again. Is it okay to push it back a couple of days? The granddaughter needs time to get here from the States."

"Exactly how many days?"

"She needs at least two days travel time."

Alain stopped and ran his hands over his face. "No more than that. You know I don't like to schedule anything too close to a race."

"I'm aware of that. But this is an exception."

"I can't afford exceptions. Photos can wait. Preparation for the race cannot." Though Alain spoke in a quiet, measured tone, his message was clear.

"I understand." Tiffany shifted from one foot to another. "I'll ask them, but I'm not sure they can accommodate your request."

"This is not a request. I must prepare. The company is the owner, so its owners should understand." Tiffany looked nervous about something. "Is there something else?"

"The marketing team changed the outfits for the shoot. They want you to go in for another fitting."

He narrowed his eyes. "Is this coming from the granddaughter? Because if it is, we have to set her straight." He'd bet she was trying to prove her worth by making changes and demands. She hadn't seemed like the type, but then, he didn't really know her. He'd seen scenarios like this play out far too many times. Egotistical owners who became intoxicated by the rarified air of Formula 1 racing. With only eleven teams in the world and requirements of $500 million plus per year for operations, it wasn't unusual for these team owners to become drunk with power and attempt to usurp control or make ridiculous demands. Owners might excel in their own businesses, but Formula 1 racing was a world unto its own.

Alain rubbed the scruff on his jaw. Under no circumstances would he let the fashion whims of a spoiled heiress endanger his team's record—or his life.

11

DAHLIA SAT BY Camille's bed in the hospital room, holding her grandmother's parchment thin-skinned hand in hers while Camille dozed. When had her skin become so delicate?

Everything about Camille had once been strong. Her determination in the beauty industry was legendary. Once, after Marshall Field in Chicago had declined her product line without even seeing it or speaking to her, Camille had gone to his office every day for two weeks waiting for the chance to personally demonstrate the line. He had finally relented, and a year later, Marshall Field's emporium was one of her most important accounts. From then on, other retailers clamored for it.

Dahlia ran her thumb over the faint blue veins on Camille's hand. Just last month, her grandmother had reigned imperiously at a fundraising gala, bejeweled and eloquent. She had showed no signs of slowing down.

Until now.

Dahlia gazed at Camille's peaceful face and measured the steady rise and fall of her chest. Frankly, it would surprise her if Camille ever retired, though there had been mumblings in the office when she'd stepped in as interim president.

This will be a temporary position, Dahlia thought. Besides, Parfums Dubois was Camille's dream, not hers. Camille had always gone after what she believed in, and she often said that she felt her mission in life was to bring beauty and joy to people through the art of perfumery. "In a world often given to suffering and ugly behavior, people yearn for beauty," Camille had once said in a media interview. "Many of our clients long for the lost art of living gracefully. My job is to infuse the world with beauty." And indeed she had. Yet, how could anyone live up to the force she'd become?

Camille's eyelids fluttered, and Dahlia stroked her hand to let her know she was not alone. She was glad her grandmother was awakening. She dreaded the day she would not.

But it was not that day yet.

"*Ma chérie,* is that you?" Camille blinked in the bright hospital room light.

"Yes, it's me, Grand-mère." She watched her grandmother inhale deeply.

"Thank heavens you've brought our potpourri. If I had to live with one more day of dreadful antiseptic odors, I think I would've died of that."

Dahlia laughed softly. "I thought you'd like the South

of France Mimosa." It was one of the company's most popular scents in its home line.

"Wish I were there now. I remember how it was when I was a girl…" Camille's eyes were drawn to the window and she fell quiet, seemingly lost in thoughts of a bygone era.

"I'm supposed to leave tomorrow, but if you need me here, I won't go—"

"No." Camille cut her off, slicing her hand through the air to make her point. "You must go. I will not have you sitting by my bedside when the company I spent my life building needs you."

"You mean more to me than the company, Grand-mère. If anything happened to you, I'd never forgive myself."

"The doctors have assured us that I'm out of danger." Camille took Dahlia's hand. "What I mean," she added, her voice softening, "is that you should not feel guilty about going, or staying longer for the race. Knowing that you have the ability to step in and lead gives me great pleasure." A smile lit her face. "Go. Have a good time."

"I love you so much." Dahlia bent her head toward her grandmother, touching her forehead with her own. Camille lifted her lips to her cheek to kiss her.

"And I love you, *ma chérie.*"

Dahlia sighed in resignation to the trip, although she didn't see any reason to prolong her stay after the photo shoot. Two-and-a-half days. That's all the time she needed.

"Is there anything I need to know before I leave?"

Camille always had special insights. To her, a meeting was never routine; there were always subtexts and agendas. She'd taught Dahlia to listen to their clients so they could understand what their customers wanted, or needed—often before they did.

"Yes, my darling, but you already have the knowledge within you." Camille pressed a button to raise the head of her bed higher. "You're ultimately responsible for the entirety of the photo shoot. If there is anything you doubt, anything that's not quite right, address it immediately. You know my philosophy and you have excellent instincts, so be alert and rely on your knowledge."

"I will." Dahlia had learned her business philosophy not in the MBA program, but from Camille. It was quite simple, really. *Treat everyone with fairness and kindness. Rely on your team, accept responsibility.* There was more, but Camille accepted the ultimate responsibility for the company and its success. She wouldn't blame an employee who hadn't performed because she had hired the management team, who in turn hired those under them. No, if there was a failure, they all had to learn from it and devise immediate solutions. Camille had raised customer service and employee morale to an enviable platinum standard in the industry. Dahlia was sure to uphold her grandmother's standards, for they were hers, too.

"There is one more thing." Camille fiddled with a tissue before continuing. "Without me there, you might hear...

stories. Pay no heed to gossip." She shredded the tissue before tossing it aside.

"People are always talking." Dahlia matched Camille's studied nonchalance. "What kind of stories?"

"Decades old gossip, really. Nothing to worry about."

Dahlia's senses went on high alert. It was unusual for Camille to be circumspect for she was generally laser direct. She helped Camille reposition herself in the bed and fluffed her pillow for her. "Then why did you feel you needed to mention it?"

Camille waved her hand in dismissal. "I hardly know why that popped into my mind. Maybe it's these drugs they're giving me."

Could it be the drugs? Dahlia doubted it. Camille seemed otherwise sharp. Was there something Camille had chosen not to share with her until now? Dahlia pressed two fingers against her temple. There was only one topic her grandmother had difficulty discussing.

"Does this have anything to do with my mother?" Dahlia spoke gently.

Camille glanced to one side. "It was so long ago," she murmured, more to herself than to her granddaughter.

Dahlia went on. "I ordered a copy of my birth certificate."

Her grandmother jerked back to her, suddenly flustered. "Why in the world would you do that? You have your passport."

"I needed it for rapid clearance through customs." Dahlia stroked her grandmother's shoulder in an effort to calm her, but she had to press on. "I'd like to know why I was born in Monaco. This is what you're afraid I might hear about on my trip, isn't it?"

Camille brushed Dahlia's hair from her face and tucked it behind her ear, just the way she had when Dahlia was a little girl. She leaned in and kissed Dahlia's forehead. "Laurel was in Europe and she turned up at the Princess Grace hospital, and then called me after you were born. I caught the next flight I could."

Dahlia took this in, disappointed, hurt, and angry that Camille had never shared this. She'd had a right to know. But Camille wasn't well, so she checked the anger in her voice before she spoke, asking as gently as she could manage, "Why didn't you tell me before?"

Camille blinked rapidly. Her eyes were glassy with tears she appeared intent on containing. "It wasn't important. Later, I was concerned that you might take it upon yourself to go to the hospital to investigate."

"And why wouldn't that have been advisable?"

"I didn't want you to be hurt again." Camille shook her head. "You've seen the birth certificate. Under *Father*, your mother wrote *Unknown*. But you know that now."

She did. Dahlia had discovered that as a child when she asked why she shared the same last as her grandmother. A nasty bully at her school had taunted with her that detail, calling her a bastard child. She'd left school crying and Camille had been forced to tell her the truth. However, knowing that and seeing it on a stark official document were two different things. She'd harbored the secret hope that her father's name might have been printed on her birth certificate. "I'd always thought that you knew something about my father. Something you weren't telling me." Dahlia hesitated. "I still think that."

Camille's eyes glazed sadly with the mist of time. "There's nothing more I can tell you. I really wish there were, *ma chére*. But please, disregard any rumors you might hear. Speculations are not facts."

Dahlia touched her lips to Camille's soft cheek. "I love you Grand-mère. I think you should rest now." Perhaps Camille didn't know anything more about her parents, but evidently other people thought they did. What gossip could she possibly encounter?

Yet, she was no longer the little girl at school who'd just made a heart-wrenching discovery. She was her own person, regardless of who her parents were.

Whatever Dahlia found, she would face on her own.

12

AFTER DAHLIA HAD visited Camille in the hospital, she asked Fianna to meet at her laboratory on the estate to discuss additions to the Fitzgerald designer line. Her Air France flight didn't leave until midnight. Before she left, she wanted to get her friend's direction on a new fragrance to keep the project on track.

Dahlia wore a white wrap shirt and slim taupe jeans with nude-colored high heels. She sat at an antique marquetry desk with an array of samples she'd prepared for Fianna, who sat across from her.

Her entire laboratory was decorated in calming shades of ivory, cream, and white. Indoor potted palms and twin braided money trees were placed strategically around the perfume lab that Dahlia had created in the former stables on the edge of Camille's property. Tropical green plants curved over stuffed furniture. Rough-hewn ceiling beams had been left exposed for a rustic effect. Behind her, a curved, horseshoe-shaped desk with stepped shelves held hundreds of tiny bottles of essential oils, the tools of her trade. The air carried a mélange of fragrant scents.

"I really wish I could go with you to Monaco," Fianna said, "but with half my employees out sick, someone has to keep the doors open for customers. But I hope you like the dress I designed. You're going to look amazing in it."

"I really appreciate it, Fianna. I know you stayed up late to finish it for me."

Fianna arched a fine auburn eyebrow. "Maybe you'll come home with a sexy race car driver."

"I seriously doubt that." Dahlia leaned in conspiratorially. "But there is a man I met in Cannes. It's not too far away."

"When you were on your elopement trip?" Fianna looked at her with mock horror, and then dissolved into laughter. "You didn't waste any time. Good for you, girl. Who is he and what's he like?"

"I met him in a cafe one morning. Later that night is when I found Kevin wrapped around another woman. This man happened to have a limo and helped me get a flight back when Camille had her stroke."

"Wait a minute. He's a limo driver?"

"No, silly, he had a driver. He was such a gentleman and I was such a mess. I didn't get his name, but I know he's an American, and he works for a company called ADR." Dahlia felt her face coloring as she spoke of him. He still had that effect on her, even a week later and thousands of miles away.

"Shouldn't be too hard to find," Fianna said with a wink. "You can check online."

They went on to discuss the new Runway candle addition before they turned their attention to the new perfumes Dahlia had been working on.

Fianna tried the first perfume. "Wow, this is perfect. I love it."

"Not so fast." Dahlia laughed and waved a white blotter strip under Fianna's nose. "Try this newer version. It still has the pikake and ginger blend, but this one is a little different. Which one do you prefer?"

Breathing in, Fianna's eyes widened with delight. "Oh, I can smell the difference. Definitely the second. It's smoother than the first one."

Dahlia smiled. "Very good, your nose is becoming more discriminating. I smoothed and rounded the bouquet with peach."

"This one is mesmerizing. Utterly magical. I feel like I'm on an island paradise, though it's more sophisticated. I'm amazed at how you can create such incredible essences."

Turning back to a neat row of small plain bottles, Dahlia reached for the next one in line.

"Can you really remember all of these aromas?" Fianna glanced toward the bottles.

"Camille made sure of it. She used to test me on my recognition when I was younger, but she really didn't have to push me. I've loved playing with perfume since I was a little girl."

Dahlia smiled as she remembered how she used to blend perfume for Camille and everyone who worked at the house. "Some of my early work was probably horrid, but Camille was patient. She taught me most everything I know about the art of perfumery." Dahlia picked up another small bottle. "Try this. It's not ready yet, but tell me if you like the direction. This is for my Dahlia D. line, which is based on my personal experiences."

Fianna inhaled and paused in thought. "It's light, warm… a summer holiday scent, but very chic. How do you get your inspiration?

"Actually, this one was inspired by a morning in Cannes. The ocean air, the jasmine and honeysuckle-covered stone walls moist with dew and warmed by the sun. Close your eyes to eliminate visual distractions and then try it again. Your mind will fill in the details."

Fianna did as Dahlia instructed. "Hmm, I can see that. I can almost feel the sun on my shoulders."

Dahlia smelled the sample again, and it transported her back to that morning in Cannes—the first time she'd met the mystery man who'd taken her to the airport. He'd thoughtfully handled every detail to help her return to Los Angeles. She would never forget his kindness—or his intense blue eyes. His manners and attention to detail in taking care of her were far beyond what she'd experienced with any man she'd dated before. She wondered if he were still there.

She could visit the airport to see if his company's plane were around.

Fianna fluttered her eyes. "It's a really nice fragrance. What do you mean when you say it's not ready?"

"You said it. It's nice, but ordinary." Dahlia tapped the plain glass bottle with her fingernail. "Each perfume should be unique. Perfume must have the capacity to form an unforgettable impression. The most iconic perfumes are not the ones that people think are pleasant, but those that have a distinct point of view and a nearly addictive quality. A perfume should entrance the wearer and those around them. The perfumer's art is to create a perfume so evocative, so vivid, so irresistible, that it transports the senses to a higher plane."

As Dahlia spoke, an idea came to mind. She recalled the scent of the coffee she'd had that morning and wondered what it would be like to introduce a note like that.

Fianna rested her chin in her hand. She'd wound her curly tresses in a messy bun to keep her hair out of her face. "Perfumery is truly an art, isn't it? We've become so jaded by the influx of fragrances pushed out by every celebrity and designer that many people have forgotten what a real artistic perfume is like." Fianna dabbed the perfume she liked on her wrist and held it to her nose.

"Parfums Dubois has created many fine designer perfumes, too. However, Camille always took care to make them as unique as the designer. It was a collaboration between them."

Dahlia reached for another sample. "Since you're from Ireland, you must remember the smoky sweet scent of peat moss bricks burned in old fireplaces in the country. That's another aroma I'd like to capture and add to a composition."

"I can smell it even now," Fianna said, a faraway look clouding her eyes.

"Think of smoky peat moss with the juicy scent of tropical mangoes, all juxtaposed with an icy element. I experienced that in a carved ice hotel in Sweden a couple of years ago and I haven't been able to capture it just yet." She sighed. "There are so many olfactory pictures I'd like to paint."

Fianna said softly, "You really are a fellow artist at heart. Why did you ever go through such a rigorous MBA program? Why didn't you focus on your art?"

"Because I wanted to develop and use both sides of my brain—my creative side and my business side. I've watched Camille run a creative business for years, so I understand what it takes to be successful. As a perfumer, I want my Dahlia D. line to reflect the perfumer's art, to evoke places and sensations. Exclusivity appeals to me. Many people cherish perfumes that are highly individual and have a different viewpoint. That's my vision."

Fianna nodded, listening intently. "Surely Camille thought you needed an MBA to run Parfums Dubois. Has that been her plan all along?"

"It's been her dream, but with a board of directors in place, my grandmother isn't the only decision-maker. She's always encouraged me to make my own way. She believes women should have knowledge and skills, no matter how well-to-do they might be."

"That's for sure. Anything can happen."

"And it does. Before she left France, Camille knew many aristocrats who, after the war, were reduced to driving cabs and working as clerks, not that there's anything wrong with making an honest living. It just wasn't how those people had imagined their lives would ever be. Some became bitter and others accepted their new stations in life, while others threw themselves into work and eventually became successful."

Fianna nodded in thought. "Even the mighty can fall. I've seen that among my clients, too. Breaks my heart sometimes to see mature women who depended on their husbands suddenly lose everything through death, divorce, or extended illness. Overnight they're reduced to poverty-level living. What's sad is that they're embarrassed by their circumstances. Society shuns these forgotten women. That happened to one of my aunts. She just moved in with my parents."

Dahlia listened and then added, "One of Camille's friends was swindled out of her life savings by Bernie Madoff, the investment crook who went to jail. Lost her retirement at seventy years of age. Things like that are scary. Scarlett is right to warn us all about the legal issues we might encounter." She picked up another sample. "Skills and education are the most important tools women have."

"We need friends, too," Fianna said. "And we need to believe in ourselves. What do you believe in, Dahlia?"

"I believe in my abilities," Dahlia said with a firm nod of her head. "You know, I never really planned to run Parfums Dubois, though I'll always be there if I'm needed." She removed a cap from a bottle. "Smell this."

Fianna closed her eyes and inhaled. "It's fresh and herbal. Lavender."

"It's some of the best I've ever smelled. It's from a farm in Provence I'm considering acquiring." Dahlia smiled with modesty.

"To live in?" Fianna grinned. "Aix-en-Provence is so charming. Davina took me there once."

"I'm more interested in it for the lavender production. Verena and I have been talking about working together to create a high-end country French line of body care. And the consulting agreement with Parfums Dubois could help pay for it."

One of Dahlia's earliest memories was of the lavender-scented linen closets Camille took pride in. As a girl, she used to open the doors and breathe in, transporting herself even then to a pastoral place. "I had planned on visiting the farm from Cannes. It's only two or three hours away, but then Verena called about Camille."

"You should definitely check it out this time."

They talked a little more about perfumery before Fianna reminded her that she needed to try on the dress she'd brought for her to wear in the Monaco photo shoot. "If you think it's appropriate," Fianna added. "You won't hurt my feelings if it's not."

"I'd love to see what you have. Do you have the dress with you?" She adored Fianna's fashions and couldn't wait to see her latest creation.

"When I arrived, your butler offered to take the dress and some other things I brought to your room. If we're through here, let's go."

They strolled across the expanse of lawn, past the tennis courts, gazebo, guesthouses, and swimming pool and into the house. As they walked, Fianna asked how Camille was doing and Dahlia filled her in.

On the second floor, the two friends entered Dahlia's suite. As soon as Dahlia saw the dress hanging in her dressing area, she exclaimed. "It's absolutely stunning." She ran her fingertips along the buttery duchess satin with reverence.

"Try it on. I have your measurements, but I brought my sewing kit in case it needs alterations." Fianna slipped the dress off the hanger while Dahlia began to undress.

"When we met with the marketing team, they said they wanted a classic look to portray the brand heritage, but with an updated edge. I thought this shade of silvery platinum would go well with your raven black hair and echo the glamor-meets-motorsports-in-Monaco theme." Fianna helped Dahlia into the long dress.

Dahlia stepped onto a round dais in front of a full-length three-way mirror. "Oh Fianna, you've outdone yourself. This is incredible."

Fianna walked around her, observing the dress with a critical eye, and making a slight adjustment here and there. "I hope the stylist likes it," she said, biting her lip.

"It's fabulous." Dahlia ran her hands over the floor length gown. It hugged her in all the right places. "I feel like Elizabeth Taylor in one of those old Hollywood glamor shots."

"You're about the same height," Fianna said. "I visited a costume exhibit that had many of her early film costumes. Few people realize how tiny she was."

"Does it need any alterations?"

"No, it's perfect on you." Fianna took a short lace dress from another hook. "I have more outfits I think you'll like. What else are you taking?"

"Not much. I won't be there more than a couple of days. I have a couple of your black dresses and two pairs of heels."

Fianna looked horrified. "You're going to Monaco, not New York. Even then, I'd hope you'd pack more. Your black dresses are chic, but you never know when you might need something fabulous."

"I'm not staying for the race."

"What if you do? The wardrobe you're taking will never do in Monaco. Not *this* weekend." Fianna sounded determined. "All the glamorous people gather there for the Formula 1 Grand Prix. You can't go around looking like you just stepped off Wall Street."

Dahlia couldn't help but laugh. "You know my style, though."

"Classic, I know. But let's jazz it up a little. It's going to be an amazing weekend. When I was there with my aunt Davina a few years ago, it was nonstop parties and yacht hopping until dawn. I don't think there's anyone in Monaco that Davina doesn't know. I had a hard time keeping up with her and she's twice my age, though she doesn't look it."

"Is she going this year?" Fianna's aunt from Ireland had been one of the top supermodels in the world before her retirement.

"No, she's having minor surgery. But if she were there, you'd be going to the palace with her." Fianna thumbed through the clothes she'd brought. "I'm sending some new pieces I've designed with you, too." She held up several chic summer dresses and a stunning tropical print maillot swim suit with sheer inserts and matching wide-legged palazzo pants. "This is from my first swim line. There's a bikini, too. Take your pick."

"I love it, but you're overloading my luggage," Dahlia said, protesting. "I'll have to check bags."

Fianna raised an eyebrow. "Oh, please. Give in to the fact that you're going somewhere fabulous." She put her hand on Dahlia's arm. "I know what you're thinking, but Camille is improving and she will be okay. She'd want you to make a splash in the name of Parfums Dubois. You have to stay for the race. Team Dubois is racing, so I'm sure Camille wants you to be there. And you'll have to have a dress for the ball."

Dahlia stared at herself in the mirror. Maybe Fianna had a point. But she hated to be away from Camille any longer than necessary. "Okay, I'll take everything in case I decide to stay longer."

As she tried on the dresses and Fianna made a few alterations, Dahlia's thoughts drifted to what she might discover in Monaco.

Somewhere out there, she had a father named Unknown.

She planned to visit the hospital while she was in Monaco to see where she'd been born. And then a thought struck her. Would there be anyone there who might remember her mother? If so, might someone remember a man who'd been with her? Monaco was a small community. She wondered what she would find.

13

NINETY MINUTES OUTSIDE of Nice, Dahlia woke to jarring turbulence as the plane flew through thunder showers. As she was jostled about, she tightened her seatbelt and gripped her seat. After a half an hour, the seatbelt sign mercifully flashed off.

She rubbed sleep from her eyes and eased her aching limbs from the cramped confines of her coach class seat, which was all she could get on short notice. With thoughts of visiting the hospital where she'd been born prevalent in her mind, she'd slept fitfully during the fourteen-hour flight.

The flight attendant served coffee, and Dahlia gulped a tepid cup. Afterward, she freshened up as well as she could in the tiny in-flight lavatory. A meeting with the Formula 1 Team Dubois representatives had been scheduled for soon after she arrived, so she tried to look her best. Or at least, not too bad.

In the back of the limousine on the way to Monte Carlo in the principality of Monaco, Dahlia dug into her large

Louis Vuitton tote. She changed from flat shoes to Louboutin heels, twisted her thick hair into a casual semblance of a French twist, and applied a perfume of Camille's creation, which was one of the company's iconic brands. She brushed wrinkles from her form-fitting, black sheath dress.

Though she was tired after the journey, she was undeterred in her promise to Camille and the board. She reviewed the marketing team's notes on her way to the hotel, trying not to think of the trip she'd just taken with Kevin and how disastrously it had ended. The only good moment of the trip had been when an intriguing stranger had shown enormous care for her well-being. She wondered how she might find him again. *Just to thank him*, she assured herself, though his magnetic eyes kept intruding on her thoughts.

Camille's personal travel concierge had managed to book a suite at the Hôtel de Paris on Camille's instruction, even though the luxury hotel on the Mediterranean had been officially sold out for months. It was exorbitantly expensive, but this was important business and well worth the expense.

As the limousine glided to a stop, Dahlia gazed out the window at the stylish crowd arriving and departing. The Formula 1 fans were out in force and the Hôtel de Paris was in a prime location at the Casino turn on the track. Barriers had already been erected around the roads for the race. She stepped from the car and as she made her way into the grand Entrance Hall, she overheard passersby talking excitedly about the upcoming Grand Prix race.

Though she longed for a warm, restorative bath, Dahlia strode through the ornately gilded Belle Époque hall to the Coté Jardin café for her meeting. She stood at the entrance to the outdoor terrace café overlooking the shimmering azure sea and breathed in the fresh scent of the sea and the magnificent cuisine.

"I'm joining Alain Delamare's table," she said to the maître d', who surreptitiously sized her up in an instant. He nodded curtly and executed a magnanimous wave of his hand toward one of the prime tables with an astounding view.

As they approached the table, Dahlia could hear the conversation in progress. The woman—Tiffany, she presumed, the publicist—was speaking in a pleading tone to a man Dahlia took to be Alain. "I'm sure you'll like Dahlia. This promises to be an incredible photo shoot for the new line."

"The answer is still no." Alain sat with his back to Dahlia, arms crossed, a crisp white shirt stretched across his broad shoulders, the cuffs casually folded back to reveal muscular forearms. "Not this week."

Dahlia's senses went on high alert and she slowed her pace, listening, just as Camille might have done if she were here.

"But she's not staying long. She's leaving on Saturday."

"Before the race?" Alain expressed a puff of air between his lips in disgust.

On the opposite side of the table from him and directly in Dahlia's line of sight, Tiffany glanced up and spied her. The blond woman's face turned a bright shade of pink.

"Looks like I've come at a bad time." Dahlia stopped behind his chair and put a hand on her hip. *I just flew fourteen hours for this reception?*

Tiffany sprang to her feet, apologies on her lips, and welcoming kisses on each cheek in the French fashion. "No, no, no, this is perfect timing." She shot a reprimanding look at Alain, who had yet to turn around and acknowledge Dahlia's presence. "Alain, I'd like you to meet Dahlia Dubois."

Dahlia steeled herself to greet this stubborn, egotistical man who clearly didn't care whether she'd just flown halfway around the world to pose for photos with him to promote *his* new men's fragrance and skincare line, a multimillion-dollar deal with Parfums Dubois for which he was also being paid quite handsomely. *How rude. I won't give him the satisfaction of—*

"Actually, we've met before." Alain stood and slowly turned around. His blazing blue eyes seemed to bore into her soul. "It's a pleasure seeing you again."

"It's *you?*" Dahlia blinked, caught off guard by the eyes that had intruded on her dreams for the past week. "Why didn't you tell me who you were?"

Alain held out his hand in greeting. "It's complicated." He gave her a sheepish half-grin.

Suddenly incensed over his nonchalant attitude, she ignored his proffered hand. "And is it *complicated* why I flew halfway around the world for a last minute photo shoot that you don't want to do?" She pursed her lips in satisfaction at his surprised look. "That's right, I heard what you said. Is this some kind of game for you?"

"You think *I'm* the one playing a game?" Alain drew his eyebrows together. "I'm not the one who demanded a wardrobe change, which pushed the shoot back to the day before the qualifying races."

"I happen to know you have Friday off from racing." Dahlia was determined not to back down. She was in no mood to accommodate an arrogant, self-centered man who was toying with her. He could have introduced himself that night. And he could have sent word that she needn't bother to fly all the way to France. Where were his manners? "This photo shoot is a high priority."

"Pardon me?" Alain raised his brow. "*Nothing* is a priority over the Grand Prix de Monaco." He spoke firmly, then turned to Tiffany. "We're through here." He threw a glance at Dahlia and then stalked away.

"Wait," Tiffany cried, starting after him.

"Is he always that rude?" Dahlia hitched her heavy tote up onto her shoulder. She was so disappointed in him. He wasn't the gentleman she'd thought he was. And he'd lied to her by omission. But then, she hadn't told him who she was either. Still, she was tired of dealing with temperamental divs. The actresses, designers, and models they worked with were often erratic and unreliable, but Alain Delamare made them look normal. And she was tired. Bone tired.

"It's the stress of the race," Tiffany said, wringing her hands. "Please sit down. Would you like something to eat?"

"All I want is to do the job at hand and leave." Dahlia watched Alain charge from the café. When she'd first met him, she'd thought he was so kind, so attentive to her needs. What an act. He was just like Kevin. The real Alain was uncouth and ill-mannered, and a race car driver—it certainly fit him. How could Camille have thought him suitable? "I had a long flight and endless security lines. I'm going to my room. Leave a message if he changes his mind by 6 p.m., otherwise I'll prepare to leave." After she visited the hospital and lavender farm, that is.

"Please don't leave. He's under pressure, but he'll come around, I'm sure."

Dahlia held up a hand. "Don't apologize or make excuses for him. I pity you having to work with an oaf like that." So far, this entire trip had been a waste of time. Then a thought struck her. Would he have treated Camille this way? Surely not, but she shuddered to think if he had.

A few hours later, Dahlia woke fully clothed in the middle of a large bed, gazing at an expanse of water outside a wall of glass. For a moment she wondered where she was, but then she remembered. Monaco. She sat up. She remembered calling Sue, Camille's secretary, and then collapsing on the bed and kicking her shoes off, but that was the extent of her memory.

Looking for a clock, Dahlia rolled over and found one. It read 7 p.m. She'd slept since noon. She hated having jet lag. Groaning, she sat up and spied an envelope that had been slid discreetly under the door. She padded to the door.

The message was from Tiffany. Although Alain was standing firm to his decision, his publicist asked that she stay until after the race, promising that he would be more amenable then. She also said that Dahlia was welcome to visit to see the race cars in the pit to, which was only open to Team Dubois members.

"Well, of course," Dahlia said to herself. "Parfums Dubois owns the team." She lowered the letter. However, Tiffany was certainly trying to make amends.

She strolled to the terrace and stepped outside to breathe in the fresh scent of the sea. The sun cast long rays across the placid sparkling water. To her right, a bevy of impressive yachts crowded the harbor like a luxurious colony of floating harems. Laughter and music rippled through the air and bikini-clad women lounged on the decks.

Her first instinct was to leave, just as she'd threatened. But this was business, and her mandate was to get the job done.

Then she thought of Camille and stories of how her grandmother had doggedly pursued the top retail accounts for her fledgling perfume line when she'd first arrived in the

United States. Camille had often sat steadfast in offices until a gatekeeping secretary would finally relent and give her a chance to show the president her perfume line. Much of the success of Parfums Dubois could be attributed to Camille's unwavering vision and fortitude.

Taking in the panoramic view, Dahlia stretched her hands along the railing. She would stay for the race, she decided, and hold Alain Delamare to the deal they'd agreed on next week. She could manage business for Parfums Dubois and her Dahlia D. line by email and phone. Camille's health was much improved. Besides, a few days of respite might be just what she needed. Alain wasn't the only one under stress.

She recalled what Fianna had said about their friend Penelope, a model who'd attended the race in the past. Maybe Penelope was here again. She tapped a number on her phone, but it went to voice mail. After leaving a message, she went back inside.

A chilled bottle of champagne in a silver bucket rested on the table. She poured a glass and wandered through the large suite to the spacious marbled bath.

After turning on music and filling the tub with a fragrant verbena oil, she slid the zipper down on her wrinkled dress and let it puddle to her feet. Stepping into the warm water, the stress of the day evaporated like the mist that hovered on the surface. She eased into the silky water up to her neck, sipping her champagne, and tried not to think of how dazzling Alain Delamare's eyes were. She was here on business, and that was all.

An hour later, sufficiently restored, she dressed in a short ivory lace dress and strappy sandals that Fianna had chosen for her. She applied her Dalia D. jasmine perfume and brushed her hair, letting the natural waves curve around her shoulders.

Dahlia made her way downstairs, pausing to admire the elaborate architecture and framed paintings. Finding the formal restaurants too stuffy, she made her way to Le Bar Américain for a light supper. A jazz pianist was playing and Dahlia found herself enjoying her time alone.

Although it didn't last long.

The waiter appeared with a bottle of Cristal champagne. "Compliments of the gentleman behind you, mademoiselle."

She turned, half-expecting to see Alain, but a distinguished man of about forty-five angled his head in courtesy. He made no move to join her or speak to her. She smiled and nodded in return. "Tell him I appreciate his gesture." Ordinarily she would have resisted such an offer, but since he wasn't pressuring her, she kept the champagne. Another glass would be nice.

While she waited for her food to arrive, she turned back in her chair to listen to the music. This is what she loved about Europe. There was a gracefulness about life on this continent with which she found herself quite naturally aligned, probably due to her grandmother and upbringing.

Dahlia had never felt part of the hipster downtown L.A. crowd that moved from one trendy nightclub to another. Or the Sunset Boulevard celebrity scene. Or even the Brentwood suburbs that revolved around private school soccer practice. Not yet, anyway.

In truth, she felt more at home in her perfume laboratory creating perfumes that spoke to her soul, or travelling through the islands of the South Pacific or the flea markets of Paris searching for inspiration. She reveled in the lush aromas that seduced her imagination.

As the jazz pianist played, she recalled the roses of Bulgaria and the lavender fields of Provence, each area beckoning with its unique scents. The more she thought of the lavender farm in Provence, the more it appealed to her, and not just for the lavender production. Though Camille had homes around the world, Dahlia had never had a home of her own. She was sure that Fianna and Niall would visit often from Ireland. It would be relaxing for Camille, too. They could spend August there. Plans began to take shape in her mind. She could be a spinster on a lavender farm.

After she'd dined on raw oysters and a seafood salad, the musician took a break. Dahlia turned to her champagne benefactor. *What was the harm in saying hello?* she thought. "*Bonsoir,*" she said to him. When the man answered with an English accent, she asked if he'd like to join her.

"My name is Lawrence Baxter," he said, taking the seat she indicated. He was courteous and proper, dressed in a navy sport coat, gray trousers, and a red tie. His deep tan hinted at a life of leisure.

"And I'm Dahlia Dubois. Thank you for the champagne."

"What brings you to Monte Carlo?" he asked. "Gambling or racing?"

"Neither. I'm in the perfume business. And you?"

"The Grand Prix. I haven't missed it in years." He poured champagne for both of them and lifted his glass to her. "To new friends and a good race."

He was well-mannered and seemed innocuous enough. "Cheers." Dahlia sipped her champagne, thinking about how not so long ago on a night such as this, she'd toasted with Kevin to their future.

"Your name is familiar," Lawrence said, pulling her from her memories. "Are you related to Camille Dubois?"

"She's my grandmother." Generations of people around the world wore Dubois perfumes.

"Ah yes, I see the resemblance." Lawrence nodded, taking in her facial features.

"Have you ever met her?"

Lawrence nodded. "It's been such a long time. We met here many years ago through mutual friends. In fact, I seem to recall that her daughter was with her. Your mother, perhaps?"

Dahlia put her glass down. "You met my mother?"

"Laurel, I believe."

Dahlia fell silent, her mind in a state of mild shock. Here sat a man who had met her mother. What could she possibly ask of him without sounding as if she were drilling him on his memory?

"Did you know her well? My mother, I mean."

"At that time we had many of the same friends. Small world, isn't it?" Lawrence ran a knuckle along his chin in thought. "How long do you plan to stay?"

"Through early next week. I have business here after the race."

"How lucky you are to be here during the Grand Prix." He went on to talk about the race and the favored teams before circling back to her family. "How are your grandmother and mother?"

Dahlia briefly told him about Camille. He was easy to talk to and he mentioned a few mutual friends that he and Camille shared. "And how is your mother doing?"

How could she possibly answer this question? Dahlia put on a smile. "Fine, I'm sure. I don't see her much."

The man accepted this without further question, undoubtedly sensing she didn't want to speak about her mother.

They listened to another music set, and then Dahlia said she was ready to turn in for the evening.

"What a pity," Lawrence said, rising when she stood up. "I hope I will see you again. Tomorrow, perhaps?"

Dahlia hesitated. His personal questions had made her

uncomfortable. But how was he to have known that? Finally, she decided she was being too sensitive. "That would be fine."

14

GAZING AT THE mirror-like surface of the Mediterranean, Dahlia leaned against the railing outside of her hotel room. She wore cropped black slacks, a sleeveless white Anne Fontaine blouse, and black ballerina flats. The morning sun was soothing on her arms and she could hear the sound of the tiny, exclusive principality awakening. Sea gulls squawked in the distance.

Her phone rang and she answered. It was Penelope, and she was in Monaco.

"Penelope, I'm so excited you're here. Fianna mentioned you might be."

Her friend's voice floated through the phone. "Fi called me, so I tried to reach you, but you were probably in route."

"Looks like I'll be staying in Monte Carlo for a few days after all. Alain Delamare refuses to shoot our ad photos before the race, so I have to stay over. But I have a swanky two-bedroom suite at the Hôtel de Paris." Being alone in the middle of a celebration made Dahlia more acutely aware of the absence of Kevin. "Where are you staying? Want to join me here?"

"What perfect timing." Penelope laughed. "I'm here on a friend's yacht, but there are so many others on board it's getting claustrophobic. I'd love to meet you there."

Dahlia turned back to the suite. The only room available had been a two-bedroom suite with a living room, dining room, and kitchen.

"Penelope, there's something else I'd like your help with, too." Dahlia clutched the phone tighter. "I requested a copy of my birth certificate. You'll never guess where I was actually born. Here—in Monaco."

The line went silent for a few moments. "I thought you were born in L.A."

"So did I. Our attorney told me he'd get a birth record copy for me to use for airport security clearance, but I had no idea it would come from Monaco." She quickly relayed her conversation with Camille. "I want to go to the hospital here to see if anyone might remember my mother. I know it's not likely, but they probably didn't have that many Americans giving birth in the hospital."

"It's worth a try." Penelope hesitated. "Was your father's name listed on the birth record?"

"It only stated 'Unknown.'" Dahlia perched on a chair on the balcony, watching sea gulls soar and dip in flight. "This is all I have to go on."

"Then I'll help. I make a pretty good detective."

"There's something else. I met a man in Le Bar Américain, a jazz bar here in the hotel. He sent a bottle of champagne to the table and as it turned out, he knew Camille and my mother."

"Did you get his number? We should definitely talk to him. He might know where she is, or how to contact her."

"I don't think so, but don't you think that's a coincidence?" Dahlia recalled the warning her grandmother had given her. Would he have actual knowledge, or only hearsay?

"No, I think our lives often unfold as they're meant to." Penelope laughed again. "Verena's grandmother Mia calls it kismet."

"Or fate. Though I'm not sure I agree. I have a hard time imagining that my mother was fated to leave me. Or that Kevin was fated to dump me at the altar of elopement."

"From what I heard, you dumped *him*. You were the lucky one, so I call that fate. Obviously you weren't meant to be with him."

"I count myself lucky now. But that doesn't mean his actions didn't hurt me, or make me angry." Dahlia paused, thinking about what she'd just said, and then she started laughing. "Just listen to me. That really doesn't make any sense, does it?"

"I know how you feel. He hurt your pride, even though you know his true nature now. I have a saying for that."

"What's that?"

"Next!"

Dahlia laughed, glad she had such an optimistic friend. "It's funny, isn't it? Everyone says that you know when a relationship is the right one, but how do you know when it's not?"

"Listen to your instincts. And *really* listen to what they say. If a man is not as enthusiastic as you are about the long term—next!" Then Penelope's voice changed, became serious. "You're a romantic-at-heart, Dahlia. But we're still young. Let's enjoy our freedom and develop our talents. You have all of us now, and you'll have plenty of time to find Mr. Right when the time is truly right."

Dahlia sighed. Her friend spoke from the heart, and her words had the ring of truth. Maybe she had been trying to create an instant relationship. She decided it was time to look at life through a different lens. Her practical side began to take charge. "How soon can you come here, Penelope?"

"You'd be surprised." Penelope chuckled.

After they said their good-byes, Dahlia hung up. She leaned back, shading her eyes against the sun, the sky an endless arc of delphinium blue. She had always been practical—a childhood psychotherapist had pointed that out, so she supposed it had something to do with her mother leaving. Yet she'd always been a romantic, a creator, an artist.

Even in the MBA program, she'd found herself yearning for a more creative path, not that she didn't take the opportunity to learn everything she could about business.

Camille had impressed upon her that an understanding of business was critical to many facets of life. Particularly for Camille, because her business was her life. Her grandmother loved what she'd chosen to do, and she thrived on it.

Dahlia wondered if she would find out anything about her mother in Monaco. Or, for that matter, her father. Her reflection in the glass window caught her eye. Who was she, really?

Just then, a knock sounded on the door and she crossed the suite to answer it. A butler held a stunning arrangement of white lilies, tuberose, white orchids, and white roses.

"Mademoiselle Dubois, this arrived for you with a note."

Dahlia opened the card and began reading.

These are the most beautifully fragrant flowers I could find for a perfumer. Would you join me downstairs at Coté Jardin? Or, your choice of another restaurant. I would be honored to escort you around Monaco. Please send a return message with the butler. I await your reply and hope to see you again. Your friend, Lawrence Baxter.

Dahlia inclined her head. Lawrence was nice, but he was a generation older than she was. He wasn't really her type, not that she'd been a good judge of men in the past. "You may put the flowers on the dining table," she said, opening the door. Seductive aromas filled the air and instantly lifted her spirits.

As she considered Lawrence's offer, she watched the butler exercise fastidious care in his placement of the flowers.

After he completed this task, he asked, "Would Mademoiselle care to send a reply?"

"Yes, I would."

The butler extracted a set of creamy writing paper and an envelope from the desk for her. "Shall I wait or return later?"

"Please wait." Dahlia wrote a brief reply, folded the note, and tucked it into the envelope. After she handed it to the butler, he left and closed the door behind him.

Dahlia strolled into her bedroom, where she fastened a strand of pearls around her neck and applied perfume on her wrists and décolletage.

Perhaps it is kismet, she told herself. Lawrence knew her mother and she should seize the opportunity to learn more—despite Camille's warnings. What could possibly be so terrible? She'd already lived with the stigma of being illegitimate and orphaned for years. There was little that surprised her now.

Another knock sounded at the door. She hurried to answer it.

"Surprise!" Penelope stood outside in the hallway wearing a short Pucci dress with an armful of thin gold bangles and flat jeweled sandals.

Dahlia embraced her friend. "That was fast. And you look gorgeous."

"Thanks, you too. I wasn't far away. But then Monaco is less than one square mile, so everything is close."

"Come in. I was just going to meet someone, but I'm sure you're welcome, too." Dahlia led Penelope into the suite toward the second bedroom. Penelope dropped the leather weekender bag she carried on the damask covered bed.

Dahlia had met Penelope at the skincare salon Verena and Mia once had in Beverly Hills. Tall and slender, Penelope Plessen was originally from Copenhagen and began modeling at the age of fourteen when she was discovered during a swim meet. She changed her looks like other women changed shoes. Today, she had magenta hair with blonde streaks framing her large hazel eyes.

When they returned to the salon, Penelope spied the floral arrangement and the note beside it. "Would that be your race car driver or Mr. Bar Américain?"

"Alain Delamare is a self-centered prima donna. Yet another man I misread the first time I met him." Dahlia put her hands on her hips. "Those are from my new friend Lawrence, the one who met my mother and Camille. He wants to have lunch today."

"Well, wasn't that a fortuitous meeting?" Penelope ran a finger along her jawline in thought.

"What are you thinking?" Dahlia lifted an eyebrow.

"Nothing you haven't thought about, I'm sure."

15

WITH HER EYES closed, Dahlia swirled a golden wine in her crystal glass, pausing to inhale the magnificent bouquet of Château d'Yquem. "This is a legendary nectar of the gods," she said, reverently touching her glass to those of Penelope and Lawrence. The afternoon sun illuminated their glasses, which sparkled like fiery canary diamonds in the golden rays.

The trio had finished lunch on the outdoor terrace at Coté Jardin café at the Hôtel de Paris, where they were now sharing the wine with a customary cheese platter.

Dahlia sipped the old vintage sauterne, discerning its silky nuances on her palate. "Apricot, cinnamon, a touch of saffron. Château d'Yquem is one of my favorite wines, and this vintage is spectacular. Thank you, Lawrence."

She also knew a wine of this caliber sold well into the four-figure range. He was clearly trying to impress them, though Dahlia wasn't sure why. He hadn't made any advances toward her, although with his proper British mannerisms he didn't seem given to displays of affection.

Still, she enjoyed the wine. She leaned back and waited to learn more.

"My pleasure. I appreciate a woman who knows her wine." He tipped his glass in tribute to her. "To two lovely ladies. What a treat."

"It's a treat to relax." Dahlia took a slice of creamy camembert cheese. "What a fine way to spend an afternoon."

"Don't even think about sleeping late tomorrow," Penelope said. "It's the first day of practice and you've never heard anything as loud as a Formula 1 car. But it's so exciting."

"Be sure to pick up earplugs," Lawrence said. "The engines are deafening."

Penelope motioned to her Chanel tote. "I'm well equipped. I brought earplugs and headphones for us."

As the sun peeked from behind the clouds, Lawrence slipped on gunmetal gray sunglasses that complemented his silver salt-and-pepper hair. "Do you ladies have any other plans while you're here?"

Dahlia looked from Penelope to Lawrence. "I've just discovered that I was born in Monaco, so I'd like to see the hospital where I was born."

"What a good idea," Lawrence said. "I remember when Laurel was pregnant with you. She looked radiant. By the way, how is she? It's been a while since I've seen her."

Dahlia wasn't sure how to respond. "Fine. But as I said, we don't see much of each other."

"That's too bad. Does she live close to you in the States? I've been meaning to visit Camille again."

His pleasant questions were discomfiting and Dahlia hesitated, taking a sip of wine, even though Lawrence said he was an old family friend. She would mention him to Camille when she called her later today. She'd opened her mouth to answer when Penelope thankfully cut in.

"Do you go to the States often, Lawrence?"

"Why, yes. New York, Palm Beach."

Penelope brightened. "A man like you must go to the theater in New York."

Suppressing a smile, Dahlia was suitably impressed. Penelope had deftly turned the conversation away from a topic she knew Dahlia was sensitive about. She'd never heard Camille speak of Lawrence, but that wasn't unusual. Camille knew many people from her childhood in Europe and even more from her years in international business.

"Theater is one of my passions." Lawrence held his glass up, admiring the wine. "There's hardly an important production I haven't seen. And I often visit Clive when he's on stage in New York."

"Do you mean the actor Clive Owen?" When Lawrence confirmed this with a nod and a prideful expression, Penelope flashed one of her most impressive smiles. "I'll bet you've seen everything I've been dying to see."

She recognized a familiar note in Penelope's voice. Her friend was an avid theater fan. Dahlia knew that when

Penelope worked in New York, she saw as many shows as she could fit in. A flash of intuition coursed through her mind.

Dahlia chimed in. "There's a spectacular new show I would love to see, but it's booked up for months ahead." She sighed and sipped her wine. "Maybe you've seen it. *Jefferson in Paris?*"

Lawrence nodded sagely. "A brilliant performance. If you'd like, I can arrange VIP tickets for both of you."

"Wouldn't that be marvelous?" Penelope's eyes flashed with mock excitement. "I do hope you'd join us, too."

Dahlia glanced across the top of her wine glass at Penelope, who was playing her role to perfection. She could hardly wait to compare notes with her friend.

After Dahlia and Penelope had thanked Lawrence and made their excuses for the afternoon—Penelope had to call in on an old friend she'd promised—the two women took a taxi to the hospital. French rock blared from the radio as they wound through the narrow streets of Monaco lined with concrete barriers and grandstand seating. Everyone was in a festive mood as the principality saw to final details before tomorrow's practice runs.

"*Jefferson in Paris?*" Penelope chuckled. "Wasn't that a Nick Nolte and Thandie Newton film?"

Dahlia pursed her lips in mock thought. "Really? Well, I could've sworn it was a new musical. When did you realize he was lying?"

Penelope lifted a slim shoulder and let it fall. "In my line of work, you develop a good B.S. monitor. When he ordered the expensive wine, I thought he was interested in you and trying to impress you. His accent bothered me, too. He said he grew up in London, although he had a Yorkshire accent. Most Americans can't tell the difference, but I worked in London. However, it was when he started asking about your mother that I really became suspicious."

"Anyone who knows Camille well knows about my mother. It's even been in the press, though not lately."

"What do you think he wants?"

"I'm not sure, but it's disturbing." Dahlia was quiet for a moment, thinking about Camille's warning. "He might be in the media, looking for a personal angle to Team Dubois."

"He should've said so." Penelope clasped her hand in a comforting manner. "You don't have to answer this, but I've often wondered why your mother is still considered missing. It's been more than twenty years. Shouldn't there be some sort of closure?"

Dalia had asked her grandmother about that once, too. "Camille said that unless evidence of foul play surfaced, she wouldn't declare her daughter dead. I thought it would help her to have a small ceremony to honor her daughter."

"And how would that make you feel?"

Dahlia laughed softly. "You sound like my old therapist. It's not like I really knew my mother. Every once in a while, a tabloid digs up the old story of her disappearance and runs

144

it again, reopening old wounds for Camille. Some even report that she's dead. I don't feel the loss of someone I knew and loved like she does, but I have felt a sense of abandonment. I grew up being called the illegitimate orphan. No amount of money can lessen that pain or make it go away. That's why I've always supported children's charities and foster care adoptions. I understand a child's need to truly belong to a family."

The taxi slowed to a stop. "We have arrived," Penelope said. She gave the driver a few Euros.

Dahlia stepped from the taxi and stood before a modern building flanked with palm trees. The sign read Centre Hospitalier Princesse Grace.

"Are you ready?" Penelope asked.

Dahlia shot her a look. "I have the strangest feeling."

The multi-story building was ordinary looking, but to Dahlia it was a view into a part of her life she hadn't known about until recently. "I wonder how my mother came to have me here."

"Maybe we can find out."

The two friends walked into the hospital and found the office of the head administrator, an older gentleman in a suit who welcomed them into his office. He indicated two chairs in front of his desk for Dahlia and Penelope to be seated.

Dahlia pitched forward and began "My name is Dahlia Dubois. I'm from Los Angeles, but I was born here. I'd like to learn more about the circumstances of my birth."

"Welcome back, although I don't know how we can help you, mademoiselle. It's certainly been a long time."

Penelope spoke up. "Her grandmother is Camille Dubois from France. She's the founder of Parfums Dubois, and her daughter Laurel gave birth here. Can't you look up her mother's medical record? It would be under Laurel Dubois."

He shook his head. "I'm afraid the mother's medical record is confidential."

"I've come so far," Dahlia said, dismayed. "Is there any way you can help me?"

"You're welcome to look at your medical records."

"Mine?"

"You were a patient here, too." He pushed an intercom button on the desk phone and asked for his assistant. "Madame Martin will assist you further."

Dahlia thanked him and she and Penelope followed a matronly gray-haired woman to the records department. They sat in a small waiting area while the woman went to retrieve her medical record.

After a few minutes, the woman returned holding an aged folder. "Here you are," Madame Martin said. She smiled and remained standing.

Dahlia opened the folder and read through it quickly. There wasn't much in it and nothing out of the ordinary. She glanced at the certificate of birth. "Nothing new here. Still Mr. Unknown."

Penelope rested a hand on her shoulder. "I'm sorry, Dahlia."

"It's okay. I'd just hoped I might find something here." She looked up at Madame Martin. "My mother disappeared when I was two years old and she's likely dead. I don't know who my father is. My grandmother is the only family I have, and she had a stroke a couple of weeks ago. For better or worse, I'd simply hoped to learn more about where I came from."

"I do understand." The woman took a breath as if to say something else, then touched her lips and stopped herself.

Dahlia looked questioningly at her. "You were going to say something?"

"Just that I can make a copy of that for you if you'd like."

"That would be nice," Dahlia replied.

After the woman left, Penelope turned to her. "Did you see anything new there?"

"Nothing. This was a waste of time. But I'm glad you were here with me."

While they waited, Dahlia told Penelope about Camille's remarkable improvement. They talked about the races and where Penelope would be traveling for her next runway assignment.

"Here you are," the woman said when she returned. She handed Dahlia a sealed envelope.

"Thank you," Dahlia replied. "I appreciate your help, Madame Martin."

"It's my pleasure." The woman clasped Dahlia's hands in hers before leaving.

As Dahlia and Penelope made their way from the hospital, Dahlia hefted the envelope quizzically in her hands. "This seems heavy."

Penelope glanced at the envelope. "Thicker, too."

"Do you think…?" Dahlia gazed up at Penelope as a feeling of astonishment grew within her.

"Oh yes, I do." Excitedly, Penelope quickened her pace. "But let's get out of here first."

They hurried from the hospital and found a café nearby. After they ordered coffee, Dahlia opened the thick envelope. She withdrew a sheaf of papers. "Look there's a note."

"From Madame Martin?" Penelope crossed her long legs and leaned in to peer at the documents.

Dahlia read the hastily written note. "'I was adopted and never knew the circumstances of my birth. I hope this brings you a measure of peace. I remember your mother; Laurel was a sweet young woman. I wish I could recall more. You should also speak to Père Renaud, who knew your mother.'"

She lowered the note and sat back in the chair, stunned. "I can't believe she did this for me. She could be fired for this."

Penelope's eyes were wide with interest. "Is there anything in the medical documents?"

Dahlia flipped through the pages, scanning them. "They're in French and most of the handwriting is terrible. I don't see any mention of a father, at least, not yet."

"We should go see this priest right away." Penelope tapped the address and phone number scribbled on the paper.

16

ON THE FIRST day of practice in Monaco, Alain arrived early at the track garages that housed the Formula 1 cars. The smell of gasoline, oil, and tires permeated the pristine garages. Once inside, he stepped into a white race jumpsuit that had sponsors' logos emblazoned on the front, back, and arms.

Alain leaned over and ran his hand over the steering wheel of one of the twin custom built V6 Formula 1 race cars that had been shipped from Silverstone, England to Monaco for the Grand Prix. As a kid, he'd admired vintage race cars with wooden steering wheels, however this was one most people would call futuristic. The steering wheel had controls that allowed him to make adjustments to the engine, differential, braking, and other systems at speeds in excess of 200 miles per hour. It was an important tool, but then, everything mattered on a Formula 1 car. No detail was too small, not when victories depended on the merest sliver of a second.

Each team built two virtually identical cars to race with

two drivers. With eleven teams, there were twenty-two drivers. Most of them had risen quickly through the junior ranks. A driver's career wasn't long. Many had retired by the age of thirty or thirty-five, so Alain was considered one of the older drivers. Still, his winning record secured his present position.

"Good morning, you're here early."

Alain turned at the sound of his brother's voice. "Hey, Jack." Older by two years, his brother had trained as an automotive engineer and worked on Formula 1 teams, but as Alain's career grew, Jack became his manager. The Delamare brothers were well known at the racetracks. They had four other brothers, but none of them were involved in racing as a business.

Jack slung an arm over Alain's shoulder. "Ready to run?"

"Ready as always. I love this race, but racing on the street sure adds an element of the unknown." Monaco was the most prestigious of the Formula 1 races. Albert II, Prince of Monaco, was a motorsport enthusiast and presided over the annual event.

"Well, try to keep your car together. One of these cars will be in a photo shoot for an ad layout." Jack ran a finger along the body of the car. "I heard Dahlia Dubois wanted you to pose on Friday. You could have, you know."

Alain rubbed his scruffy jawline. The Monaco Grand Prix ran on a different schedule than other Formula 1 races, which had practice on Friday, practice and qualifying runs on

Saturday, and the race on Sunday. Monaco had practice on Thursday, a quiet day on Friday, practice and qualifying on Saturday, and the race on Sunday. Friday was a day Alain and other drivers often mixed with media, fans, and team owners. "I'm staying with Monday."

"This would've been a great background here at the race. Why did you cancel it?"

"You know I have to be on top of my game, Jack. I don't need any distractions before the qualifying rounds."

Jack stared, studying him. "You were once the king of overcoming distractions, but now you've become Mr. Enigma. What gives? You weren't yourself last night, either. It's not a woman, is it?"

Alain shot Jack a look. "Not how you think."

"Ah-ha. Knew it. Is it that hot Dubois woman?"

"Back off," Alain said, lightly punching Jack in the arm. He found Dahlia attractive—distractingly so, in fact. She was the real reason he didn't want to shoot the layout before the race. He needed to focus on the race—without feminine distractions taking up space in his brain. However, he'd been looking forward to seeing her again at lunch, but she'd arrived at precisely the wrong time.

"Then you *are* interested," Jack said.

Alain shrugged. "Not really. Turns out she's kind of a nut. Got all bent out of shape because I wanted to push the shoot back. Miss High-and-Mighty, she was. Acting like she calls the shots." She was so sure of herself and her position.

He found that fascinating, too.

"Yeah, I know. Tiffany filled me in." Jack slid him a sidelong glance. "You sure are complaining a lot."

"She means nothing to me," Alain muttered, but as soon as he spoke, his gut tightened. Actually, he wasn't sure what she meant to him, but she was different from other women he'd been with over the years. "Jack, when you first met Tanya, how did you know she was the one?"

Jack's expression turned serious. "I knew Tanya was special from the moment I met her. She understood me from the beginning."

Alain put his arm across Jack's shoulders. "We all miss her, Jack."

Jack could only nod for a moment. When he spoke, his voice was husky. "Two years she's been gone and it still seems like yesterday." He gave a sad chuckle. "She liked you an awful lot. Always said that when you finally fell for someone, you'd fall hard."

"Did she?" Alain had been fond of Tanya, too. He was shattered when she died in a random accident. She'd been driving though thunderstorms in Austin, Texas, right after the Formula 1 race there. Weighted with water and buffeted by high winds, a tree limb had cracked above her car, crashing through the soft convertible top and killing her instantly. The two families had been devastated, especially when it was discovered that she'd been two months pregnant.

When the engineering team and pit crew arrived, Alain

and Jack met with them. Leading up to the race on Sunday, they would spend time analyzing road conditions and optimizing the vehicles, as well as forming strategies for the race. The Formula 1 teams were limited in their Thursday practice runs. The rest of the time was spent talking to media. Alain preferred to leave much of the media work until Friday, the quiet day—though it was hardly quiet.

On Friday, teams continued to strategize and make adjustments in advance of the qualifying runs of Saturday. Special events were held for fans and media to meet the drivers. Alain had always enjoyed this day—it gave him time to relax and recharge, as well as make important career connections. He'd met several new sponsors in Monaco in prior years. Most of all, it gave him time to strategize for the challenging race ahead.

Alain watched the other drivers take their turns on the large screen monitor. By the time his turn at practice came around, he would have to be ready. He would have two ninety-minute practice sessions, so during that precious time it was vital that he focus and relearn the nuances of the Monaco roads—or the track, as it became during the week of the race. Except for the new race in Azerbaijan, this was the only Formula 1 race conducted on streets, rather than a racetrack. It was an enormous undertaking for the principality, requiring six weeks to set up grandstands and barriers prior to the race.

Racing on streets was more dangerous, but Alain found

it exciting. The race required more finesse than outright speed. Uneven roads and irregular curves demanded unwavering attention. More than any other race, Monaco separated the drivers according to sheer driving skill. It was the ultimate test of the drivers' skills and judgement. Which was why he never took the chance to drink too much or stay out too late, the way some of the younger drivers did.

The parties here were legendary, but Alain was here to become a legend. His goal was to make racing history.

When his turn to practice came, Alain eased himself into the Turbo V6. He secured the steering wheel, which had to be removed each time he got in or out, and then his helmet.

He started the engine and it responded with a rumble. After leaving the starting line, he concentrated on putting the car through its paces. The engineers and mechanics had done well calibrating the team cars for this race. As he drove, he made adjustments on the steering wheel to improve performance.

The engineers and pit team were wired into the same frequency in his soundproofed helmet, so they could receive his feedback. However, only if he were in terminal trouble could the team offer suggestions. Once on the track, the race was up to the driver.

The cars were so loud that everyone had to wear protective headgear to protect their hearing. Alain took many other safety precautions, too. There had been only one fatality in the Monaco Grand Prix. The cars were safer than ever because of technical advances, but he was still aware of the hazards.

Alain concentrated on maintaining a fluid line, whipping around curves with precision and gaining speed in the short straightaways. He felt good; he was at the top of his game. He loved racing and wished he could do it forever, but at thirty, he had more racing years behind him than in front of him. Now it was his turn to make history, to become one of the winningest drivers of all time.

Anything could threaten his record. A misjudged turn, an accident, or a younger, hungrier driver who took more risks that paid off. The stakes and rewards were high, but so was the level of danger.

After Alain completed his practice laps, he wheeled into the pit and met his teammates with back slaps and bro-hugs.

"You're looking good out there," Jack told him, grinning.

"Not bad, but the Casino turn is tricky. There are a couple of things we can improve on." Alain removed his helmet and wiped sweat from his forehead.

Just then, he caught sight of Dahlia, who was speaking to one of the engineers. A tall woman with deep red and blond streaked hair stood next to her. She looked familiar, but he couldn't place her. He frowned. "What's Dahlia doing here?" He didn't try to hide his consternation because he hated distractions in the pit.

"Dubois owns the team and she's a Dubois." Jack cocked

his head. "What's wrong with that?"

"Everything. She's… she's demanding." He turned away from her and loosened the collar of his racing outfit. A prickly sensation curled around his neck. "I've got a job to do, Jack. Just get her out of here, would you?"

As he was speaking, Jack widened his eyes, indicating someone behind Alain.

Before Alain could turn around, he heard Dahlia huff behind him with displeasure.

"Well, I *was* going to compliment you on the race."

Not again, he thought, turning around to face Dahlia. "So you heard that, but I'm not going to apologize for it. You must understand the importance of what I do." He paused and waved his arm, encircling everyone in their pit area. "Of what we all do. Your company bought the team because we have an excellent record. We can't have distractions if we're going to win. And we plan on winning."

Dahlia jabbed a hand onto her hip. "First of all, it's not *my* company," she said, her voice icy. "My grandmother founded it, and while she might be the majority shareholder, the company is run by a board of directors, which has empowered me to make sure this advertising campaign is delivered on time for the fall launch of *your* signature line. If you think I'm hindering you, let me assure you, I have no such intention. I am here to do my job, just as you are."

Alain took a breath to speak, but he was so taken by her stunning beauty and commanding presence—all five feet of her, he'd guess—that he was momentarily at a loss for words, which certainly wasn't like him.

When he'd given her a ride and helped arrange her trip from Cannes to Los Angeles, he'd felt like he was rescuing a princess, but this woman could stand on her own. How had he misread her? Yet, her independence was exactly what intrigued him about her. How was he going to get rid of this interference? Especially when all he really wanted to do was take her in his arms.

Jack nudged Alain with his elbow, but when he didn't respond, Jack spoke up. "You've got to excuse Alain. He's got his head in the game right now."

Dahlia stared at Alain, obviously waiting for his reply, but he was still at a loss for words. She huffed and muttered something in French, and then spun around. The tall woman with the unusual hairstyle followed her out.

Alain drew a breath, her perfume distracting his focus. Before a race, he had to be entirely focused on the car, the race, and the strategy required to win. He turned to his brother. "I mean it, Jack. I can't have her around here."

17

"WHAT A JERK," Dahlia said, fuming as she and Penelope left from the Team Dubois pit. "Alain Delamare is another example of what a poor judge of men I've been. When I first met him, I was so impressed. Now he's showing his true nature—egotistical, rude, and uncouth. I'm the team owner representative and that's how he greets me? By throwing me out of the pit?"

Penelope hurried behind her. "He was brusque, but they seemed awfully intense in there."

"I don't care how busy they were. Where were his manners? Camille will definitely hear about this." Dahlia frowned and folded her arms.

Penelope put a hand on her arm. "I'm not taking his side, but before important runway shows I don't particularly want to talk with strangers either."

Dahlia stopped and whipped around to face Penelope. "I am *not* a stranger. And he's going to have to get used to me. Or I'll make his day miserable during the photo shoot next week."

"Take it easy," Penelope said, holding up the palms of her hands. "What's got you so fired up?" She arched a finely shaped eyebrow. "I sense there's something else you're not telling me."

"If you must know, he was rude to me yesterday, too." Dahlia told her about the brief meeting she'd had with Alain and Tiffany the day she'd arrived.

Dahlia hailed a cab, opened the door, and slid into the back seat. "Hôtel de Paris, *s'il vous plaît.*"

Penelope slid in after her. "You sure were interested in watching his practice runs this morning."

That much was true. Dahlia had been eager to watch the practice runs and learn more about Formula 1 motorsports. With her consulting agreement signed, she was officially engaged by Parfums Dubois. She'd also wanted to observe Alain Delamare, now that he was the spokesman for the new masculine line. What she saw was impressive.

"In my professional capacity, I needed to watch his performance." Dahlia shrugged. "I merely wanted to congratulate him and wish him luck for the race ahead. But could he even be civil? No, he's such a lout." She glowered at Penelope. "And you are clearly taking Alain's side."

"He *is* a world champion. In my line of work, I've met many people at the top of their game, whether it's fashion, sports, or business. They're all hyper-focused and have more than few eccentricities. They've earned them."

"Not you," Dahlia said, leaning back in the taxi. "I wouldn't call you eccentric, and you're a top model."

Penelope laughed. "Look at me. I tower above most men, my hair changes color faster than prime time pilot shows, and I'm mad about fishing. Yes, fishing. Let me tell you, I get my fair share of looks on the opening day of bass season in the Sierras. But I love it. My dad and I always fished together when I was a kid growing up in Denmark. So yeah, I'm eccentric."

Despite her anger toward Alain, Dahlia had to chuckle at the thought of Penelope mixing with the Cabela's crowd in their camouflage and beards. "Eccentric, is that what you call it when a man acts like that? All right then, I'll give him that."

Penelope poked her playfully. "And he's certainly easy on the eyes."

Dalia sighed. "That's what I thought the first time I saw him, too."

"Yesterday?"

"No, a couple of weeks ago. I met him in Cannes and he helped me return to the States when Camille had her stroke." Dahlia told her the story. "But I was on the rebound from Kevin, so anyone who was kind to me then would've made an impression."

"Oh, I think Alain Delamare makes quite an impression anytime. Though he's not my style," Penelope added quickly. She gave Dahlia a sidelong glance as a slow smile curved her lips.

"What?" Dahlia pointed to herself. "You think he's my type? Absolutely not."

The next day Dahlia left Penelope at the spa while she stepped into a taxi to meet with the ad team and stylists in charge of the photo shoot for the legends ad. She arrived at the high-rise building and made her way to the penthouse level. She stepped into the airy flat that faced the Mediterranean Sea on one side and spanned the mountains on the other.

"Leigh Percy," the ad agency owner said, extending her hand. "I'm so pleased to meet you."

"The pleasure is mine," Dahlia replied, shaking her hand. She noted the woman's artistic air, evident in her avant-garde Kenzo ensemble, which was a stylized fusion of Japanese and French couture. Camille had also told her this was Leigh's private residence, which she'd had for many years. "I've admired the campaigns you've done for Parfums Dubois."

"Your grandmother and I have had a good working relationship for many years." Leigh led her into a well-appointed living area where white leather mid-century modern divans and light bamboo floors created a light canvas to showcase splashes of modern art. Dahlia spied a grouping of four Warhol paintings on one wall and a surrealist Miró and a drip-style Pollock on another.

"Dahlia, it's really good to see you again."

"You've done a great job steering the marketing committee, Cynthia." Dahlia had enjoyed working with Cynthia Bartlett before.

Cynthia seemed anxious. "Hope it all goes smoothly on Monday."

"Of course it will." Dahlia had never seen the Dubois director of marketing nervous before.

Just then, Cynthia's phone buzzed with a text and she frowned. "Excuse me, my assistant needs to speak with me about something important."

"You go on," Dahlia said.

Other members of the Dubois marketing team and Leigh's colleagues were milling around a long, highly polished table that was a slice of a massive tree. Those Dahlia hadn't met introduced themselves.

Leigh Percy was one of the founders of Percy + Galant, one of the world's foremost advertising companies. She was one of the great advertising minds of all time and had trained under the legendary David Olgilvy in New York. Leigh had such insights to consumer desires and conveyed brand stories so well that her clients' taglines often became part of the English vernacular. With her trademark style of cropped silver hair and heavy-rimmed round black glasses, she stood in complete command of the room.

Dahlia admired Leigh's style. She had studied her company in business school and she was well aware of the hardships Leigh had faced in her career. Through persistence and vision, Percy + Galant had become innovative leaders in advertising.

"Hello, Dahlia."

Dahlia turned to face George Wilstead, the consultant that reported to the Parfums Dubois board of directors. "George. You didn't say you planned to attend this meeting." She was sure that Sue McGregor, Camille's secretary, would have told her if she'd known.

"Didn't I?" A smug, superior look was etched on his face.

"You might have told me." Dahlia's instincts went on high alert. George was domineering, but he was also smart. Why hadn't he told her he was coming to Monaco? More important, what did he expect to gain? Glancing at other members the Dubois marketing team, she saw they looked uncomfortable, too.

Cynthia stood in the corner on her phone. When she saw George, she hung up and shot him a look of distaste. Dahlia figured she hadn't known he was coming either.

It's on, Dahlia thought. George was definitely up to something and she didn't like it. Whatever George was planning, she would handle. Dahlia narrowed her eyes while offering him a tight smile. *Oh yes, I will.*

Leigh cut in. "Dahlia, you'll sit by me." She gestured toward the table, where her assistant was distributing briefing documents.

After sitting down, Leigh turned to Dahlia. "First, let me

say that we all hope Madame Dubois makes a rapid recovery, but it is also our pleasure to work with you. When we were working with the Dubois creative team and floated the idea of having you in the campaign, the response was nearly unanimous."

Although Leigh was speaking in a direct, forthright manner, Dahlia detected a subtle undercurrent. *Nearly* unanimous? Why had it been important to Leigh to make such a distinction, or why mention it at all? This was a woman who dealt in the power of words.

Dahlia glanced around the table. George looked positively delighted. Coincidence? Camille's warning rang in her mind. "And I look forward to working together as well. I understand we have a tight schedule on Monday, so let's get started."

At that, the door opened and Alain's director of publicity hurried in and took a seat. Leigh turned to Dahlia, who was seated to her right. "I believe you and Tiffany have met."

"Yes, we have." Their meeting had been brief, so Dahlia hadn't formed any opinion of Tiffany, but she knew she held a responsible position with direct access to the heads of all the companies Team Dubois worked with, as well as important media contacts. "You have quite a lot on your hands," she said. *Alain Delamare, for starters.* She pitied the woman that task.

"I enjoy it, though," Tiffany said. "I get to work with a great team."

Dahlia nodded. The word *team* had a broad definition. Team Dubois had more than a thousand people based in Silverstone, England, along with those who travelled with the racing team to twenty or more Grand Prix circuits each year.

As Leigh began to outline the campaign concept and long-term vision for the new Alain Delamare Lifestyle line, Dahlia listened intently and made mental notes.

Camille was a rare entrepreneur who had made the leap from her kitchen table startup to a world-class multinational organization. As Parfums Dubois grew, it had also acquired a number of small fragrance brands and helped them grow into larger companies in the Dubois portfolio. Others brands had licensing deals, while still others were a joint venture arrangement. Camille had also arranged the acquisition of a chain of exclusive perfumeries in Europe to insure retail distribution, with a long range view of bringing the concept into the United States. The deal with Alain Delamare was a master license with broad and deep plans for the future that encompassed more than fragrance and men's skincare.

Leigh was discussing the long term vision and how the introductory campaign would set the tone for the business. "We envision Alain Delamare Lifestyle as a champion brand, where a man is the champion of his life. He's real and accessible, as comfortable in his ski chalet with his wife and children as he is in a boardroom half a world away. This is an aspirational statement for men who are dedicated to discerning the finest in life."

Dahlia nodded her approval to Leigh. This brand positioning fit well with the Dubois philosophy. A brief discussion followed about specifics of the photo shoot on Monday before Leigh continued.

"Above all, we appeal to a man of quality. A man who will pass down his knowledge of exceptional grooming, fitness, and style to his sons. Formula 1 represents the best of the best, the most innovative and cutting-edge racing in the world. Every time Alain Delamare steps onto the track, he is determined to make history. Formula 1 is an exclusive family of only eleven teams, a family that cuts across borders and languages to pursue the common goal of excellence in motorsports."

Leigh paused to take a breath and look around the room. "Alain Delamare is the gentleman of racing. Consumer tests reveal that he is perceived as a little aloof, so our challenge is to turn this into a mystique."

The gentleman of racing? Dahlia certainly wouldn't have described him that way.

George cleared his throat. "Leigh, don't you think this campaign positioning will alienate the average man? I'm all for sophistication, but let's talk profit. I would prefer a broader appeal and let's face it, there are a lot more average Joes out there to sell fancy smelling, high-priced stuff to. Look, if they're buying, we're selling." He laughed smoothly. "Doesn't take much to sweeten up rubbing alcohol, does it?"

Dahlia was appalled. He had just reduced their polished

brand heritage to drugstore swill. Her grandmother would be flabbergasted.

"This is a luxury brand and will be positioned accordingly," Leigh said coolly. "I appreciate your opinion, but we have conducted extensive research and we know consumer advertising. This campaign has already been approved, by Camille Dubois, as well as the Dubois board and marketing team. We have not approached this task lightly."

Dahlia felt like applauding, but from George's dismissive expression, she sensed he wasn't finished making his point.

"As for Dahlia being part of the ad," George said, "this is a man's line. What business does she have in this campaign? I mean, I wouldn't buy a cologne from her." He looked around the table and laughed. Pointing to other men, he added, "Would you? Or you?"

Leigh's tone turned icy. "The ad will be shot on Monday as it is planned. If there are any changes, we will be happy to oblige, but in the absence of instructions from our pre-established contact and written approval, we will proceed as per our agreement."

George stood up. "If your point of contact is Camille Dubois, then you should know that she stroked out and she's in the hospital. Right now the board is meeting to determine interim leadership." A superior grin flashed across his too-perfect features. "So you see, we may be continuing this conversation shortly."

George stepped away from the table and strode to the door.

After he had gone, people turned anxiously toward Leigh. "We will proceed as agreed unless we receive other instructions," she said in a calm voice. "In the meantime, familiarize yourselves with Monday's schedule." She rose, signaling the end of the meeting. "Thank you all for coming. I trust that whatever is discussed in this room will not leave this room."

Dahlia thought about Camille and her health. Should she trouble her with George's behavior? On second thought, she had been engaged to oversee the campaign, so that's exactly what she would do. George could jump into the Mediterranean for all she cared.

Before she left, Dahlia thanked Leigh. "I'm sure the campaign will be spectacular and I'm looking forward to the photo shoot."

Leigh motioned to her to follow her into a private study. Closing the door, she sighed. "You're a class act, just like your grandmother. But why is that vile man becoming involved at this late date?"

Dahlia didn't know any more than Leigh did. "Rest assured, I'll get to the bottom of it. The photo shoot will go as planned."

"I've seen plenty of ambitious, ruthless men like him. Watch him. With Camille in the hospital, the company could be put into play."

A chill slithered down Dahlia's spine like a serpent's tongue, just as it had the first time she'd met him.

Leigh gave her a pointed look. "Just be aware."

18

DAHLIA STOOD CLUTCHING her phone in front of the long expanse of glass in the hotel suite. Camille had called to see how the meeting had gone.

After Dahlia made sure that Camille's health was still improving, she said, "I really enjoyed meeting Leigh. I can see why the two of you have had such a long relationship." Dahlia could just see the two women together, planning the campaigns that had helped catapult Parfums Dubois to the top of the bestselling charts.

"She's rock solid, Dahlia. Now, I just spoke to Sue and she told me the travel agent called her to confirm return flights for you... and George. Was he there?"

Trapped with a direct question, Dahlia had to respond. "Yes he was." She bit her lip to keep her anger from spilling out. She had wanted to give Camille a respite from her worries.

"Such impudence. Watch your back, Dahlia. He's trouble."

"I sensed that. Has he done anything specific that I should know about?"

Camille responded slowly with deliberate care. "He's very careful, mind you. But he's made small mistakes and careless comments. I believe he's working for someone who's planning a hostile takeover of the company."

Dahlia lowered herself onto the couch, stunned. "How can you be sure?"

"The truth will come out. It always does. I imagine he's using this opportunity—my being in the hospital, that is—to lay groundwork."

"But that would mean he has board support."

"Certain directors do support his work. But I'm more concerned about the ones who appear disinterested. They are the ones who are most dangerous, the most insidious."

Dahlia clenched her jaw, angry that people would take advantage of Camille's hospitalization to gain control of the company. Such greed and avariciousness—was it any wonder to her grandmother why she didn't want any part of it? Dahlia paused to compose herself. "What will you do?"

"I will wait. Sue is making observations and I want you to do the same. George is not as clever as he thinks. He will slip, and we will be ready."

Dahlia agreed and ended the call. Through the years she'd observed how people sometimes underestimated her grandmother. Although Camille carried herself regally, some saw only a woman of a certain age; they did not understand the keen intellectual fire that burned within her, nor did they recognize the razor-sharp strategic reasoning faculty she possessed. Camille had taught her that when opponents underestimated her, it gave her the advantage because they became careless. She'd watched her grandmother bide her time on countless occasions.

Dahlia leaned back on the sofa and laced her fingers behind her head, thinking. She realized now why George was here. An ad campaign centered on legacies would transmit to the world that she was the heir apparent to lead Parfums Dubois.

Camille was absolutely correct.

Dahlia wondered how far George would go to win his prize.

19

"THAT'S IT, MATE. Now lean over the railing, look to the left, chin up, and hold it."

Alain held the pose while the Australian photographer's camera whirred. Tiffany had scheduled journalist interviews in fifteen-minute time intervals on the team's enormous floating hospitality motorhome anchored in the bay. At this time in his motorsports career, he was as practiced in the art of striking a pose as he was in handling a sophisticated Formula 1 race car.

The photographer checked his digital screen. "That's it, mate, ta. This side was better without shadows from the sun. Thanks for moving."

"No problem, mate." Alain bumped the man's outstretched fist before moving on to the magazine's attractive young freckle-faced writer. In the background, a DJ played the latest French hits, adding to the party atmosphere on the boat.

Alain and the journalist sat down at the new table while

she fumbled with her recording device. Alain noticed her fingers were trembling. He hated that his presence sometimes made people nervous. In his mind he was still just a regular guy, though he did appreciate the opportunity to use his status to help others when he could.

"Here, I can help you with that." Alain picked up the miniature device and tapped a couple of buttons to turn it on. When he was satisfied it was recording, he said, "This is Alain Delamare in Monaco."

The woman's fair complexion reddened as she murmured her appreciation. In his younger days he might have asked the sunny young woman to the apartment he'd once kept in Monaco, but he was past that stage. He left that to other drivers on the circuit who were eager to indulge in the sweet spoils of fame. He was here to win and nothing would distract or dissuade him from his goal.

The young woman tucked her hair behind an ear and quickly regrouped. "So, what's it like being in the cockpit of a Formula 1 car?"

Alain leaned across the table. Staring into her eyes, he lowered his voice, spinning the story as he'd done so many times before. "Imagine that you're slithering into a cocoon. Your eye-line is at knee level. The cockpit is constructed around you and you're tightly constrained. You become one with the car, unable to move anything but your feet, hands, and arms. You're strapped into the seat with a six-point harness that's so tight you can crack a rib on a hairpin turn.

The helmet limits your visibility, so you must be alert to every movement, every shadow, every smell on the track and around you. At the starting line, the engines blast your eardrums and your adrenaline pumps. Your heart rate triples, blood pounds through your veins." He paused for effect. "It's the most intense and exhilarating feeling you can imagine."

The reporter gaped at him with wide eyes, mesmerized by his story. "I see," she said, sounding a little breathless. She jotted some notes and studied her list of questions. "How do you feel about the Monaco circuit?"

"It's the crown jewel of Formula 1 racing, the most challenging and demanding course there is. It's my favorite." He folded back the sleeves of his casual white linen shirt, exposing his tanned, muscular forearms. Gripping a steering wheel at the fastest speeds on four wheels kept his arms in shape.

"Will you win this year?"

"I intend to."

"That's awfully cocky, don't you think?"

"I intend to win every race I'm in." A movement caught his eye over the reporter's shoulder. He jerked his head up and his heart quickened. It was her. Dahlia. Was he destined to run into her everywhere?

Dahlia was sitting with her back to him, but he'd know the slope of her neck and the line of her shoulders anywhere. She wore a pale pink sundress that left her golden shoulders bare. He lifted his nose, detecting her perfume on the light sea breeze. *What a striking woman*, he thought, his gut tightening. Her memory had invaded his thoughts every day since they'd met.

Alain dragged his attention back to the young reporter. "Excuse me, do you have enough?"

Taking his cue, the woman shot a look at Tiffany, who was seated at the next table. "May I contact you if I need anything else?"

"Please do," Tiffany replied.

Alain thanked the journalist and rose when she got up to leave. Tiffany escorted her to the exit.

Staring at Dahlia, Alain rubbed his jaw in thought. He could ignore her, acknowledge her, or sit down and talk. Before a race, especially the Monaco race, he needed to keep his wits about him and remain focused. Maybe talking with her for a few minutes would alleviate the stress he felt whenever he saw her. He had to get her out of his mind. She couldn't possibly be as perfect as he'd imagined. Actually, she wasn't at all, though he'd found her anger incredibly attractive, too.

When Tiffany returned, Alain said, "That's the last interview, right?" He had been giving consecutive interviews for three hours, and he needed a break before he was scheduled to meet the fans. "I thought I'd say hello to Dahlia Dubois. I might have been a little rude when she stopped by the pit."

"Oh, you think?" Tiffany expressed a puff of air and

shook her head, but she looked relieved. "Go ahead, we have about twenty minutes before the fan event. I have to check on it, but I'll be back for you."

He stood to make his way to Dahlia's table. The Team Dubois floating hospitality center was outfitted with sleek chrome and glass. Anchored at the shoreline next to the Red Bull Refueling Station, the party boat's onboard guests could watch the race waterfront.

When Alain touched Dahlia's bare shoulder, a spark seemed to fly through his hand. "Hi, mind if I join you?"

She turned her face up to him, her vivid green eyes illuminated by the sun. She was bathed in a golden beam of sunlight, reddish glints sparkling in the black hair that tumbled down her back.

"Go ahead." She shrugged in a noncommittal fashion.

"What are you having?" Alain eased into the chair across from her.

"A citron pressé."

"It's the best. Reminds me of the homemade lemonade my mother used to make for us when we were kids." He raised a finger to a server and asked for the same.

Dahlia's unwavering gaze put him on edge. Maybe this wasn't such a good idea. "Look, I owe you an apology."

She waited, coolly appraising him while he fumbled for the right words to say.

Chastising himself for coming to talk to her, he scraped his teeth over his lower lip. "What I mean is... aw hell's bells, look, I'm sorry if I growled at you. That's what I came to say."

She started laughing. "Hell's bells? Where'd you get that phrase?"

Alain grinned, relieved at her laughter. "My grandma. That's as close as she ever got to swearing. If any of us spouted off with anything stronger, she'd wash out our mouths with soap."

Dahlia raised her brow. "She sounds like a stern soul."

"Guess she had to be to help my folks keep eight kids in line. Six of us were rowdy boys. My father loved motorsports and got us involved in karting—that's a type of junior racing—to keep us out of trouble. But we still caused plenty of trouble." He caught himself rambling, although he was beginning to relax around her.

Dahlia lifted her chin. "Is that where you get your tough guy attitude?"

From her accusatory tone, Alain couldn't tell if she was insulting him or teasing him. "I suppose so. We fought like hell between us, but we were always united if someone picked on any one of us." He chuckled as he thought about his brothers and sisters. They traveled to watch him race when they could, but they all had busy lives. They sent family news through his brother Jack when he was busy. The truth was, having Jack on the Formula 1 circuit helped keep him sane despite the crazy schedule and media circus.

A hint of a smile flickered on Dahlia's lips. She cast her

eyes down, sipping her citron pressé.

Alain reached across the table and touched her hand with his finger. "I meant it when I said I was sorry."

Dahlia raised her eyes to his. "Apology accepted. I realize you're under a lot of pressure. Since we have to work together, we might as well be on friendly terms."

"Thanks, that means a lot to me." Alain expressed a breath of relief. The tension that had knotted the muscles between his shoulder blades melted away.

Dahlia moistened her lips. "I don't think I properly thanked you for helping me return to the States when Camille had her stroke."

"I didn't know who you were at the time. Had I known you were Camille's granddaughter, I would have taken you to L.A. myself," Alain said earnestly. "I think the world of her. She's one smart, accomplished lady."

"Thank you. She's had a huge impact on my life."

"How is she doing?"

"She's improving, thank goodness. Still as determined and forceful as ever. The doctors say that most likely she'll continue to improve, given that she sought medical attention so soon after the stroke occurred."

"Give her my best when you speak to her. I'd like to visit her when I can."

"I'll tell her. She'd like that." Dahlia's face lit with kindness and sincerity.

The waiter served his citron pressé, and Alain was glad

he had an excuse to linger with her.

"I spoke to a few media people earlier, too, as the owner representative." Dahlia looked at him quizzically. "But they asked questions about the race that I couldn't answer. I'd really like to learn more about Formula 1. What makes the Monaco Grand Prix so challenging?"

"It's run on the street, of course, not on a proper track that's built for high speed racing."

"Is every track the same?"

"No, they're different. This race begins with a short, tight run to the first corner at Ste. Dévote, followed by a ninety degree turn. Imagine twenty cars racing to a bottleneck and you're already going about 150 miles per hour when you make the turn." Back in familiar territory now, Alain relaxed a little more in her presence.

"Tell me more." Dahlia propped her elbow on the table and cupped her chin, focusing her full attention on him.

She seemed intrigued, so Alain pressed on. "The Fairmont hairpin turn is tight, too. Watch that one during the race. It's tough to overtake there, but if you can, you do it."

"I've heard the tunnel is a problem."

He nodded. "That's true, the tunnel is risky. You go from broad daylight into darkness. You don't see much for a couple of seconds, which is an awfully long time in a Formula 1 car."

Dahlia seemed to take this in and consider it. "You really

have to maintain focus, don't you?"

"When I'm driving, I can't lose concentration for even a split second. Your sensory perception is magnified. Everything is flying at you and you have slivers of a second to react. It's two of the most intense hours you can imagine." He grinned. "And I love every second of it."

"I can see that."

Alain decided to risk veering off course. "Is there anything you're that passionate about?"

Inclining her head, she replied, "Perfumery. That's my first love. Perfume has the power to connect with the soul. Transforming emotion into an ephemeral scent is the perfumer's artistic alchemy." She inhaled deeply and nodded toward him. "Camille told me you had final approval on your signature fragrance." Her eyes twinkled. "You must like it. You're wearing it today."

He couldn't help himself; he watched her chest rise and fall. Forcing his eyes back to hers, he said, "You have a good nose." As if responding to a magnetic pull, he inched his fingers closer to hers. "What are you working on now?"

"Besides filling in for my grandmother, I have my own brand called Dahlia D. I'm also considering acquiring a lavender farm in Provence for a new skincare project."

"Busy woman. I like that." He saw Camille's influence on her, and he admired that. He'd met his share of heiresses who weren't interested in anything but partying their way through life, or spending their inheritances as fast as they could. Dahlia had depth and intelligence.

A smile spread slowly on Dahlia's face. "I'm glad we had this talk before the photo shoot on Monday. I have to admit I was dreading seeing you there."

Alain expelled a breath. "I really made a bad impression on you, didn't I?"

"We all have our bad days. Don't worry about it. Just go out there and do your best in the race. Then we'll have a good time on Monday."

"I don't race to do my best. I race to win." He gazed at her luminous eyes, her delicate features. He lowered his voice. "I like winning."

Dahlia demurely sipped her citron pressé. "So I would imagine."

From the corner of his eye, Alain saw a redhead in a tight dress heading directly for him, cocktail in hand. Just when he was getting on with Dahlia...

"You were amazing in the practice runs yesterday," the redhead cut in, gushing. She held out a hand. "I'm Ruby. Ruby Stone."

"Thanks. Glad you enjoyed watching." Alain shook her hand.

Ruby giggled. "Oh, I like to watch. Bet you do, too," she added in a provocative tone.

Alain saw Dahlia staring at the woman. "I appreciate your stopping by, Ruby, but we're in the middle of an important conversation. Would you mind giving us some privacy?"

Ruby pressed her hand to her fiery red lips. "Oh, I didn't notice, sorry."

"That's okay. Hope you have a good time this weekend."

"You know I will," Ruby said with a wink before strutting away on her stilettos.

"Sorry about that," Alain said, touching Dahlia's hand. There it was again, that electric spark between them. It was all he could do to keep from leaping across the table and sweeping her into his arms.

"No need to apologize." Dahlia laughed. "You managed that with grace. Does that happen often?"

"I'm afraid so. Comes with the job, but I do appreciate the fans. However, I want you to know that I'm quite discerning about who I choose to spend my time with." He held her gaze as his heart beat so loudly he imagined she could hear it.

"I see." She lowered her eyes.

Over Dahlia's shoulder, Alain saw Tiffany approaching. "I've really enjoyed talking to you, but I have to attend an event for fans. Would you like to come along?"

"Thanks, but I'm meeting a friend soon." She adjusted a thin strap that had slipped from her shoulder.

Alain watched her graceful motion, aching to help her. He could hardly bear to leave her. He had to see her again. *Soon.* "Are you free for dinner tonight?"

"No, I'm having dinner with one of our European

retailers."

Tiffany was pointing to her watch and nodding toward the door. Alain kept his focus on Dahlia. "Tomorrow we have practice and qualifying runs. I hope you'll stop by in the morning."

"Then all is forgiven?" Dahlia reached out and touched his hand as she spoke, her sparkling green eyes connecting with his.

Alain thrilled to this small contact she initiated. How had he thought that talking to her would alleviate his tension? But he didn't mind the feeling now. In fact, he felt energized. "Of course. And I'd really like to see you again."

"Then tomorrow it is."

20

THE NEXT MORNING Dahlia and Penelope dressed for the Paddock Club, where VIPs mingled and watched the racing. Dahlia chose a coral linen sundress with matching bracelets and earrings for a chic, summery look. Penelope opted for a lemon yellow dress that brought out the accents in her hair.

When Dahlia and Penelope entered the exclusive Paddock Club on the bay, Dahlia saw Alain with a small clutch of VIPs. As soon as he spotted her, he excused himself and strode toward her. Dahlia watched him, admiring the way he carried himself with the grace of an athlete. He was oblivious to the glances of wealthy fans who'd traveled from around the world to mingle at the most glamorous venue on the Formula 1 circuit.

"I hoped you'd come early," he said, greeting her with the customary kiss on each cheek.

"I wanted to wish you luck." Dahlia brushed her face against his in response. She noticed he lingered beside her a little longer than usual, lightly squeezing her shoulders. His breath was warm on her neck, and she caught the scent of his signature fragrance—a sensual mélange of fresh citrus with patchouli and oud wood—which blended so well with his natural masculine scent. She closed her eyes and drank in this heady aroma, certain that no other man would ever wear the fragrance as well as he did.

Alain drew his hands down her arms and clasped her hands, gazing at her with eyes that melted her will.

Dahlia heard Penelope clear her throat behind her. "Alain, I'd like you to meet a good friend, Penelope Plessen."

"The pleasure is mine," he said, greeting Penelope.

They spoke for a few minutes before Alain told them he had to go prepare for practice. Sliding his arm around her shoulders, he kissed Dahlia on the cheek.

After he left, Penelope tugged her arm. "I don't believe what I just witnessed. What happened while I was having a massage and facial yesterday? Clearly things have changed between you two. Last time I heard you talk about Alain, you were describing him as rude and uncouth."

Dahlia gazed after him. "He apologized for his behavior. He's under a great deal of stress."

"That must have been some apology." Penelope wagged her head in disbelief. "He's a hunk, that's for sure. But watch yourself, Miss Dreamy Eyes. You're not the only woman who's fallen for Alain Delamare. From what I hear, he's left a trail of broken hearts."

"I'm sure he has, but just for once let me live in the moment, Penelope. It's not as if we'll be eloping." She turned back to Penelope, remembering Ruby Stone, the woman who'd flung herself at Alain yesterday. "I know other women are crazy about him. He's a celebrity, and he has his choice of women falling at his feet. But I know there's a real man under the bravado. And I plan to enjoy his attention until I have to return home." There. She'd said it. And that was exactly what she planned to do, even though she hadn't realized it until this moment.

"Well, you go, girl," Penelope said, laughing. "What a change of heart."

"Maybe it's Monaco. Look around, everyone is having such a good time. I might as well join in." Dahlia winked at her and the two women shared a knowing smile before turning to check out the people nearby. "I love seeing how everyone is dressed. Fianna should be here, too."

"Well, well, look who I spy. Over there, almost behind that carved Indonesian folding screen." Penelope indicated a spot over Dahlia's shoulder. "You can see them better if you step over here by me."

When Dahlia turned, she could hardly believe what she saw. Lawrence Baxter and George Wilstead were standing slightly behind a folding screen that shielded the server's entry. They appeared to be having a heated conversation. "How about that?"

Penelope narrowed her eyes. "I don't think Baxter is

with the media."

Dahlia took out her phone and snapped a photo of the pair. Her mind whirred, considering the possibilities, none of which she liked. A slow anger grew within her. "Let's move on. I don't want them to know we've seen them together."

The practice runs were beginning, so Dahlia and Penelope sat down to a champagne brunch at a far table. Everyone was in a festive mood, and many people who knew Camille stopped by their table. Dahlia kept an eye out for George and Lawrence.

After they finished dining, Dahlia met the owner of the world's largest chain of duty free stores and spent time talking with him about the expansion of Parfums Dubois products in their airport locations. Penelope was soon swept into conversation with other models she had worked with over the years, comparing notes on designers they'd worked with in recent runway shows.

After Dahlia finished talking business, she turned her attention to the practice laps. As she watched Alain hurtling around the track, adrenaline coursed through her. She could only imagine how Alain felt. Her heart raced as he braked hard going into a corner, and she nearly dropped her glass when another car clipped his.

She wondered how the drivers' wives and families lived with the danger of the sport. Alain had told her that Formula 1 racing was much safer than it had been in years past. Still, accidents did happen, so she sent up a little prayer for the safety of all the drivers.

Dahlia was watching Alain when she heard a familiar voice by her side. Steeling herself, she turned. "Hello, George," she said in a pleasant manner that belied what she really thought of him. He was so sunburned he looked like he'd spent the remainder of the day before on a yacht. Lawrence had been sporting a dark tan, too.

"Dahlia, I've been trying to reach you. About the photo shoot on Monday—"

"We went over that at the meeting, and we came to an agreement. The campaign stays as it is."

"I don't agree. Look here, while we're at it, let's shoot some photos with Alain on his own. That will give us the most flexibility."

Dahlia raised her brow in dismissal of his idea. "That defeats the campaign message."

George wasn't one to give in. "When Camille returns, she can be photographed and Photoshopped into the layout."

Dahlia doubted that he wanted Camille in the ad either. He was saying this to placate her. Did he realize how transparent he was? Or did he care? "We won't have time. The shoot will probably take all day as it is."

George's mouth curved into a semblance of a smile, but it didn't reach his deadened eyes. "Leigh Percy is out of touch with consumers. She had her day, but we've got to stay on the cutting edge."

"Who have you been speaking to, George?" Dahlia's

tone turned icy. Camille was not going to like this.

His face reddened with anger. "I spoke to another ad man yesterday, and he had some valid points. It's not too late to make a change."

"It is and we're not." Dahlia was growing impatient with his games. "Don't ignore my question. Who are you talking to?" Besides Lawrence, she thought.

"Carson Phillips. He's young and hot, just what we need."

"And did you know he was fired by our largest competitor?" She and Camille had had a long discussion about Carson Phillips. Camille didn't trust him or the management at his advertising agency. This was too close to be a coincidence. Dahlia's intuition charged into overdrive. Corporate espionage was still thriving in the upper echelons. "You shouldn't be talking to him, George. Does the board know?"

"You can't give me orders," George bellowed, pointing his finger at Dahlia. "You're not running the company, Dahlia."

"And neither are you. You're way out of your league. You shouldn't have called Carson Phillips." Camille was going to be furious. From the corner of her eye, Dahlia noticed a security guard watching their heated exchange.

"He contacted *me*," George shot back. The veins in his forehead were bulging out.

"Lower your voice. I don't care if he sent an engraved

invitation by carrier pigeon. And I certainly hope you're not divulging confidential information about our advertising plans."

At that, George's face darkened. He narrowed his hooded eyes. "I'm warning you, stay out of my way or you'll regret it. The old lady is on her way out, and it's time for new talent to step in."

"Are you saying you're planning a takeover? A coup? I doubt you have the support or the guts to do it. And how dare you take advantage of Camille's *temporary* health situation to even think of staging such an underhanded move. You're despicable."

The security guard was making his way toward them.

George looked as though he wanted to strike her, but Dahlia stood her ground. She would not be intimidated, nor would she allow George's devious behavior to go unchecked.

"You're an imbecile. You have no idea who you're dealing with." George slammed his drink down and stormed away, rudely wedging his way through the crowd. People slid curious glances in her direction, while the large security guard strode after George.

Dahlia heard a commotion. Through a parting in the crowd, she spied George. The security guard was holding him by the arm and guiding him from the club.

"Good riddance," Dahlia muttered to herself. Searching the crowd, she spotted Lawrence hurrying after George. He was playing a part, too. She sighed in disgust. She hated to disturb Camille with more bad news, but she'd have to tell her about George and his activities. He was certainly trying to sabotage Camille.

"What happened?" Penelope returned, her eyes wide with curiosity. "I left you alone for two minutes and suddenly you're having a man removed from the Paddock Club."

"Actually, George accomplished that on his own." Dahlia told her what had happened.

For the next few hours they continued mingling with other VIP guests and watching the practice runs. Then the qualifying segments began.

During a break, Dahlia and Penelope left the Paddock Club to visit Pit Lane. Dahlia spotted Alain, who was busy speaking to fans and signing autographs. She admired his friendly, engaging manner with the fans. *He has such presence*, she thought. No wonder his fans loved him.

When Alain saw them, he cut through the throng of fans, beaming at Dahlia. "I'm so glad you came, but I'm afraid I won't have much time to talk," he said, putting his arm around her. "I hope you stay in the pit wall."

"We will, but we won't stay there long," Dahlia said, enjoying the feeling of his arm across her shoulders. The pit wall was a shaded area under an awning where the team managers and engineers had set up communications and computer monitoring equipment. "You all have a job to do and I don't want to interfere."

"You're not interfering." Alain's electric blue eyes were

mesmerizing, and they crinkled at the edges when he smiled at her. "I've been looking forward to seeing you."

Dahlia was pleased to hear his words. "Just keep your mind on the race," she said, tapping his chest. When she did, Alain caught her hand and brought it to his lips, kissing her fingertips. Heat gathered around Dahlia's neck.

"When I'm out there racing, that's all I can do." After another kiss on her cheek, he left to sign more autographs.

Penelope whispered to Dahlia. "He's definitely into you."

A little later, Dahlia and Penelope visited the pit wall and watched the qualifying runs from there for a while. The team owners often watched the race from the pit wall. Dahlia spoke to the chief racing strategist, engineers, and managers, and they were all pleased to meet her and share their insights on the cars and some of the strategy they were following. Afterward, Dahlia and Penelope returned to the Paddock Club to join the party with Penelope's friends.

At the end of the day, Dahlia was delighted that Alain finished fairly well in the qualifying rounds, although he'd had technical problems that placed him farther back in the starting grid than he probably wanted.

The next day dawned sunny and clear, perfect conditions for the arduous Monaco circuit. Most everyone in the crowd had turned out in glamorous style. Standing trackside by the starting grid, Dahlia could see celebrities, royalty, aristocrats, and motorsport enthusiasts. Everywhere she looked, bright advertising banners touted trappings of the good life: Chandon, Rolex, Heineken, and Emirates Air.

The drivers' track parade began just after noon, and the race would begin about an hour later. The truck carrying all the drivers snaked through the crowded raceway. As it approached, Dalia could see all the drivers dressed in their racing gear waving at the fans. She waved at Alain, and he blew her a kiss as the truck passed.

"All the drivers are so handsome," Penelope said. "But Alain is definitely the best-looking one." She quirked an eyebrow at Dahlia. "He sure likes you."

Dahlia watched Alain until he disappeared with the other drivers around a curve. The race hadn't started yet, but already her heart was pounding. "He's a lot different from what I expected a Formula 1 driver would be like."

Penelope turned to her with interest. "What did you think he'd be like?"

"Arrogant, egotistical, a real ladies' man. That's the way the media sometimes makes him sound. But he's not like that at all."

"You've been searching for him on the Internet, haven't you?"

Dahlia grinned. "So what if I have been? A woman has to do her research."

"Don't believe everything you read in the media. Tabloid journalists are always digging for the sensational story, even if it's not exactly true."

"Oh, I know that. A lot of service people sell false stories to tabloids, too. It's practically a profit center in L.A. Now even gardeners have to sign confidentiality statements." Dahlia shook her head, wondering if Camille had ever asked their groundskeeper or housekeeper to do that. "I don't want to live that way."

"It's a little late for that, girlfriend." Penelope slung her arm around Dahlia. "You are a Dubois."

"My grandmother made the choice about how she wanted to live. She's always worked hard and enjoyed the spotlight."

"You don't?"

"Not so much. I'm a creative at heart. I'd like a simpler life." Dahlia thought about the lavender farm in Provence and the type of life she would have there. But she liked this excitement, too.

The director of marketing for Parfums Dubois stopped by to talk to Dahlia about the race. Cynthia said, "If Alain wins or places, you'll be on the podium, too. The media will want to talk to you, especially as the granddaughter of a female owner. That's a great story angle." She crossed her fingers and grinned. "We want a lot of photos. Be ready for the cameras."

"I've been going over all your instructions. If one of our Team Dubois drivers make it to the Winner's podium, I'll be ready." Team Dubois had a driver for each of its two cars, but

Dahlia hoped that Alain would win.

She chatted a little longer with Cynthia, who still seemed on edge, though she appeared to be handling herself well. As Dahlia had suspected, George did not tell Cynthia he was coming to Monaco, and Cynthia had not been happy about it. She told her that he was condescending to her, which Dahlia could well imagine.

At last it was time for the drivers to line up. Alain had the fourth position in the starting grid behind the Mercedes team driver in the pole position. Ferrari, Red Bull Racing, and Williams were ahead of him.

Fans screamed out the names of their favorite drivers: *Alain, Lewis, Sebastian, Nico.* The engines were so loud that even with headphones on, Dahlia could still hear little else. The rumble vibrated around them, and Dahlia thought she'd never seen anything so exciting.

The starting light flashed and the drivers were off. Dahlia held her breath as she watched Alain accelerate, hurtling toward the first sharp turn. Her heart thumped, and she couldn't hear anything but the roar of the engines. The smell of burning rubber filled the air.

"Go, go, go!" Dahlia cheered Alain on, joined by Penelope and Cynthia.

Reaching speeds of 100 miles per hour on the short sprint, drivers jostled for position. Alain wedged his way in between two other cars to capture third position going around the curve.

Laughing, Dahlia and Penelope gave each other a high-five. Everyone around them was excited, too. With seventy-eight laps to go in the nearly two-hour race, Dahlia knew it was going to be an adrenaline-filled afternoon.

Pressing a hand to her chest as she caught her breath, Dahlia remembered what Alain had said about having to be hyper-focused on this challenging, dangerous track.

21

DAHLIA WAS DIZZY from watching the race. The whine of the engines was omnipresent, adding to the stress she felt watching the race. Yet it was exciting, and she could understand why Alain loved it. The chance to race among the best drivers in the world, alone on the track, was a heady feeling, she imagined. To be among the best in anything was such a feeling of accomplishment.

Having grown up in the shadow of Camille, Dahlia understood the mindset required to be the best. That was the way she felt about her talent, too. She wanted to create excellent perfumes that would stand the test of time. Though she didn't crave the enormous success that Camille had, she still wanted to perform at the highest level. In this way, she understood Alain's passion.

As she watched, a car lost control on a sharp turn and spun out, clipping another car. Everyone in the crowd gasped when the car crashed into the safety guardrails. Track marshals waved yellow caution flags around the track warning drivers of the danger and requiring them to maintain their positions, while the driver clambered from the damaged car to safety.

Nearly midway through the race, Alain pulled into the pit and Dahlia watched as the perfectly synchronized fourteen-member pit crew changed all four tires and had him back on the track in seconds. It was an amazing feat.

The announcers were calling the race over the loudspeakers. "Nico Rosberg finding clean air in the lead... strategy is everything... big on the steer... struggling a bit with a light wind... Delamare's tires lasted a bit better than expected... car has performance... unleashing it now."

Dahlia leaned in toward Penelope and asked, "What does *clean air* mean, I wonder?"

A silver-haired man behind them answered. "The cars are so fast that air coming off the back of cars is turbulent. Drivers try to avoid that by finding air that is not disturbed, or clean air. Turbulence affects the aerodynamics."

Dahlia looked back at him. "And the large wing on the back? What purpose does that serve?"

"Wings exert downforce, forcing the car into the ground so they can take corners faster."

The announcer continued. "Delamare is closing the gap... Hamilton locked a brake in a turn... who will be worthy of the win today?"

As the final lap began, the roar of the crowd reached a dizzying crescendo. During the race, Alain had dropped to sixth position, then moved up slowly to second position. Now he was battling for first position as the two cars careened around the track.

"Go, Alain, go!" Dahlia yelled. Penelope and Cynthia echoed her enthusiasm. They were at the finish line, where others had gathered, too. Between the thundering engines and the crowd's chants and screams, she could hardly hear anything else. Her pulse raced and she was glued to each turn. Giant screens placed around the track showed the action happening on the far side of the track.

And then the chequered flag came out, ready to wave the winner in. Alain and the Mercedes driver were locked in a race to the finish. Seconds crept by before the two cars rounded the last curve and sped toward the finish line.

The Mercedes pulled ahead slightly, sparks flying from its wheels and chassis. Dahlia could see Alain's helmet and hands on the wheel and she could almost feel his intensity. All around her, people cheered them on.

In the final seconds, Alain surged ahead and the chequered flag whipped in the wind. The announcers cried out, "Alain Delamare is the winner!"

Dahlia and Penelope flung their arms around each other. Alain slowed, and the pit crew ran out to congratulate him. The engineers and managers raced to meet him, too, though Dahlia hung back to let the team enjoy its win. The yachts in the Monaco harbor blew their horns, and all around her everyone was cheering and calling to Alain.

Alain was helped from the car and he removed his helmet. When he saw Dahlia, he raised his arms to wave and blew her a kiss. He motioned for her to join them, so she ran onto the track to join in the jubilant melee. Penelope and Cynthia followed close behind.

"Congratulations," Dahlia cried when she got close to Alain.

"This win was for you," he said, sweeping her into his arms.

Dahlia could hear the whir of cameras and people yelling for him to look this way or that, but he ignored them all as he kissed her on the lips. She could taste the salt in his kiss and feel the thrill that coursed through his body as he embraced her and lifted her off the ground. They were both laughing when he set her back down. Dahlia had never known such an exhilarating first kiss.

The celebration continued with the team members slapping him on the back. His record time had put the team in good standing. Soon he was swallowed by waves of well-wishers and media.

"That was a great shot," Cynthia said to Dahlia. "You know that's going to be plastered on social media around the world in two seconds."

Dahlia hadn't thought about that, but right now she didn't care who saw it. She was so happy for Alain, and for Camille, who was watching the race in the hospital. She'd call her as soon as she was in a place where she could hear her.

Finally, the winning drivers stepped onto the podium, framing Alain in the middle. The national anthems began to play in turn for the three drivers and teams. Alain raised his hands in a sign of victory to the cheering crowd that pressed toward the podium.

His Serene Highness Prince Albert of Monaco and Princess Charlene congratulated Alain and presented him with the Winner's trophy, which was designed in the shape of the racetrack. After the trophy presentations to the drivers and teams, enormous bottles of champagne were brought out.

"Watch this," Alain called out to Dahlia, winking at her. He shook the champagne and spewed it across his team members and fellow drivers, who also had bottles of their own.

Everyone was laughing and cheering. Dahlia was pushed into the crowd, where the media began to jostle for her attention. Cynthia stood beside her, ready to assist.

"Mademoiselle, Miss Dubois," the television announcers called out. "Are you pleased with Team Dubois? Where is Camille Dubois? How long have you and Alain Delamare been dating?"

The atmosphere was festive and celebratory. All the reporters were friendly, so Dahlia answered their questions easily, except for those who asked how long she and Alain had been dating. "We're not dating," she told them.

"But we all saw him kiss you," one female reporter

insisted. "It's the kiss seen 'round the world."

"We were just celebrating," Dahlia said, laughing. "Alain got caught up in the moment." Though she couldn't help but wonder what Camille would think, especially after her recent debacle with Kevin. Right now, all she wanted to do was celebrate Alain's win and give the team kudos.

"Watch out behind you!"

Dahlia screamed as Alain lightly sprayed her with champagne, then grabbed her and kissed her again. The crowd cheered them on, and someone passed champagne flutes to them. Alain poured two glasses and handed one to Dahlia, who flipped her damp hair over her shoulder.

Alain leaned over and whispered to her, "Come with me to the ball tonight. I have to give some interviews, but I'll call you and come for you later."

"I'd love that," she said.

Later, at the Hôtel de Paris, Dahlia relaxed in her warm, verbena-scented bubble bath, thinking about Alain. She was so happy for him and could hardly wait to see him this evening.

Popular French love songs blared through the suite. Penelope had put herself in charge of music.

Dahlia was glad that Fianna had insisted she bring more clothes Monaco, so she was prepared with a dress that she'd had designed. Dahlia knew Fianna would receive good press coverage, and she was pleased she could do that for her friend.

Feeling revived, Dahlia stepped from the bath and wrapped herself in a fluffy white bathrobe. She padded to her bedroom, sank into the soft, goose down duvet, and picked up her phone to call Camille.

"Dahlia, is that you?"

"Yes, did you watch the race?" She clutched the phone, relieved that Camille's voice sounded stronger. She'd been calling her twice a day since she'd arrived.

"Alain was magnificent," Camille said. "I'm so proud of him and the team. This is perfect timing for the launch and the advertising campaign. To win the Monaco Grand Prix is the highest Formula 1 achievement."

"And tomorrow we'll shoot the ad. Everything here is under control and the ad is going to be fabulous." As much as Dahlia had once been dreading the photo shoot, now she was looking forward to it.

The line was quiet for a few seconds. "Grand-mère, are you there?"

"I saw Alain kiss you after the win."

Dahlia swallowed. Camille's tone was distinctly different. Worried, even disapproving. "Yes, he did."

"What's going on between you?"

"Nothing, really. He was caught up in the excitement." It was too soon to tell her grandmother how she felt about Alain. She hardly knew herself. Other than the crazy tingle that raced over her skin every time she thought of him, that is.

"You must be very careful, dear. You're dealing with the international media and some of the tabloids in Europe are out for blood. Remember how they hounded Princess Diana?"

"I'm hardly in her league."

"I'm only cautioning you about how a relationship might be perceived in the media. Please don't do anything to jeopardize the launch."

Dahlia bristled at her grandmother's words. "I fully understand what's riding on this debut. I assure you that I will do nothing that might damage that."

Another pause. When Camille spoke again, her voice sounded softer. "Dear, I'm also worried about you. I know I was the one who suggested you meet Alain, but things seem to be moving awfully fast between you. I suppose that's acceptable these days, but please be careful about having a relationship that plays out in the media. It can be disastrous. Not only for the company, but for you, too. Your heart's been broken before."

Dahlia raked her teeth over her lower lip in thought. "I appreciate your concern, really I do." After a moment, she added. "I'll be careful."

After Dahlia hung up, she thought about what her grandmother had said. She and Alain had developed feelings for each other quickly. But then, what else should she expect from the fastest man in the world?

Penelope tapped on the door. "I can help you with your

hair and makeup after you dress."

"Come in," Dahlia said, glad that Penelope was with her.

Penelope was already dressed in a long, aqua-colored dress with a chunky aquamarine necklace at her throat.

"You look gorgeous," Dahlia said.

"It's a Dior gown I modeled for the spring collection. I fell in love with it and had to have it." She skimmed her hands over her narrow hips. "What are you wearing?"

"One of Fianna's latest designs. It's the ivory dress in the closet."

Penelope crossed the room and took the dress from the closet. "This is going to look amazing on you. It's the perfect shade to complement your skin tone and hair. What kind of accessories do you have?"

"Wait and see." Dahlia dried her hair.

When she was finished, Penelope studied her in the mirror. "Why don't you wear your hair up tonight? I can style it for you. And I'll do your makeup."

The two friends chatted while Penelope transformed Dahlia. Penelope knew the latest trends, and she worked with a deft hand. After a while, she said, "There, turn around and look."

Dahlia gazed into the mirror. "I feel like Cinderella going to the ball."

Penelope dabbed blush onto her brush, using it to contour Dahlia's face, accenting her fine bone structure. "I'll add a little gold and shimmery olive green to bring out your eyes even more."

Dahlia held her face still while Penelope worked her magic. Then she smoothed Dahlia's hair into a sleek style, which further accented her eyes.

Next came the bias-cut ivory dress suspended by thin twin straps and dipping to a V in the back. Dahlia added elongated canary-yellow diamond earrings and a matching bracelet she wound around her wrist. Not wanting to overdo her accessories, she left her neckline bare. Turning around to Penelope, she asked, "What do you think?"

"Elegant and tastefully sexy. Alain should be pleased."

"And he should be here any minute."

Dahlia paused on the red carpet on the way into the black tie gala, striking a pose for the media cameras as Cynthia had coached her to do. Alain held her close to him, offering friendly grins and chatting up the press people he knew on the circuit.

The reporters called out to him. "Who's your date, Alain?"

"Dahlia Dubois," Alain answered, pride evident in his voice. "She's part of Team Dubois."

Cameras whirred and flashes popped as Dahlia struck her poses with Alain. Blue spots floated in her field of vision, and she tried hard not to blink them away. In his custom-made tuxedo, Alain looked as he had the night he'd rescued her and helped her return to Los Angeles. Knowing him better now, he was even more attractive to her.

A reporter called out to Alain. "How'd you manage to win today, and what's next?"

Alain answered, saying, "Good strategy, good pit stop. Overall, timing was good. We'll continue to improve collectively as a team, and we'll keep pushing onward to Montreal."

More flashes popped in their eyes, and Dahlia finally blinked against the bright lights.

Noticing this, Alain said, "That's enough, thank you all." He gave a final wave to the crowd before they went inside.

He had an easy, respectful way about him that Dahlia liked. She glanced behind at Penelope, who was also posing for the red carpet media. They made their way into the ACM Ball hosted by the Automobile Club de Monaco and presided over by His Serene Highness Prince Albert and Princess Charlene.

When they stepped inside the Salle des Etoiles, Dahlia caught her breath. Tiny lights sparkled throughout, reflecting the brilliance of women's shimmering jewels and evening dresses. All the team drivers and VIPs were there mingling with celebrities from around the world. The gala was an international affair, and Dahlia caught snippets of French, Italian, German, Russian, and other languages rippling across the glamorous crowd.

Dahlia spotted Cynthia and George, who immediately

made their way toward them. "Hello Cynthia. What an amazing party. I hope you're taking full advantage of the evening."

"Indeed I am." Cynthia had wound her long chestnut hair into a braided chignon, and she wore a sleek, black lace dress. "I've made some important European media contacts that are interested in the new Alain Delamare line. I've arranged interviews for both of you tomorrow before and after the photo shoot. But I have to warn you, they all want to know about your relationship."

Dahlia and Alain looked at each other with raised brows. They barely knew each other, after all. Yet what Dahlia knew, she certainly liked. Finally she said, "Sounds like a long day."

"Then I'll have to put you to bed early tonight," Alain murmured to her.

"Hey, slow down. You're not on the racetrack anymore." Dahlia hadn't expected such a forward reaction from him. She took a step away from him.

Crestfallen, Alain immediately took her hands in his. "I only meant that I promise not to keep you out all night. These people party until dawn."

Dahlia had to laugh. He looked so injured. She realized she'd read more into his comment than he'd meant. Still, it wouldn't be a bad idea, just not yet, she promised herself. Camille's words rang in her ears. She was now standing on the world stage, and she'd have to watch herself.

A waiter offered champagne, so Alain took two glasses.

He gave one to her and raised his glass. "To the most beautiful woman in Monaco tonight. I'm a lucky man to have met you not once, but twice. After you flew away to Paris, I thought I'd never see you again." He gave her a sheepish grin. "I tried to find you through the hotel in Cannes, but they didn't have any Dahlias registered."

"I was staying with my ex-fiancé. I'm glad the universe conspired to bring us together again. My friend's grandmother would call this kismet."

They toasted to kismet, while other guests stopped to congratulate Alain on his victory. He posed good-naturedly for photos with everyone who asked and took countless selfies.

Everyone was in high spirits and having a wonderful time. In fact, Dahlia couldn't remember when she'd had so much fun. She was glad she'd stayed in Monaco and hadn't returned to Los Angeles before the race. Fortunately, Camille was recovering well, but she wished her grandmother could have been here, too. Now she could understand why Camille loved motorsports. It was exciting and attracted the most interesting people.

In listening to conversations, Dahlia learned that many people met their friends and business associates year after year in Monaco for the Grand Prix. Others followed the teams to different venues around the world. There were generations of racing enthusiasts, too. It was as if she'd been dropped into a large, extended family that thrived on excitement and traveling.

After a while, Dahlia and Alain were seated at places of honor while the Prince spoke of the history of Monaco and racing. After dinner, one of the top French recording artists took the stage to perform. When people began to dance, Alain took her hand and led her to the dance floor. He was as smooth on the dance floor as he was on the track. Dahlia felt cherished in his muscular arms.

True to Alain's word, he escorted her back to the Hôtel de Paris by midnight so they would both be fresh for their photo shoot at eight o'clock in the morning. He walked her to her suite and paused outside.

Encircling her with his arms, Alain nuzzled against her neck, dragging his lips across her décolletage and up her neck until he reached her lips. "You are the most exquisite woman I've ever met," he murmured before he kissed her.

Dahlia arched her neck to him and closed her eyes. It was the most passionate, loving kiss she'd ever known. It seemed as if their souls had merged into one. When their lips finally parted, Dahlia was left yearning for more.

Alain's eyes glowed with adoration for her. He kissed the tip of her nose and opened the door to her suite for her. "I'll see you right here in the morning," he said, his voice husky.

"With coffee, I hope." Dahlia moistened her lips, still tasting him there.

Alain's eyes sparkled with mischief. "And a lot more kisses."

Essence

22

"PLACES, EVERYONE," the photographer's assistant called out. "Let's try that pose again."

Alain took his place next to Dahlia, who was seated on a stool looking utterly delicious. It had taken all of his willpower to leave her at her hotel room last night. He could only imagine how good it would be waking up next to her sometime. But not yet. Dahlia was special, and he didn't want to do anything to endanger what they had.

"Hey, handsome," she whispered.

"Hey, gorgeous." They were keeping their relationship on a professional level. Alain could tell by the way the photographer grinned at him, he suspected there was more between them. The camera lens didn't lie.

He'd shot with this photographer before. Nils Andersen was a genius in capturing moods and subjects. He was one of the world's foremost photographers, having shot everyone from Pulitzer Prize to Academy Award winners.

While jazz music filled the air, people scurried around

adjusting lighting until Nils was satisfied. The makeup artist and hair stylist were on hand and alert to the hint of a shine on a face or a stray hair out of place.

While he waited, Alain rolled his shoulders and stretched his scapular muscles. He was accustomed to photo sessions for sponsors and media. But today, his body ached from the rigorous Formula 1 race. High engine heat, G-forces, and dehydration severely impacted the body. Drivers remained in top shape with extreme endurance training, along with reflex training and hand-eye coordination exercises.

"Just relax," Nils told them. "Have fun with this. I want to try different attitudes and lighting. You'll be haughty and sexy one moment, or laughing hysterically the next. Get loose, get out of yourself. Be the champions you both are."

Alain saw Dahlia expel a small breath. She seemed a little nervous, but she was still extremely professional. He admired the way she handled herself with such poise and presence. Now he understood why Camille had spoken so glowingly about her when they'd had lunch in New York.

Hot lights were trained on them. Alain ran a finger around the neck of the racing suit he wore, loosening the collar from his sore neck. "How are you doing, Dahlia?"

She smiled up at him from her perch on the stool. "I'm okay, but these lights are awfully hot." She blew on his neck to cool him down.

The photographer spoke to his assistant, and the young woman clapped her hands. "More air, please. Would someone turn on the air conditioner?"

Assistants rushed to adjust the air and lights, while a black-clad makeup artist powdered Dahlia's face again. The woman dipped her brush in a pot of lip gloss. Dahlia held her lips open while the makeup artist dabbed on a glossy finish with a fine brush.

Alain watched with interest. "You look absolutely sensational."

Dahlia could only wink in response. She was wearing a long, elegant dress in a sexy shade of platinum that she'd told him her friend Fianna had designed—who'd also designed the dress she'd worn last night. He needed to learn more about her and her life before they parted. Regrettably, that time would come far too soon.

Everyone was going about their jobs when a deeply tanned man in an expensive custom suit strode onto the set toward the photographer. "Mr. Andersen, I'd like a word with you."

"Damn, it's George again." Dahlia rolled her eyes.

Alain bent toward her. "Who's George?"

"Trouble," she answered. "He's the one they threw out of the Paddock Club."

Every head in the room swiveled. The assistant looked horrified at the intrusion.

Clearly irritated, Nils glanced at George. "I'm busy. Who are you and why are you here?"

George puffed out his chest with self-importance. "I'm

overseeing the Parfums Dubois advertising campaign." He surveyed the room, his gaze landing on Dahlia. "We need to make changes." He snapped his finger toward Dahlia. "You, out. We need Alain in these photos alone."

Alain placed his hand protectively on Dahlia's shoulder.

Cynthia charged toward George. "Absolutely not. We're firm on this." The vice president of marketing hurried toward them, too.

Nils threw his hands up in frustration. "What's going on here? I cannot work with these interruptions. Who's in charge?"

"I am." Dahlia strode toward George. She stood next to Cynthia and the other woman, the three of them united against him. "We've discussed this, George. This is the campaign that's been decided upon, and it's going forward."

George curled his lip. "The board will hear about this."

Dahlia put her hands on her hips. "Oh, I assure you they will. In fact, Camille can call an emergency meeting right now, even though it's after midnight in L.A. I'm sure they'd all be delighted to know that you're willfully interfering with a legally contracted activity." She lifted her chin in defiance. "And they're sure to have questions about your relationship with Lawrence Baxter, if that's his real name."

George's face reddened, and he let out a string of expletives.

Dahlia crossed her arms. "Leave now or I'll have security remove you. Again."

This was her fight, and Alain was secretly cheering her on. Men who bullied women disgusted him. However, George didn't move. Alain shook his head. Time for intervention.

"Hey, you heard the lady." Alain walked toward him. He could easily take this soft corporate guy, but that wasn't his style. *Still, if I have to...* He stopped inches from George's face. The man reeked of liquor, even at this hour. "Move on or I'll throw you out myself." He thumped him in the chest with the back of his hand.

George stumbled back, cursing. As he left, he shouted over his shoulder. "You're all going to regret this."

Cynthia, Tiffany, and the marketing team traded looks of disgust, while Nils turned back to his crew, clapping his hands. "The show is over. Let's get back to work."

"Thanks," Dahlia said to Alain as she repositioned herself on the stool. "That man is more than rude. He's trying to damage the business. But he's gone too far this time. I'm going to have an attorney review the terms of his consulting contract. Then I'm going to request that the board terminate him and consider filing a lawsuit against him."

"I'd hate to be on the other side of you," Alain said, grinning. "You fight smart."

She quirked her lips to one side. "I'm not the granddaughter of Camille Dubois for nothing. I will always protect my grandmother and what she's spent her life building, especially from despicable men like George

Wilstead."

What a woman. Alain beamed his approval as the makeup artist and stylist closed in on Dahlia again.

When Nils called for order, Alain hit his mark and the air conditioner blasted on. The photographer peered into his camera lens and went to work, calling out directions as the camera whirred under his expert touch.

Several hours later, after multiple wardrobe and set changes, Nils finally announced that he was satisfied. As the crew talked about where to go for cocktails, Alain pulled Dahlia aside.

"Want to ditch the party and go somewhere on our own?"

"I'd love to, but I made an arrangement to see someone after the shoot today." She blushed. "That was before, you know…"

"Before I apologized for being such a jerk?" He couldn't believe how he'd acted toward her, but now she'd given him a new reservoir of strength. "May I at least offer you a ride?" His driver and car waited outside.

"That would be nice, thanks." She hesitated a moment and then said, "You're welcome to come along. It's kind of personal, but I don't mind. In fact, I'd like you to be there."

"Where are we going, then?"

Dahlia curled a strand of hair around her finger in what Alain had quickly come to realize as a nervous gesture. "To see Father Renaud."

Alain chuckled and offered her his arm. "That's not quite what I'd expected, but I'm game." This was a woman full of mystery, and he intended to find out everything about her.

23

DAHLIA AND ALAIN sat at a round teakwood table with Father Renaud in his modestly furnished office. Clasping Alain's hand, Dahlia said, "Thank you for seeing us, Mon Père." She hoped he'd remember something about her parents.

The elderly priest steepled his fingers and leaned back in his chair. A crucifix hung on one wall, and a hint of incense spiced the air. A brilliantly colored parrot in a large cage in the corner chattered to himself, saying "Our father, our father. Who art in heaven. Amen. Awk, awk. Amen."

Alain grinned. "I've never seen a parrot that knows the Lord's Prayer."

Father Renaud chuckled. "He can probably lead mass as well as I can. Now, how might I help you?"

"I'm looking for my mother and father." Dahlia withdrew a large envelope from her tote and removed her record of birth from it. She gave it to the priest. "My mother's name is Laurel Dubois. It's there on the birth record. As I mentioned on the phone, she gave birth to me here in Monaco."

The priest studied it, passing a hand over his graying head. Finally, he raised his rheumy eyes. "I'm not sure I can be of much help."

Dahlia leaned forward in her chair. "Madame Martin from the hospital suggested I speak to you. My grandmother is a perfumer. Camille Dubois of Parfums Dubois."

"Perfume? I do recall something. Ah, yes." Stroking his chin in thought, Father Renaud's gaze settled on a point past them. He answered slowly. "That was many years ago, yet it seems like yesterday."

"Then you remember Laurel?" Dahlia held her breath as she awaited his reply. The ticking of the clock on the desk thundered in the interminable silence. Even the parrot fell silent, seemingly to await his master's reply.

Father Renaud studied Dahlia's face. At last, he said, "You favor her. She was a kind young woman."

"How did you know her?"

"She used to attend mass and confession, but she—." Father Renaud stopped himself from saying more.

Dahlia squeezed Alain's hand. She knew better than to ask the priest to divulge anything her mother might have said in confession. But what else might he recall? She moistened her lips. "Unfortunately, my mother disappeared two years after I was born, and she hasn't been heard from since. I'm hoping you might remember some details about her. Maybe even something that might help me find out what happened to her."

"Some things are better left alone, my child."

"Laurel is my mother, regardless of what she might have done. My grandmother raised me. She is quite ill. She had a stroke, and…" Dahlia's voice trailed off, and tears burned in her eyes. She lowered her eyes and blinked several times. What did she really wish to accomplish? If she could do anything for Camille right now, this would be it.

Alain stroked her hand, renewing her strength. Dahlia continued, "Father Renaud, I grew up without a mother or father—orphaned and illegitimate. But it was my grandmother who bore the heaviest burden. Laurel was her only daughter, her only child. To know what happened to Laurel would give her closure—good or bad. I realize my mother is probably dead, but my grandmother still holds out hope."

Father Renaud seemed to consider this. He picked up the birth certificate, adjusted his reading glasses, and ran his spidery veined fingers across the birth record. After a few moments, he peered at Dahlia over his half-rimmed glasses. "You have no idea who your father was?"

"No, I don't know. As you can see, the record states 'Unknown.'" Dahlia felt her throat constricting with nervousness. "But I would like to know who my father is, too."

"You ask many questions." Father Renaud looked at

Dahlia with a mixture of sorrow and curiosity. "But you must first ask yourself a question. Are you prepared to accept the truth? Once known, this new knowledge cannot become unlearned. What will you do with it?"

"I would like for my grandmother to see her daughter, and I would like to meet my parents. That's all. Nothing more, if that's the way they want it." It hurt her to think that her mother might shun her, but she had to know. Whatever happened, she would accept it.

The priest seemed to weigh her words for truth. "Parents are human and as such, may be given to sin. You must ask yourself that if you found the truth—and your parents—to be less than ideal in your estimation, could you find forgiveness in your heart for them?"

Dahlia drew an unsteady breath. She thought she could, but a seed of doubt sprouted in her mind. "I believe I could." She paused, her lips parted, and her gaze fell on the simple carved crucifix on the wall. "I will pray on this, Father, but I am ready to learn about my family, regardless of what I find."

Father Renaud took her hands and turned them over in his. "You have delicate hands, but they are capable and strong. As your heart must be."

Alain put his arm around Dahlia. "I promise to support her any way I can."

Father Renaud nodded to Alain and then turned back to Dahlia. "I must ask for guidance in this matter. Leave your telephone numbers. Give me a few days." He got up and shuffled to the birdcage. The parrot sidestepped on a bar to nuzzle the priest's finger through the cage.

"*Merci, mon Père,*" Dahlia said, as they wrote their phone numbers on a piece of paper. She and Alain rose to leave.

The priest turned and added, "Madame Dubois is a fine woman. When you speak to her, tell her I pray for her, too."

As they were leaving they heard the parrot call, "Amen, amen."

Dahlia and Alain stepped outside into the bright sunlight. All around them, workers in the principality were removing street barriers that had been erected for the Grand Prix. The grandstands were being dismantled, too.

"He knows something," Dahlia said, frowning. "What if he won't tell me?"

"Then we'll find another way. You deserve some answers."

"I've wondered for so many years." However, she hadn't expected what Father Renaud had to say. Why would she need strength to face the truth about her parents? "From what he implied, I might be very disappointed."

"Then it's your choice. I'll support you whatever you decide." Alain draped his arm around her shoulder and hugged her to his side. "For now, how about a massage and a casual supper? I'm pretty beat up from yesterday's race."

"I'd like that," Dahlia replied. "Penelope tells me the Hôtel de Paris has marvelous massages." A relaxing massage would help calm her racing mind. She had to be patient, at least until Father Renaud was blessed with the guidance he sought.

They slid into the back seat of Alain's car, the one that had taken her to the airport on her return to Los Angeles. Only this time, Alain held her hand. "We're going back to her hotel," he told his driver.

Dahlia tilted her head and gazed at him from beneath her lashes, a slow smile spreading on her face.

He caught her eye and leaned over, kissing her softly. "You have no idea how lonely I felt in this car after we drove you to the airport the day we met." He touched his lips to the palm of her hand. "I have two weeks until the next race in Montreal. I'd like to spend as much time together as we can."

"I would, too."

"Maybe you could come to Montreal." He trailed a finger along her cheek.

"Perhaps." Dahlia cherished his small gestures of affection. She had to be smart this time, but her heart was saying full speed ahead. The feeling she had about him was unlike any she'd had before. "Would you like to come with me tomorrow to look at a lavender farm in Provence? I'm considering buying it for a new skincare project I'm working on with a friend."

"A road trip into the country. I like the sound of that." Alain's smile creased the fine laugh lines around his eyes. "Now, about those massages. Let's call ahead."

Essence

24

ALAIN MANEUVERED HIS white McLaren roadster through the narrow twisting streets and tall buildings of Monaco on the same roads he'd rocketed through just a couple of days ago. After a massage and steam bath the evening before, he'd mostly recovered from the beating his body had taken during the Monaco Grand Prix.

Today he was looking forward to cruising through the French countryside to Provence with Dahlia. No other woman had ever affected him like she did, so he wanted to get to know her better. He might be on top in his career now, but it would not last forever.

Was Dahlia the one he could spend his life with? It was too soon to tell, but she seemed like a woman who could be a partner, not a trophy wife, although she was certainly attractive enough to be mistaken for one.

As he tapped on the door, Dahlia answered the door to her suite.

"Good morning," he said, taking her in his arms and

kissing her. He wanted her so much he could hardly stand it, but he wanted the time to be right. She was worth waiting for.

She was a stunning vision in a turquoise sundress with a thin gold and turquoise necklace and earrings to match. Her glossy black hair fell in soft waves around her shoulders, and the perfume he loved so much on her surrounded her like a magnificent aura.

When he released her, she laughed and said, "Now that's the kind of good morning I like." She looked so fresh and inviting, with a natural beauty that needed no make-up or skin-tight clothing to enhance it. She was the kind of woman who'd look just as good with a ponytail and blue jeans.

"Would you like some coffee before we go?" Dahlia motioned to a table near the terrace that held a silver coffee pot and croissants. "Help yourself. I'll get my purse."

"Good morning, Alain," Penelope called from the terrace. She stood in a thick terry cloth robe, her hair in a turban, cradling a cup of coffee.

"Hi Penelope. What are you up to today?" He poured a short cup of coffee.

"I'm joining a friend of my dad's on his yacht. It's a family gathering." She yawned. "I needed a break from the party scene. Too much champagne,"

Alain laughed. "You have to be in shape to keep up with Grand Prix week parties."

"I know. But great networking, too." Penelope folded

her arms and glared good-humoredly at him. "You'll take care of Dahlia today, won't you?"

"I'll do my best," he said, gulping his coffee.

"She's a special, genuine lady." Penelope peered around the corner to see if Dahlia was coming. "She just came out of a bad relationship, so don't hurt her."

"I understand. And I couldn't agree more." Alain was amused that Dahlia's friend was looking out for her, but it was sure nice to have friends like that.

Dahlia appeared behind him and slid her arms around him from behind. "Well, I'm glad you're in agreement about whatever."

After they left, Alain eased the sleek car along the scenic roads of rural France. The city fell away, and farmland spread out on either side of them.

"I thought you'd be a faster driver," Dahlia said.

"I get enough of that on the track. When I'm not racing, I like to take my time and enjoy the journey." He glanced at her. "Would you like to put the top down?"

"I'd like that a lot. It's a gorgeous day."

He pulled into a side road and eased to a stop. When he pushed a button the hardtop automatically retracted, leaving them open to the wide cerulean sky above. "How's that?"

"Perfect. Mmm, I smell nature…farms and livestock." She tilted her face up. "And the sun feels so good. We'll get our share of vitamin D today."

Laughing he said, "You're full of surprises."

"I have lots more." She teased him with a smile.

"I'll bet you do." He pulled out onto the main road, the light breeze lifting a few strands of her hair. She smoothed it back into place with a small, delicate hand.

He reached over and took her hand, kissing her fingers. "So tell me about this farmhouse and why you're considering it."

Dahlia's green eyes glowed with excitement. "It's an old farmhouse, but it's been renovated and enlarged. And it comes with quite a lot of land that's in active production of lavender. It's high-grade quality, which is perfect for a new skincare project I've been talking to a friend about. Verena's family has a legacy in skincare, so she'd manage the marketing and distribution while I'd source ingredients and oversee product development."

"You'd be willing to leave L.A.?" As he curved around a bend, a pasture with goats came into view.

"Part of the time, yes. My grandmother is there, and I have a close group of friends there as well. But I've always wanted to have a place to get away from it all. And I love Aix-en-Provence and the surrounding region."

Alain was pleased to hear this. "It's not far from Cannes. That's where I spend a lot of time, when I'm not on the road or visiting my family in San Diego."

"Really, San Diego?"

"That's right. My mother is from France, but my father is from San Diego. We spent a lot of time in both places.

Most of my family lives in southern California now, though we have a couple of other nomads like me. We're a big rowdy bunch, like the Kennedy clan on the west coast."

She turned slightly in her seat to face him. "I'd love to have a big family, but it's just me and my grandmother rambling around a large home. I've dreamed of having my own place, where I can have a laboratory to blend my perfume and watch things grow outside. But I also love to get dressed up and go out, so being close to Paris or Cannes or Monaco would be fun, too. And I'll have lots of room for friends to visit."

"Or for children someday?" He spoke lightly, but he wanted to hear her answer.

"Someday, I hope. I love children. But I'm not going to rush things." She smiled and added, "I've learned my lesson. I'm going to be patient next time around."

He squeezed her hand in approval, thinking about what Penelope had said.

They drove on for the next two hours enjoying the drive and chatting amiably about their goals and families, where they'd traveled, and where they still wanted to explore. They talked about what they wanted to accomplish in life, and Alain shared thoughts with her that he'd never told anyone else. She was a good listener, and he appreciated that. By the time they arrived at the farm in Pays d'Aix, the outlying area of Aix-en-Provence, Alain felt even closer to her.

Dahlia peered through the windshield. "Turn here."

Alain did, and expansive, purple-rowed lavender fields came into view. "What an amazing view." A rambling stone cottage anchored the property. Pink and white roses rested on a low wooden railing in front of the house. A middle-aged man stood on the front steps.

"This must be the place." Alain shut off the engine. "Is that the person you're to meet?"

"Yes, he's the probate attorney. The owner passed away, and the heirs are selling the farm. None of them wanted to run it or live here. The attorney is a friend of a friend, so that's how I learned of it. It's not really on the market yet."

Alain walked around to the passenger side of the car and opened her door, offering his hand to help her from the low slung car.

Accepting his hand, she swung out of the car. She breathed in deeply with her eyes closed. "I can smell the lavender from here."

She had such a lovely expression on her face. Alain cupped her face in his hands and touched her lips with his. "Welcome to Provence."

Dahlia shivered with a look of sheer delight. She grabbed his hand. "I can't wait. Let's go inside."

The attorney introduced himself as Claude Rouvier. "*Bienvenue*, welcome to La Maison de la Lavande."

Alain let Dahlia enter first and he followed behind, greeting the congenial man, who recognized him at once. "What a surprise, Monsieur Delamare. Congratulations on your victory in Monaco."

Alain thanked him, and Claude quickly replied, "Don't worry, we have many people who live quietly here, away from the prying eyes of paparazzi. You will enjoy the peace and tranquility here."

Dahlia looked at Alain and they both burst out laughing. Dahlia said, "Oh, but we're not really…"

"Not yet," Alain said with a wink.

Smiling, Dahlia pressed a hand to her mouth, feigning surprise, but her eyes sparkled with the light of a thousand stars.

"You make a lovely couple. I'm sure you'd be very happy here, whatever you choose." Claude waved his hand. "Let's have a look, shall we?"

Alain held Dahlia's hand as they meandered through the house. It was a charming country home with beamed ceilings, wooden floors, and white-washed walls. The kitchen had been enlarged and the appliances were modern stainless steel. Intricate hand-painted tile surrounded a fireplace in one corner.

"The tilework is lovely, and it looks original," Dahlia said, touching the antique tile. "They're in very good condition."

"They are original." Claude ran his finger along a grout line. "The owner wanted to keep as much of the original ambiance as possible. The pieces were removed one at a time, cleaned, and replaced with fresh grout."

"The kitchen is so inviting." Dahlia stopped to admire a long, wooden farmhouse-style table. "I can just imagine our friends and family gathering around this table."

Alain loved watching her explore the house. He imagined how relaxing it would be here for her and hoped he'd have a chance to share it with her someday. Though he was the kind of man who wanted to provide for a wife, too.

"Come see the bedrooms." Claude started upstairs and they followed. "There are several rooms that are ideal for guests...or children." He turned back to them, grinning with mischief.

Alain looked into the rooms. He chuckled and put his arm around Dahlia. "Yes, those look perfect, don't they, Dahlia?"

"They certainly do," she said, her face flushing.

Claude swung open a door. "And this is the large renovated bedroom I told you about. The owner added a luxurious spa bathroom."

Dahlia spun around in the bedroom, which was decorated with French antiques and creamy white linens. A fireplace flanked one wall. "This would be so cozy in the winter." Then she walked in to the bathroom and exclaimed. "Oh, this is so romantic."

Alain peeked around the corner. A tub large enough for two was positioned under a wide window framed with orchids of every hue. A separate rock-walled shower could also accommodate two. "Wow, this is amazing." He'd never had anything more than a bachelor home. His home built into the hillside of Cannes was small, but the large balcony and oversized garage he'd made served his single needs. However, this was a true home meant for a couple. A loving couple.

Claude was showing them how the rain shower feature in the ceiling above the shower worked when Alain's mobile phone rang. He pulled it from his pocket, but he didn't recognize the number in Monaco. Just as he was to send it to voicemail, he remembered they had given the old priest their phone numbers. "Excuse me, I need to take this." He stepped out onto the balcony and closed the French-paned door behind him.

"Hello?"

Father Renaud immediately asked, "Are you alone, my son?"

"Yes, I can talk."

The priest began haltingly. "I have prayed over this matter, and I feel instructed to share the information I have with Dahlia. I wanted to speak to you first so that you can prepare your lady friend. She will need you with her."

Alain thought Dahlia was strong enough to handle most anything on her own, but he was touched by the priest's concern for her. "What is it, Father?"

Father Renaud spoke in a grave tone. "I would like for both of you to be here tomorrow. I will tell you the details, as I know them, at that time."

"Can you tell me if her mother or father are still living?" Alain clutched the phone to his ear, hoping for Dahlia's sake that she would have the chance to meet them. He knew how much it meant to her.

"Her mother is alive and doing the Lord's work. Her father died last year." The priest hesitated before telling Alain her father's name.

When Alain heard the name, he sucked in a breath. "I, I understand." A chill swept through him.

Father Renaud continued in a world weary manner. "So I will see you both tomorrow, yes?"

Alain agreed and tapped off his phone. He remained rooted to the spot as he sought to make sense of what Father Renaud had told him. How would Dahlia take this? He ran a hand over his hair, trying to assimilate the news. Did Camille know? Is this why she had never told Dahlia about her parents? His hand slightly shaking, he shoved his phone back in his pocket and expelled a breath.

Alain turned, watching Dahlia through the glass door. She looked so happy, so pure. How could this be true? Now he understood why Father Renaud wanted him to be with her. He swallowed hard. More than anything, he had wanted this to be a perfect day for them. And it will be, he promised himself, masking his emotion. Dahlia deserved a day of happiness before what was to come. He turned the doorknob and stepped inside.

"We're going to see the lavender operation and fields

now," she said in a lilting voice. "Is everything okay?"

"Yes, yes, of course. Let's have a look at that lavender." There would be time later to tell her about their meeting tomorrow, once he was over the shock.

25

DAHLIA SAT BESIDE Alain and across from Father Renaud. Alain held her hand tightly. He had been so attentive to her this morning, protective even, in an odd way. Still, she was glad he was here with her. The familiar scent of incense still hung in the air.

"Awk, awk, amen," the parrot squawked. "Amen."

"Bless you, but hush." After Father Renaud admonished his parrot, he turned back to them. "My child," he began, his rheumy eyes focused on her. "I have prayed on this matter and I am guided to convey what I know to you. You are a strong young woman, and it is time you knew about your parents."

Dahlia pulled the large floral scarf she'd covered her bare shoulders with more tightly around her arms. She wore a white sleeveless sundress because they'd planned to go for another drive this afternoon, but Alain wouldn't tell her where they were going.

This was the moment she'd longed for, but now a

strange sense of foreboding filled her. For some reason, she almost dreaded the knowledge the old priest was about to impart to her. Why did she feel this way? Perhaps it was how Father Renaud spoke about secrets and strength, or maybe it was how Alain gripped her hand like he was clutching the steering wheel of a Formula 1 car.

Dahlia touched Alain's white-knuckled hand and smiled at him. "Easy there." His brow shot up in a silent apology, and he eased his iron grip. She lifted her face to the priest who'd known her mother and nodded with conviction. "Go on, I'm ready."

Father Renaud laid his hands palms down on the table. "I first met your mother when she was pregnant with you. Laurel came to me seeking sanctuary. She was a lovely young woman, so much like you in appearance. But she was very much afraid." He shook his graying head. "She had reason to be."

"Why? What had happened?" Dahlia leaned forward, anxious for him to share his story. However, she knew she must be patient and let him relate his story. To do otherwise would be disrespectful. She sat back and waited. The clock on the wall ticked loudly, measuring the seconds.

The old priest drew a breath. "Laurel was here attending university classes for a year and met your father at a party. Only later did she learn the truth about your father, but it was too late. He was not a good man, and she did not want to subject you to his influence. Or that of his family."

"You speak of them in the past tense. Are they no longer living?" For some reason, Dahlia couldn't bear to say the word *dead* about her mother. Not yet. Her heart pounded faster. Alain squeezed her hand, and she met his eyes. She was so thankful he was with her.

"Your father passed away last year. His name was Luigi Abandonato. He was the head of one of the deadliest crime families in Europe. In your country, you call these people mafia."

Dahlia sucked in a breath. She vaguely recognized the name from the European news broadcasts she'd heard over the years. Her head began to throb, and she pressed a finger to the pulsing vein in her temple.

A wistful smile turned up a corner of Father Renaud's thin mouth. "You were an impatient one. You arrived two months early in the middle of the night. I was the one who called your grandmother."

Dahlia noticed the slight deviation from Camille's story, wherein her mother was the one who'd called. Had Camille purposefully edited the story? The room grew warmer and wavered around her. She felt as if she were entering an alternate reality.

"Laurel and her mother left when you were strong enough to travel. I did not hear from them for two years, so I assumed all was well." The priest's hand trembled as he swept it across his mouth.

"And then Luigi was arrested for a murder he'd

committed while they were dating. Your mother was called to testify against him in the case. If she refused, she would be charged as an accessory. So she came. Alone. Laurel told me she wanted her mother to stay with you."

Dahlia began to piece the events together. "That's when she disappeared. So my grandmother must have known."

"Perhaps not at the time. She did not tell me when she first returned. I did not know of Laurel's plight until after her accident." Father Renaud sighed, but went on. "Before Laurel's testimony, she received an urgent note from a school friend to meet her. Laurel was driving a car she had rented. When she came to a road closure, she followed the signs. But she was too late to stop and the car crashed down a hillside, exploding on impact. She was presumed dead."

"Presumed?"

"Actually, she was thrown free into a thicket of bushes. From where she was, she recognized the men who stood on the edge of the hillside above her, laughing among themselves as the car burned. She waited hours until she crawled away and called me for help. It was not safe for her to return, so I called a trusted person who had a great deal of authority. Your mother was immediately taken into custody for her protection."

Dahlia pressed a hand to her face. "Protection? I don't understand."

"She gave valuable information about Luigi and others, so she had to be protected. You must understand, threats had been made not only against Laurel, but also her family. Against you and your grandmother. And so it was determined that Laurel should be presumed dead. A death certificate was issued and you and Camille were safe, just as she wanted. After that, Laurel was given a new identity and warned not to contact her family."

"She never did. At least, not to my knowledge." Dahlia thought about the risk her mother had taken to protect her and Camille. Picturing herself in such a position, she could now appreciate what her mother had done out of love and protection, however difficult it had been.

As Dahlia considered this, fragmented memories came rushing back. Surely her grandmother had known something about her father. "My grandmother had bought a large, secluded home when my mother returned with me. We still live there. It's surrounded by a high wall and an electric fence. When I was young, we even had armed security guards. I once asked my grandmother about them, and she told me that when *Forbes* published her net worth, she'd become concerned about safety. But now, I question whether that was the real reason." She bowed her head. "My mother paid a steep price to ensure our safety." Her prior resentment toward her mother dissolved, replaced by compassion for what she'd endured.

"Because of her courage, many evil men were put into prison, including your father. He still continued to run his organization and give orders from prison, so Laurel had to remain in hiding." The priest paused, his eyes glistening. "Now that Luigi is dead, Laurel would like very much to see you."

"Oh, she's alive!" Dahlia turned into Alain's arms, collapsing and sobbing with relief after a lifetime of questions. He supported her in strong arms, rubbing her back and wiping her tears with his handkerchief. A jumble of questions raced through her mind. Did Camille know?

Wiping tears from her face, Dahlia said, "My mother gave me up to protect me. I'd like very much to see her."

"I'm glad you can forgive her, my child." Father Renaud beamed through his own tears. "She is waiting for you on Malta."

"There it is." Dahlia stood at the edge of a grave, a chill wind blowing against her back. As the sun dipped behind the clouds, Alain held her closer. She stared at a flat marker on the dusty hilltop. Here was her father. An evil man, a murderer devoid of compassion, even for his own child. Her stomach twisted in revulsion.

Alain put his arm around her, and she rested her head on his shoulder. "I thought you might want to see where he was buried," he said. "Get some closure."

"Or spit on his grave." Dahlia had no tears for her father. "He threatened to kill me and my grandmother. What kind of man would kill his own child?" She kicked a rock onto the marker, and it clanged against the metal. "He deprived me of my mother and her of her only child. I hope he rots in hell."

"I'm sure he is." Alain kissed the top of her head. "Ready to go?"

Dahlia nodded, and they made their way back to his car. She was so grateful Alain had been with her today.

The sun peeked from behind the clouds as they drove back to the hotel. They talked about her mother and the instructions Father Renaud had given them to find her.

Alain looked over at her. "We can take my plane to Malta tomorrow."

"I remember that plane." Dahlia drummed her fingers on the center console. "During my private flight to Paris, I asked the pilot and flight attendant who owned the plane. They told me it was ADR, Inc."

"Did they now?" He flashed a smile at her.

"I looked that up on the Internet and found a medical company with those initials, so I thought you were a corporate executive."

"Actually, I am."

Looking at him from the corner of her eye, she said, "ADR... I'll bet that stands for Alain Delamare Racing, doesn't it?"

"Sure does." Alain turned into the hotel. "I'll give my pilot notice today so we can travel in the morning."

"I'd like that." Feeling a measure of relief, she gazed from the window across the vast Mediterranean Sea. Somewhere out there was her mother. And she would meet her tomorrow.

Dahlia and Alain went to a casual café for a light supper before returning to the hotel. When they returned to the suite, Dahlia asked him in and they sat in the living area.

"I have to call my grandmother," Dahlia said. "Would you mind waiting?"

"Not at all." Alain leaned back against the sofa, stretching his arms along the top. "Are you going to tell her you found your mother?"

Dahlia took her phone from her purse. "Not yet. I want to see how she's doing. This could be a shock to her. Besides, I'd rather tell her in person."

Dahlia stepped outside onto the terrace and dialed Camille's cell number. When her grandmother answered, she asked her how she felt.

"Feeling much better." Camille's voice sounded stronger. "I won't be in the hospital much longer. When the doctor makes his rounds in the morning, he'll tell me whether I can leave. Of course, I've already told him I plan to."

Dahlia smiled to herself. That was the Camille she knew. She had to stall for time to see her mother. "That's good news, but I'm not sure I can get a flight back that soon."

"Don't worry, Cynthia will be back at the office tomorrow. She said the photo shoot went well. Have you seen any more of Alain?"

"We had supper tonight." Which technically

correct. Dahlia turned and a seagull landed on the railing. "Shoo, shoo." She waved her hands at the large, smelly white bird.

"Don't tell me you're shooing him away." Camille sounded mildly alarmed. "What's going on there?"

The seagull shuffled aside and then lifted off, flapping its great wings, only to land on a neighboring terrace farther down. "A seagull landed on the terrace. It's gone now."

"Stay a little longer. The Memorial Day weekend is coming up anyway. You should take the opportunity to get to know Alain."

"Okay, I'll try." Dahlia paused. "I visited the hospital where I was born."

The line was silent for a few seconds. "You did?"

"It's just a hospital, really." She tried to sound nonchalant. "Still, it was interesting."

They spoke a little longer before Dahlia hung up. She gazed out at the sea, trying to sort out the questions racing though her mind. *How much did Camille know?* And, if Camille had kept this information from her all these years, how did she feel about this now? Could she forgive her grandmother? She sighed. She didn't have the answers. Not tonight, anyway. A sudden weariness overtook her. Stretching and yawning, she heard Alain behind her.

"I thought you could use this." Alain handed her a crystal snifter.

Dahlia raised the glass to her nose and drank in the rich

bouquet. "Cognac. Hennessy. XO, if I'm not mistaken."

Alain whistled. "That's a damned fine nose you have there."

"It's also my favorite." She lifted the glass to her lips and drank, enjoying the fiery sensation in her chest as the cognac flowed through her. "I have a favor to ask of you."

He leaned against the doorjamb. The light from inside formed a halo effect around his head. Lifting a hand, he stroked her arm. "Anything, just ask."

Warming to his touch, she turned into his muscular embrace. "Today has been emotionally exhausting. Will you stay with me?"

He caught his breath, and she quickly added, "I'd like for you to just hold me. I'm not really ready for—"

"I know," he murmured, finding her lips.

26

DAHLIA AWOKE TO find herself cradled in Alain's arms. She wore black silk pajamas, while his torso and legs were bare except for his underwear. She snuggled into his broad arms, his steady breath warming her neck.

The night before they'd left the exterior door open to listen to the lapping waves and distant foghorns. The air breezing in from the ocean was cool, and birds chirped their morning song. While he was still sleeping, she drew her leg along his, surreptitiously exploring his body under the duvet covers. His frame was lean, his muscles long and well-defined. He had the body of a thoroughbred built for speed. The more she explored, the more delighted she was that he was sharing her bed.

After a few blissful minutes, Alain stirred, tightening his hold on her. "You'd better watch out," he murmured, his deep voice rumbling against her back. "If you keep that up, you'll be sorry. Or not," he added in an enticing voice.

Dahlia paused with her leg entwined with his. "I didn't

know you were awake."

"I was asleep, not dead." He'd kept his promise to her, holding her throughout the night when her emotions had overwhelmed her.

She couldn't stop thinking about the story Father Renaud had told her. She had a real, live mother. *A mother.* After all these years.

And they were on their way to meet her today in Malta. What would she say to her?

Dahlia turned in Alain's arms to face him. "Thank you for staying with me last night. And for not pressuring me to make love yet."

He opened a sleepy eye, revealing a slit of ocean blue. "That's the first time I've ever been thanked for *not* making passionate love to a woman. I must be losing my touch."

She brushed her lips against his, lingering. "Not a chance."

At that, he whipped the covers off. "That's it. If we stay here any longer, we'll never leave and you'll be in for a big surprise."

Dahlia screamed playfully. "Hey, it's chilly in here."

Alain shoved off the bed and made his way to the closet. He returned with two robes and wrapped her in one of them. "Never let it be said that I don't take care of a woman."

Dahlia watched him put on his robe. That handsome body, the long muscular legs and narrow hips, the chest that broadened out in all the right places—all those well-proportioned parts were being swathed in terry cloth. She sighed with regret and belted her robe. Now was not the time for the thoughts he'd brought to the surface in her.

"What will you wear?" she asked as she was choosing her clothes for their trip to Malta. "You don't have anything with you."

He grinned. "I always keep extra clothing and toiletries on the plane."

"Smart man." She decided on a pressed white blouse and black jeans with woven loafers for comfort. "That's life in the fast lane, I guess."

Alain grabbed her from behind, lifting her from the ground and kissing her neck. "Do you know how many times I've heard that old line? Never, ever say that to me again."

"Or what?" She laughed, kicking her feet in mock consternation against his shins.

They fell onto the bed and Alain rolled on top of her, holding himself above her. As his face grew serious, he stopped laughing. "Miss Dubois, do you have any idea what you're doing to me?"

She lay pinned under him, staring up into the most handsome face she could ever recall. "I hope it's along the line of what you're doing to me."

He bent toward her, nuzzling her neck and burying his stubbly face in her thick hair. All at once, he rolled over, bringing her on top of him. "We have got to stop this. We'll miss the flight."

She teased his lips with her tongue. "Isn't it your plane, Mr. ADR?"

"There's a flight plan that's been filed. I like to stick to it." He picked her up and put her on her feet. "And you're making it awfully hard to keep my promise to you."

She turned around and plucked her clothes from the closet. As she was walking to the bathroom, she paused by the door and glanced over her shoulder. "Then we might have to amend the terms of that promise someday."

Before the plane lifted off, the flight attendant brought Dahlia and Alain coffee and croissants, along with thick Greek yogurt, ripe red strawberries, and soft boiled eggs. Dahlia ate sparingly; she was too nervous to enjoy the warm, buttery croissants.

Alain gave her a quick kiss. "I'm going to freshen up and change. Relax and try to eat something. It's going to be a long day."

He disappeared into the lavatory and Dahlia eased back in the same beige leather seat she'd sat in on the way the Paris. She smoothed her fingers across the cabin wall's burl wood trim, thinking about what was in store for her in Malta. Was her mother as nervous as she was? Dahlia wondered what her mother expected in terms of a future relationship.

A troubling thought struck her. What if her mother hadn't wanted to be found and was only seeing her out of courtesy or curiosity?

Her mother had been living on her own under a different identity for more than twenty years. Did she have another family? And would she want to see Camille?

Dahlia came to the conclusion that she really had no choice but to accept whatever terms her mother proposed. Still, she hoped Laurel would agree to see Camille. She closed her eyes, recalling the photos of her mother that she'd seared into her memory. She wondered how much her mother had changed before she drifted to sleep.

Sometime later, she woke to Alain gently rubbing her arm. "Time to wake up, we're almost there. Custom officials will be coming on board after we land."

Blinking, Dahlia sat up. "You changed," she said. He'd shaved, too. He was dressed in gray slacks and an open collar dress shirt. A herringbone sport coat hung on a hook next to his seat. "I like your style."

"I thought I should look nice to meet your mother." He tugged his French cuffs, checking his discreet black ebony cufflinks.

They flew across the high rocky coastline of Malta and landed in an arid region. After they'd answered the custom official's questions and had been cleared to enter the country, they made their way to a car Alain had hired.

As they wove through the Maltese countryside, Dahlia gazed out over modern homes and low-rise buildings. She spotted older homes and stone churches that must have been a few centuries old. Once they reached the town, the driver slowed, looking for the address.

"We have arrived," the driver said, parking near an older building that had paint peeling from the rafters.

Dahlia checked the address that Father Renaud had given her. They were at the right place. It looked like a private school. Young children played on a playground filled with older, makeshift equipment. The children wore pressed uniforms, but their clothes looked faded.

Slowly Dahlia got out of the car. Her stomach tightened, and her mouth felt dry. This was the moment she'd longed for, but she was as nervous as a Chihuahua at a fireworks show.

They went inside. A receptionist at a nondescript desk with an ancient typewriter looked up. "May I help you?"

"We're here to see..." Dahlia faltered, stumbling over her mother's new name.

Alain spoke up. "Marie Brittain."

"Oh, are you family? You favor her so much," the woman said.

"No," Dahlia managed to say. She hadn't been prepared for questions, even from a friendly, chatty receptionist. Then she remembered what Father Renaud had told them to say. "Tell her it's the Johnsons from an American charity. We spoke earlier."

"I see." The woman picked up the phone and punched an intercom button. "Marie, you have a couple to see you from an American charity. May I send them back?" The woman hung up and smiled. "It's lunch and play time for the children, so she has time to speak to you."

The woman led them down a hallway. Crayon artwork lined the walls, and the sound of children's laughter rang through the open windows.

They stepped into a small office decorated with photos of older children and young adults. Former students, Dahlia surmised. A trim, neat woman stood in front of the desk, her hands tightly clasped in front of her. She was a youthful-looking woman of about fifty.

Alain closed the door behind them.

Looking for signs to confirm their genetic relationship, Dahlia noted Laurel's appearance—no, her name was now *Marie*, she reminded herself. Her mother was dark-haired and her petite stature was similar to Dahlia's. She had the same high cheekbones, which gave her face mature sophistication. Her mother still looked as she did in the photographs, only older and wiser.

Dahlia stood rooted by the door, unsure of what to say. "Marie?"

The woman nodded and held her arms to her. "Dahlia."

Hesitating, Dahlia took a step toward her. Laurel met her, enfolding her in her arms.

"You've probably forgotten all about me," Laurel said, "but I'm so glad to see you." With tears welling in her eyes, Laurel ran her hand along Dahlia's face. "Can you ever forgive me?"

Dahlia found it difficult to speak. Blinking back her own tears, she said, "Father Renaud told us everything."

Laurel's eyes settled on Alain. "Is this your young man?"

Alain stepped forward and introduced himself.

"Please sit down." Laurel motioned to a table and chairs. She sat, still clasping Dahlia's hand. "I missed you so much. Leaving you was the hardest thing I've ever had to do. But you survived. You are alive."

"I missed you so much." Dahlia's voice wavered. She could hardly believe that after all these years she was actually talking to her mother. In light of Father Renaud's explanation, the anger she'd harbored against her mother for leaving was gone.

"I have prayed for you every day." Laurel clasped Dahlia's hands, running her fingers over them as a mother would a child's hands. "I'm so sorry. I hope you understand the decision I was forced to make."

"I do. It must have been so hard for you." Dahlia glanced around. The school was modest, as were Laurel's plain white shirt and navy skirt. She had clearly given up any inheritance she might have had.

Laurel followed Dahlia's gaze around the room. "When I first came to Malta, the Sisters sheltered me. In time, I began teaching the village children and found that I enjoyed helping them. Now, I run this school for underprivileged children." She nodded toward the photos on her walls. "We've had great success in elevating their learning skills.

Some have gone on to become doctors, engineers, and artists." She ran a thumb along Dahlia's hand. "But none of them could take the place of you."

So many questions burned in Dahlia's mind. "Did you ever marry or have other children?"

"No, my life was not really available for sharing. I was frightened for such a long time. More for you and Mom than for myself, though."

Mom. Dahlia had never heard Camille called that.

"I love you so much." Laurel wrapped her arms around Dahlia again. "I can't believe I'm finally holding you in my arms." Her voice cracked with tears of joy.

"I love you, too, Mom." It felt as though the part of her emotions reserved for her mother had been on ice and were now thawing. Underneath, her feelings were like new pink skin—tender, but destined to grow back.

Laurel dabbed her eyes. "How is your grandmother doing?"

Dahlia shot a questioning look at Alain, who nodded in response. *Tell her.* She turned back to Laurel. "You'd be so proud of all she's accomplished."

"I've followed her career," Laurel said, smiling. "Are you still living in the same grand house in Holmby Hills?"

"We are." Dahlia moistened her lips. "The reason I was in Monaco was that I came to take her place for business. You see, she had a stroke."

"Oh, no." Suddenly stricken, Laurel pressed a hand to

her mouth. "How bad is she?"

Touching her mother's arm to reassure her, Dahlia explained. "The doctors kept her in the hospital for rest and observation. Thankfully, she made remarkable progress and is being released today." She paused, a hopeful feeling welling up within her. "Do you think you could come to see her?"

Laurel furrowed her brow. "I have someone in the government already checking for me. That man—unfortunately, your father—never had any other children. All his brothers met with untimely deaths, too. I hope there is no one left to care about avenging my deeds, or me. But you never know." She clicked her tongue. "I couldn't endanger you or her. I never thought we'd ever meet again, so this day is a precious gift to me. I don't know if I dare hope for more."

A thought struck Dahlia and it saddened her. Would Laurel even want to visit? "You have a life you've built here. You must have friends, people who mean a lot to you now."

Laurel's face brightened. "The children needed me, and I needed them. While this was not the life I'd once imagined I'd have, it has been rewarding in many ways." She looked down at her hands. "I have been of service to others. Isn't that the best we can say in the end?"

Her mother sounded so resigned that Dahlia's heart ached for her. "But this is not the end. It's our new beginning," she said fervently.

However, Dahlia understood that Laurel had made the best of her situation. Malta had been her home for half of her life. She had become Marie. Perhaps she had left behind her true identity as Laurel forever.

"I have learned to live each day as it comes and not to expect too much." Laurel seemed philosophically reconciled to her life as it was. "The mistakes I made in my youth forever changed the course of my life. And yours. That is my deepest regret for which I pray you will forgive me."

"I already have." Dahlia grew silent, thinking about the mistake she'd nearly made with Kevin. She glanced at Alain, who was proving himself worthy of her love in so many ways. Would he break her heart, too? She wondered how a person knew for sure when love was real, or if it were possible to ever know. Even if love were present between two people, many other difficulties could destroy a relationship. Yet, many people built strong unions, finding love and laughter despite their difficulties. Although marriage might be a compromise between habit and desires, honesty and loyalty were nonnegotiable.

They talked a little more until the children began returning to class.

"I wish I could invite you to my home," Laurel said, rising from her chair. "But I'm afraid that my neighbors would ask about you. In my little village, the residents find strangers fascinating. They'd find a reason to knock on the door and then they'd want to learn all about you. I never have unknown visitors."

Alain nodded in agreement. "Until we learn if you're safe

now, we wouldn't want to raise suspicion or cause you harm."

"Thank you for understanding. It's for Dahlia's protection." Laurel ran a hand over Dahlia's hair and embraced her. "I'd never forgive myself if something happened to you."

"We'll see each other again, I promise." Dahlia pressed her lips against her mother's smooth cheek.

Laurel cradled Dahlia's face as if to memorize every feature. "If we can't, know that I will cherish this day as long as I live."

They said their tearful good-byes and left, but Dahlia vowed she would find a way for her grandmother to see her only daughter again.

27

THE PLANE THUDDED on the airstrip, waking Dahlia.

Alain was seated next to her. She had looked so peaceful while she slept, and he'd had to resist the urge to wake her with a kiss. "You had a nice nap. Do you always sleep on a plane?"

"When it's as comfortable as this." They were taxiing past other private planes on the airstrip.

Since he and Dahlia couldn't stay to talk with her mother, and they'd both spent time on Malta before, they'd decided to return.

Dahlia stretched like a panther, her glossy black hair flowing around her shoulders. "So what's this surprise you have planned this evening?"

Alain took her hand. "I hope you don't get seasick."

Her eyes widened with delight. "Are we going out on a boat?"

"My captain brought mine over from Cannes. I thought you might like to get away and relax before you return to the

261

States."

"I'd love that." She leaned over and kissed him. "Do you take it out often?"

"In the off-season and sometimes between races. I like to go out to sea and get lost. Really clears my head." He hoped she'd like it. Being on board his yacht was one of the pure getaways he had. The yacht had been a splurge, but he'd never regretted it.

By the time the sun was low in the sky, they were on board the *Formula Win*, Alain's sleek ninety-foot beauty. When Dahlia stepped on board, she exclaimed. "I love it. I could live here."

Secretly, Alain was pleased. That was just the reaction he'd hoped she'd have. Though he had a couple of vacation homes and a pied-à-terre in New York, this was the place he felt most at home. He could sail into any port or escape any time he wished. It was the ultimate floating fort. "Come on, I'll take you on a tour."

As the captain eased from the harbor, they roamed about the *Formula Win*. Alain showed her the lounging decks and hot tub, several staterooms and galley, and lounges with large screen televisions. He swung open a fine crafted wooden door. "And here is the master suite." The full beam cabin was outfitted in shades of white, taupe, and aquamarine. Light gleaming maple wood lined the walls. The entire effect was one of tasteful comfort.

He didn't broach the subject of which stateroom she

would choose. He decided to leave that to fate and let the lady have her way. Although he hoped she'd choose to stay with him.

Taking her in his arms, he said, "There's a bottle of champagne chilling on the upper deck, along with a light supper. If you'd like to change, we can relax in the hot tub and watch the sunset."

"Sounds yummy." Dahlia looked around. "Where is my bag?"

Alain had forgotten about that. "Ah, the crew might have put it in the dressing area." He walked around the corner and spotted her overnight bag. A crew member had indeed been too presumptuous. He hoped it wouldn't put her off. "Here it is. But if you'd like to change in another cabin—"

"No, this is fine."

He could hardly contain his relief. "Then I'll chat with the captain and be right back." He gave Dahlia her privacy.

When he returned, she was lounging in a chair waiting for him. He let out a low whistle. "You look like a gorgeous goddess of the sun." She wore tropical print bikini and sheer wide-legged cover-up pants. He quickly changed into his swimsuit, and then the two of them went above deck.

Dahlia tented her hand above her forehead against the sun's slanting rays. "I love the scent of the ocean." She inhaled deeply, filling her lungs.

Alain watched, glad she was enjoying herself. He had

asked for the champagne and supper to be put out for them. The small crew on board was very discreet, although Alain hadn't used the yacht for romantic interludes in a long time. The crew knew not to intrude on his privacy in the evening.

They slipped into the hot tub and leaned back against warm pulsating jets. "This feels wonderful," Dahlia murmured, reaching a hand to him. "I love everything about this evening."

He grinned as he handed her a glass of champagne. "Even me?"

"Especially you." She raised her glass to him.

"You have no idea how much I've wanted to hear you say that." Alain kissed her forehead, her nose, her lips, and then touched her glass with his. "I promise you an evening you'll never forget."

"Nor you." A mischievous smile played on Dahlia's lips. She cast her eyes down as she sipped the champagne.

"What am I going to do with you?" There was more truth in that line than he cared to admit. His lifestyle wasn't the most conducive to relationships. He'd dated plenty of great women—from actresses and models to heiresses and self-made business women. Most of them tired of his nomadic, peripatetic work schedule—one week here, two weeks there.

But here was a fine woman who was everything he'd dreamed of—and more. His feelings for her were deeper than he'd ever imagined. He thought they had a real chance of making a go of it. His playboy era was behind him. Ultimately he wanted a life and family like his parents had created.

"I have another surprise for you," he said, reaching for something tucked into the silver ice bucket. "Turn around and close your eyes."

"What for?" When he gave her a stern look, she laughed and did as he asked.

Alain reached into a small pouch and withdrew a diamond-and-emerald encrusted platinum necklace fashioned in the shape of two entwined hearts. It was an original piece styled by one of Monaco's most talented jewelry designers. He'd been fortunate to find a stunning piece that also had meaning to him. Draped it around her neck he said, "I thought this would go with your eyes. Open them."

When Dahlia opened her eyes and looked down at the double hearts—one rendered in diamonds, the other in emeralds—she gasped. "Why, this is exquisite. Oh Alain, you shouldn't have, but I adore it. And I adore you, too." She threw her arms around him, smothering him with kisses. He couldn't have been more pleased by her reaction.

Alain and Dahlia held each other, watching as the sun kissed the horizon, casting fiery hues of plum and magenta across the waves. As twilight encroached, the lights of Monaco sparkled across the bay, illuminating the mountains that rose behind it. The glittering principality grew smaller as the sleek yacht glided across the water, leaving the complexities of the world behind.

Their bodies feeling warm and supple, Alain and Dahlia left the hot tub and slipped under a light-weight down throw on one of the pillow-strewn lounge beds on deck. High above them, stars shimmered against the velvet night sky.

"My onboard chef is quite good," Alain said, lifting a silver dome from a platter on a low table beside them. "This is one of his specialties. Seared foie gras in a cognac reduction sauce with crystalized walnuts and poached apples and pears." He lifted a forkful to Dahlia's lips, and she moaned with pleasure.

"That's delicious." In turn, Dahlia put a thin, crispy slice of toasted nut bread spread with creamy Camembert cheese into Alain's mouth and then licked her fingers.

Alain was mesmerized by her every movement.

"What else do we have?" Dahlia leaned over him and as she did, loose strands of hair from her thick bun trailed across his chest. He caught a whiff of the perfume he loved in her hair.

He shook himself from his trance. "We have an assortment. There are marcona almonds in olive oil and sea salt, steamed artichokes with herb sauce, chilled shrimp with mango and avocado chutney, fire roasted squab, and seafood paella with the chef's special saffron blend."

"That's quite a menu.' Dahlia's eyes shone like emerald orbs in the glow of a rising full moon. "Sounds like you come here often."

"Every chance I get. I'm awfully glad you like it, too." Alain positioned pillows in back of them and Dahlia rested in the crook of his arm. Switching from champagne, he poured a glass of light, buttery yellow wine for her. "Try this."

Dahlia accepted the glass and inhaled the aroma. "This is Chassagne Montrachet, isn't it? Another one of my favorites." She swirled and drank. "Peachy, some oak, and an earthy mineral finish."

"You're right again." Alain was impressed and intrigued by her refined sense of smell and taste. "To us," he added, raising his glass to her. "May this be the beginning of a wonderful relationship."

Dahlia murmured her agreement and pressed the glass to her lips. "Where is your next race?" she asked, looking up at him over the rim of her glass.

"Montreal is next week. We usually have one or two weeks between races. And we're free from the end of November to the middle of March." He paused. "Could you come to Montreal?"

"I think so. Could you come to L.A.?"

"I'd like that," he said, smiling.

Dahlia raised herself on her elbow. "I'd like for you to meet some of my friends."

"And I'd want you to meet my family. Well, most of them." He chuckled softly. "You know Jack already."

As they talked, they fed each other from the tray of delicacies. Their voices rose and fell against rhythmic waves slapping the bow, punctuated by soft laughter. This was just as Alain had envisioned the evening unfolding. The two of them, alone, making love and planning their future. Though the night wore on, Alain felt energized by her presence.

He trailed a finger along her arm, threaded his fingers through hers, and brought her hand to his lips. She responded with a feathery caress to his chest that swirled to his abdomen, where she stroked the fine definition between his muscles.

Responding to her touch, Alain took Dahlia in his arms. He stroked her neck and bowed his head to press his lips to her soft curves. With every movement, he waited for her response before pressing on. They took their time with each other, enjoying the feel of the cool evening air on their warm, moist skin, and sharing the wonder of exploring new delights.

The moon rose higher in the sky, bathing them in glowing sepia rays. As the craft rocked beneath them, their bodies came together naturally, united with desire and soaring with love. Dahlia responded fully to him, transporting Alain to a plane of passion he'd never known before.

Sated at last, they lay together under the stars, catching their breath and listening to the sound of waves that filled the cool night. Alain stroked Dahlia's skin, his heart full with emotion. "This is heaven," he murmured.

"Yes it is." She curved into him, their bodies melding as one.

The rhythm of the waves rocked them to sleep. They woke to the pale of dawn and then made their way to the master cabin. Falling into the downy soft bed, they made tender love again and then drifted back to sleep cradled in each other's arms, their legs entwined as a vine.

28

"IS THAT EVERYTHING, mademoiselle?" A bellhop had carefully placed her luggage on a trolley.

Dahlia glanced wistfully over her shoulder at her suite at the Hôtel de Paris. When she'd arrived, she'd only wanted to do her job and return to Camille and Los Angeles as quickly as she could.

"*Oui, merci.*" Dahlia closed the door to the room and the bellhop went ahead of her. Penelope had left while she and Alain were aboard the *Formula Win* to work a runway show in Paris.

Dahlia strolled down the hallway, considering how much her life had changed in the course of a little more than a week. Alain, who had gone ahead of her to talk to his driver, was already downstairs waiting for her. She touched the double heart necklace nestled in her décolletage. They'd become a true couple after the intimate days they'd spent on board his yacht.

She'd also made an offer on the lavender farm, La

Maison de la Lavande, and was waiting to hear if it had been accepted. And she'd discovered her heritage and met her mother.

However, reuniting her mother and grandmother remained to be seen.

When she stepped into the grand Belle Époque Entrance Hall, she spotted Alain walking toward her, moving with masculine grace and confidence. He had his phone pressed to his ear. Dahlia watched as he passed other women. Though these stylish, attractive women smiled at him, or turned to size him up, he was oblivious to them and looking only for her. A warm feeling grew in her chest. He was so different from Kevin.

Knowing the feeling that she had found with Alain, she wondered how she could have ever thought Kevin was the one.

As he approached her, he grinned and tapped his phone, ending the call. Alain met her with a huge hug. The feel of his arms encircling her waist filled her with longing.

"Great news," he said with a broad smile. "That was Charlie on the phone, the number two driver who was injured in a crash. He woke from his coma and he's on the mend. What a relief for his family and the team."

Dahlia remembered the story he'd told her about the young driver he'd mentored. "That's wonderful. Do you think he'll race again?"

"Charlie is already making plans to return to the track."

He laughed. "There's another young hotshot I'll have to worry about on my tail."

Dahlia thought about the danger Alain faced every time he ventured onto the track in a Formula 1 car. He'd assured her that the cars were safer now than they'd ever been. She would just have to accept that the man she was in love with was one of the fastest men behind a wheel in the world.

Alain steered her through the crowded lobby. "The Bombardier is ready, flight plan filed—the only thing missing are its two passengers."

On their way through the hall, a few people recognized Alain. He stopped to pose for selfies with two fans, and exchanged fist-bumps and high-fives with a few others. Once out of the hotel, a few lingering paparazzi raised their cameras.

"You caught us," Alain said, giving them a good-natured smile.

Dahlia smiled beside him, admiring the way he dealt with the photographers. This, too, came with the man she adored.

"Thanks for being a good sport about that." After the photographers turned their attention to others, Alain tilted Dahlia's chin up and kissed her. "You have no idea how that's angered other women. And then there were those who dated me solely to get their pictures in the tabloids."

Dahlia tapped his chest. "Doesn't bother me, I grew up with it. But sometimes you have to draw the line to your privacy."

Alain touched her nose with his and kissed her forehead. "This is just one more reason to love you. You can't imagine how relieved I am that you understand my complicated world."

"That works both ways."

As they relaxed in the back of Alain's car, Dahlia thought about the trip ahead. She'd told Camille that she was returning to Los Angeles on Alain's private plane, but she hadn't shared their new relationship. She wanted to see her grandmother's reaction in person. She squeezed Alain's hand.

He leaned toward her, grazing her lips with his. "Are you sure you can make it to Montreal?"

"I wouldn't miss it. Besides, it's my job, remember?" Alain only had a few days in Los Angeles before he was scheduled to race at the Canadian Grand Prix on the Gilles Villeneuve Circuit in Montreal. Cynthia had asked that Dahlia appear at the race and speak to the Canadian media on behalf of Parfums Dubois.

After Monaco, re-entering the reality of Los Angeles now seemed almost foreign to Dahlia. She wondered if the relationship she and Alain had developed would survive with her in Los Angeles and Alain traveling the world. Not to mention the feminine competition he was bound to encounter along the way. The image of her former fiancé with another woman was seared into her memory. But that was Kevin. She drew her fingers over Alain's muscular forearm.

Alain was different; she was sure of that.

After the long flight, which Dahlia found much more comfortable on a private airplane, they touched down in Los Angeles. Camille's chauffeur, Thomas, met them at the airport. Dahlia introduced Alain, and Thomas told him he'd enjoyed watching the race in Monaco. The two men spent the drive home talking about Formula 1 racing, giving Dahlia time to think about her mother and Camille and the myriad questions she had. When would Camille be well enough to travel, or would it ever be safe for Laurel to visit?

When they arrived at the grand Holmby Hills home, Winnie met them in the entrance foyer and Dahlia embraced the older woman.

Everything here was as it had been when she'd left. A large floral arrangement with the heady scent of white bouquet of tuberose, lilies, and roses sat on the skirted entry table. Camille's outgoing correspondence was neatly stacked in an Art Deco silver tray inlaid with ebony. Strains of Vivaldi emanated from the central music system speakers. All remained the same, yet Dahlia felt profoundly changed after her trip to Monaco.

"Alain, I'd like you to meet Winnie." She introduced Camille's house manager to Alain. "And how is Grand-mère doing?" Dahlia knew Camille had been released from the hospital.

"She tires more easily than before, but she's improving every day." Winnie inclined her head with a slight smile. "She's been on conference calls, and files have been couriered to the house for her review so she can continue to manage business. But the staff is making sure she gets plenty of rest and eats well."

"Her mind seldom rests," Dahlia said. "Where is she?"

"She's waiting for you in her salon." Winnie turned to Alain, her hands folded in front of her pastel blue twinset. "In the meantime, I'll have your luggage taken to a guest room."

Dahlia noted Winnie's quick glance and nearly indiscernible tug of her mouth, a subtle sign that she approved of Alain.

Dahlia grasped Alain's hand, and they climbed one side of the curved twin staircases that led to a landing. She tapped on a door. "Grand-mère, are you decent? I have someone with me."

"Dahlia, dear, do come in."

She opened the door. Camille was seated in her private sitting area that adjoined her bedroom suite, both of which were decorated in serene shades of dove gray and muted mauve. A tray set for tea was on a table beside her.

Camille was dressed in a celadon green knit dress and wore her collection of apple green jade jewelry—a necklace, earrings, and bracelets. Her hair was styled away from her face, pulled back with a gold clip. Dahlia was surprised and relieved at how well she looked. Camille held her arms out to her.

"Grand-mère, I'm so happy to be back." Dahlia sat beside her on the sofa and hugged her. "How are you feeling?"

"I'm perfectly fine now. The doctors have overacted by insisting on special diets and so on." Camille waved her hand, minimizing her recent stroke. "But we have more interesting things to talk about. Alain, it's lovely to see you again."

"And you. You're looking well." Camille extended her hand to him, palm down.

Dahlia watched as Alain took Camille's hand and executed a gentleman's kiss a hair's breadth above her hand.

Camille's face lit with pleasure. "Such distinguished manners. Please sit here." She touched the arm of a tapestry covered wingback chair next to her, and he sat down.

"Would you care for more tea, Grand-mère?"

"Thank you, yes." Glancing between Alain and Dahlia, Camille spread her hands and tapped her fingertips together. "First, I'd like to know how you think the photo shoot went." She looked directly at Alain.

"Nils Andersen is quite talented," he answered, conversing easily. "I've worked with him before. He got so many great shots that I think you'll have a hard time choosing." Alain looked at Dahlia. "Of course, he had an excellent model in your granddaughter."

"I agree. I've seen some of the shots." When Dahlia

looked up in surprise from the tea she was preparing, Camille clarified for her. "Nils emailed a few shots to me, dear. And Alain, I'm sorry you had to witness that dreadful scene with George Wilstead."

As Dalia placed a teacup before her, Camille said, "Thank you for being so observant and alerting me by phone. When you saw George and Lawrence together, it confirmed my suspicions. I hadn't any proof of his actions before. A major crisis was averted due to your prompt action, Dahlia."

Camille shook her head and continued. "George thought I was a little old lady with one foot in the grave. I might have had a slight stroke, but I'm certainly not too weak to defend the company I built from his greedy grasp. He was conniving with that Lawrence Baxter, who was representing the acquiring group. They were trying to weaken me any way they could. Including through you, Dahlia. Lawrence was trying to distract you, but you have good instincts. No doubt George was trying to determine who might be inheriting my stock so they'd know who they had to deal with. I know how they think."

"And will this shake up the board, too?" Dahlia knew certain directors had backed George. She wouldn't be satisfied until she was certain Camille had uncontested control of the company again. Parfums Dubois was the most profitable company in its industry due to Camille's superb governance.

"I'm sure it will. We're looking into that now.

Nevertheless, George has been terminated and our attorneys are looking into the matter further. And I do hope you'll stay on at the company, dear."

"I appreciate the opportunity." Dahlia took Camille's hand. "I will always be there to help when you need me, but I have my own company to run and a new venture as well. The money I made from this engagement I hope to use as a down-payment on a lavender farm in Provence. I'm waiting to hear if my offer will be accepted."

Camille radiated pride. "Mia shared your plans for a lavender-based body care line. With Verena's new infomercial distribution, she has developed quite a valuable customer mailing list. I imagine this will be a successful partnership."

Dahlia slid a sideways glance at Alain, who was sipping his tea and listening. "Actually, there is one part of the job I'd like to continue doing."

"And what might that be?"

"I'd like to represent Parfums Dubois in media relations at Formula 1 venues."

Camille's gaze travelled to the ceiling, and she nodded thoughtfully. "Well, that would make sense. Especially if you plan on traveling with Alain."

Alain sputtered his tea, while Dahlia asked, "How did you know?"

"There isn't much that happens in the company without my knowledge." Looking satisfied with herself, Camille lifted a shoulder and let it drop. "However, photos of the two of you *were* on the front page of *Fashion News Daily* and in major sports sections. All over social media, too. I have media alerts set up on my computer." A smile spread on her face. "I knew you two would make an attractive couple."

Alain wiped his chin with a napkin. "I'd hoped I could discuss Dahlia with you first, Camille."

"You're both adults. You don't need my permission." Camille's eyes twinkled. "But I want you to know I definitely approve."

"I thought you might," Alain replied, matching her expression. "The first time I met Dahlia, I overheard a conversation she was having with you. I believe you were the one playing matchmaker."

Dahlia gaped at him. "I remember that you overheard that part, but how did you know we were talking about you?"

"You mentioned my name in conversation with Camille," he said, relishing her astonishment. "My ears generally perk up when I hear my name bandied about."

"So you knew all along."

Alain laughed. "Ladies, it's not the first time friends have set me up." He lifted his cup toward Camille. "And for a while there, it looked like nothing would come of it. Your granddaughter can be pretty bossy."

"Me?" Dahlia feigned shock.

Camille raised her tea cup. "I taught her well, didn't I?"

While they were laughing, Dahlia couldn't help but

think of Laurel and how nice it would be if she were here with Camille.

Her grandmother placed her tea cup on the table and sighed with happiness as she looked between them. Dahlia noticed she was looking a little tired.

They could always talk about Laurel another time. Dahlia wondered again how much Camille had known about her daughter's situation. And if she did, why hadn't she told her? A daughter had a right to know.

29

AFTER RISING EARLY, Dahlia and Alain went for a morning swim, followed by coffee and croissants by the estate pool. She wore her tropical print swimsuit and cover up, while Alain sported swim trunks. They shared a wide chaise lounge, stretching and basking like felines in the morning sun. Nearby, gardenia bushes sweetened the summer air.

Alain touched his lips to hers. "This almost reminds me of being on the *Formula Win*." He winked at her. "Almost."

"Hmm, I miss that." Dahlia felt heat gathering in her as she recalled their passionate lovemaking. Out of respect for Camille, Alain had not visited her during the night.

He ran a finger along her arm, sending chills through her. "Looks like I need to have a place here. What do you think about a condo or an apartment nearby?"

She rolled into his arms. "Now that's the best idea I've heard in a long time."

"We fit so well together. I can't bear being away from you for long." He caressed her cheek. "Besides, you're my lucky charm now. How soon can you come to Montreal?"

"I can leave when you do. As long as I have my laptop computer, I can work from most anywhere. Unless I'm creating new perfumes."

Alain kissed her forehead. "That's what I want to see. Your laboratory. I want to understand how you create the bewitching perfume you wear."

Dahlia was pleased he was interested. "How about now?" He followed her to the stables she had converted into her laboratory.

"This is where the magic happens." She waved her hand, inhaling the familiar fragrances that lingered in the air. While she explained the process, she showed him what she was working on.

"Is this how your grandmother began her business?"

"She started in a similar manner." Dahlia leaned against her desk. "However, when a perfume line reaches a certain scale of distribution, the process must by necessity change. Now Camille works as creative director and employs perfumers."

Alain nodded, taking it all in. "I'd like to see how perfume is made."

"It's all high-tech, but I can show you sometime. The perfume is stored in giant stainless steel vats. But the raw materials are still sourced from our company-owned fields. We're one of the few companies in the world of this size that are vertically integrated to maintain exceptional quality throughout the process. Camille insists on this."

Alain's attention turned to her collection of essential oils. "I'm curious about the raw materials you use. Mind if I smell a few?"

"Go ahead," Dahlia said, gesturing toward her curved work station. "That's called a perfume organ. The essential oils are arranged like notes and chords."

As she watched Alain explore, she wondered if her mother had also shared the family passion for perfume-making. It was strange that she didn't know. Now that she had met Laurel, she wanted to know so much more about her.

She'd also have to find the perfect time to tell Camille that she'd met Laurel. The doctor had warned her about the risk of overexciting her grandmother, but Camille seemed much stronger now. She would tell her later today, Dahlia decided, unless Camille seemed too tired. She was afraid Camille would want to book an immediate flight to Malta, which would be too risky for her health.

Alain opened and closed several tiny bottles, carefully smelling each one. "Here's one I like." He held out a bottle.

"That's sandalwood. It suits you well." She pressed a finger to her nose in thought. "I'm going to make a fragrance for you."

He raised his head. "Besides my line with Parfums Dubois?"

"Something just for us to share."

Deepening his voice, Alain asked, "And where is your special perfume?" He stepped closer to her, desire evident in his eyes.

"Which one? I have so many…"

"You know the one. The one you were wearing in Monaco. The one that is the essence of you."

Alain stood in front of her now, so close that she couldn't resist. Dahlia pulled him toward her, hungrily kissing him.

After a few minutes, Alain groaned. "I have to find a place fast. Maybe I could rent a yacht in the harbor in the next fifteen minutes."

She thumped him on the chest. "If we don't leave now, we're going to end up on the floor."

Alain waggled his eyebrows and she laughed. "I want to introduce you to my friends. We're going to meet them at Bow-Tie for lunch."

Penelope had called Fianna from Monaco, and everyone had seen their photos in the media. Dahlia had already received calls from Verena and Scarlett, too.

After they changed from their swimwear, Dahlia and Alain drove by a few condominium complexes on the west side that would work for the lock-up-and-go situation Alain needed. Some were even furnished. Alain saw two units he liked and asked that the rental applications be sent to his assistant for completion.

"You make decisions fast," Dahlia said as they left the high-rise complex and waited for the valet parking attendant to bring her car.

"I learned to be decisive at 200 miles per hour." He grinned. "But seriously, I don't want us to lose any time together. I have fallen completely in love with you, Dahlia."

His words were sustenance to her soul. "And I with you," she murmured.

When they arrived at Bow-Tie, Dahlia saw her friends waiting for them. Except for Penelope, most of her closest friends were there.

Johnny met her at the front of the outdoor patio, which was in bloom with a riot of red, pink, and purple bougainvillea. "Dahlia, welcome back." He shook hands with Alain and said, "You have no idea how much our friends want to meet you. We live near Hollywood, but you'd think they'd never seen a celebrity before."

Scarlett joined them and poked Johnny in the side. "Just because you guys have gone all fan-boy on him, doesn't mean we will." She brushed her coppery blond hair over her shoulder and turned to Alain. "I think the guys just want to test drive your car. I'm Scarlett, Dahlia's business attorney. Come join us."

They made their way to a large umbrella-covered table. Dahlia noticed a number of eyes following them. However, the clientele here was accustomed to well-known people and no one approached them.

When they sat down, everyone began talking at once, welcoming Alain and making comments on the recent race.

Dahlia began to introduce her friends.

"This is Fianna and Niall," she said. "Fianna designed the dress I wore for the photo shoot, and several other outfits I wore in Monaco."

"We're the Irish contingent here." Fianna caught her wild red mane and pulled her hair to one side.

Niall reached over and shook Alain's hand. "Niall Finley. I'm known to carry a few tunes."

Alain grinned. "Love your music, man."

Scarlett laughed. "Now it's mutual fan-boy time."

"And here is Verena, the one I'm working with on the lavender body care project." Dahlia leaned toward Verena, her excitement growing. "And guess what? I got a call from the probate attorney while we were looking at the condos."

Verena clasped her hands to her chest. "And?"

"You're looking at the new owner of a lavender farm in Provence. It's time for us to start work on our new body care line." Dahlia motioned to the man in chef's garb approaching their table. "And here's Verena's other half, Lance, who will be whipping up delicious fare for us today. Johnny and Lance own Bow-Tie."

Lance greeted Alain. "Welcome to the gang. This is a tough crowd, especially when they're hungry."

"Hey, we're starving over here," Fianna said, chiding Lance.

"I'm really glad to meet you all." Alain put his arm around Dahlia. "You're going to be seeing a lot more of me around here. I'm renting a place to be close to this fabulous woman." He gave Dahlia a light kiss, and everyone around the table cheered and clapped. Alain laughed along with them. "You've got a great group of friends, Dahlia."

"Didn't I tell you?" She looked around the table. Her cherished friends were beaming at them, and she could tell they were truly happy for her.

Dahlia thought about how much she and her best friends had been through together. Verena, Scarlett, Fianna, and Penelope were like sisters. The men were getting along well, too. She looked forward to the fun times they would have together, but most of all, she was looking forward to sharing her life with Alain.

Lance's team in the kitchen sent one of Bow-Tie's signature appetizers, empanadas, to the table. He'd created a special menu for their lunch, filled with new Asian-French fusion dishes he was trying out. After they ate, Alain asked to be excused. Johnny directed him to the men's room.

Scarlett spoke up. "We really like him for you, Dahlia."

Verena and Fianna nodded.

"He sure seems like a good guy," Johnny said. "I looked him up online, but couldn't find anything too awful about him."

Dahlia glared at Johnny. "How dare you search him online?" She narrowed her eyes at Johnny, but burst out laughing a few seconds later. "Actually, Penelope beat you to it."

Verena asked about the lavender farm, and Dahlia told her all about it. After they talked for a while, Dahlia began to wonder what had happened to Alain. Curious, she got up to look for him. Maybe he needed rescuing from an overzealous fan.

As she made her way through the bar crowd on her way toward the men's room, a reflection in a mirror caught her eye.

Alain was standing at the bar, his arm around a young, slender brunette. They were speaking, their heads bent toward each other as if sharing secrets. The woman gazed at him, laughing, and then he kissed her forehead and hugged her. Recognizing the endearing movement, Dahlia blanched.

She was shocked, hardly comprehending what she was seeing, and yet, on a basic level she immediately understood. The moment Alain was out of her sight, he was seducing another woman. Like Kevin, he could not be trusted. Her heart hammered and blood rushed to her head. How could she have entrusted her heart to him?

She took a step toward him, but a wave of dizziness overtook her. Touching a chair for support, she breathed deeply, summoning the courage to do what she must. Why today, with all of her friends here? A part of her still couldn't accept this—she had trusted him completely—and yet, the evidence was before her.

Walking toward him, Dahlia lifted her chin, ready to confront him.

The brunette saw her first. "Alain, is that her?"

The woman was actually giggling. Dahlia seethed with anger.

Alain whirled around. "Dahlia, look who I found. My sister, Giselle."

"Sister?" Dahlia's lips parted and relief surged through her. With her emotions on a roller coaster, she touched Alain's arm to steady herself. "You might have told me she was coming," she managed to say.

Alain frowned for a moment. Then, comprehending the look on her face, he flung his arms around her. "Sweetheart, I didn't know she would be here. I know what you must have thought, but I assure you—"

Giselle broke in. "I'm so sorry, you must have thought I was some groupie fan. I couldn't believe he was here. This was a total accident. I often meet my L.A. friends here. It's one of our favorite places."

"Giselle is from San Diego," Alain said.

Now that Dahlia could see the resemblance—they even used some of the same gestures—she was embarrassed for having jumped to a conclusion. "Giselle, the apology is all mine." She looked sheepishly at Alain. "I was actually coming over to tell you exactly what I thought of you."

Alain feigned fright. "I would have liked to have seen that."

"It wouldn't have been pretty." Dahlia shook her head, her emotional rampage having dissipated.

"I find it kind of sexy," Alain said, kissing her forehead. "I've seen you in action—remember George? No, ma'am, I don't plan to get on your bad side."

Dahlia put a hand on her hip. "Hey, I don't have a temper, except when it's well-deserved."

"Even though he's my brother, I can tell you that he's one of the most stupidly loyal guys I know." Giselle made a face at Alain.

"Let's not go there," Alain said. "I'm sure Dahlia will hear that story and many others when she meets the rest of the family." Alain sighed and playfully tapped Giselle on the shoulder. Turning to Dahlia, he added, "I was hoping to gain your complete confidence before letting my family at you."

Dahlia smiled, finally feeling secure again. She chastised herself for jumping to a conclusion. Kevin had shattered her trust, but Alain *was* different. Promising herself that she wouldn't impose an expectation of misconduct on him that would only damage their relationship, she took a step toward Alain and grazed his lips with hers.

"Bring on the stories," she said, laughing again now. "I can handle them." And she could. She vowed she would trust him, until such time as he proved himself untrustworthy. Not all men were like Kevin. She owed herself the opportunity for happiness. Alain had his hand on the throttle of life. And she was right there beside him with dreams of her own.

After they left Bow-Tie, Dahlia and Alain drove back to her home. Lance had prepared a special healthy meal for

Camille—today it was a spinach and salmon salad with a light honey Dijon dressing and fresh blueberries and raspberries. Dahlia knew Camille loved Lance's salmon—it was so moist and tender, many professional restaurant reviewers had lauded him for it.

Dahlia led Alain into the kitchen where they found Winnie preparing a pot of tea. The kitchen was spacious, with professional-grade stainless steel appliances flanked with modern cherry wood cabinets. Camille had gutted the original kitchen and set up the new one to serve the large parties she often held on the estate. After recently losing her last chef, who'd moved for family reasons, Camille had employed a part-time chef who came to the house, but he wouldn't arrive until later to prepare supper.

Dahlia slid onto a kitchen barstool next to Winnie. "How was Grand-mère while we were gone?"

"Today she's irrepressible. She's so happy you're home—and with Alain." Winnie removed a kettle from the burner and poured it over loose tea oolong leaves in a Chinese teapot. "Much stronger and sharp as ever, too. She spent the morning reviewing the best photos for the ad that Nils emailed and conferring with the marketing vice president."

Dahlia hoped she hadn't overdone it today. She really wanted to talk to Camille. "Alain and I had lunch at Bow-Tie, so I told her we'd bring her lunch. I know she likes to eat later." She walked to a cabinet and reached for a large floral painted tray.

"What can I do?" Alain asked.

"Keep me company," Dahlia said with a light kiss. Alain leaned against the Italian granite countertop, looking entirely at ease in the domestic setting.

Dahlia transferred the food to a gold-rimmed white china plate. "If that tea is for her, I can take it up."

"Would you?" Winnie put the teapot and three cups on the tray. "Thanks, I have several calls to make for her."

"You're amazing the way you run this house and plan all her events." Dahlia added silverware and a white linen napkin. When she went to pick up the heavy tray, Alain placed his hand on hers.

"I've got this," he said. "Lead the way."

Dahlia and Alain went upstairs. When they opened the door to her private salon, Camille was talking on the phone. She was dressed in a chic navy knit tunic and pants with one of her favorite Chanel scarves that bore her namesake flower, camellias. Dahlia often gave Camille one of these scarves on her birthday.

Alain arranged the tray on a table next to her. Camille nodded her appreciation.

After Camille hung up, she exclaimed over the dish Lance had prepared. "He really is an excellent chef. Everything he creates is delicious. Now, tell me all about the race while I dine." Dramatically unfurling her napkin, she looked pointedly at Alain, a bemused smile on her face. "And I want a full report on how the two of you began dating."

While Dahlia poured tea for everyone, Alain told Camille about the race. He was recounting their trip to Provence when Winnie opened the door and then shut it quickly behind her.

"Hello, Winnifred." Camille put her tea down. "Was that the front door I heard a few minutes ago?"

"It was," Winnie began uncertainly and then halted, biting her lip and fiddling with a handkerchief.

"What is it, Winnie?" Dahlia asked, suddenly alarmed. "You're pale as moonlight. Why, you've been crying. What's happened?"

Winnie pressed her handkerchief to her mouth in an effort to compose herself.

"Get the chair by the desk for her." Camille motioned to Alain. "Now tell me what's wrong, Winnie."

"It's good news." Winnie waved off the chair. "But you must prepare yourself, Camille." With a shaking, tearful smile, she opened the door behind her.

Laurel stood in the doorway, a hand pressed to her heart. "Mom, it's me."

Tears sprang to Camille's eyes and she brought her hands to her face, her entire frame shaking. She let out a strangled cry, and then threw her arms open as she rose from the sofa. "My child!"

Laurel raced into Camille's arms and the two women clung to each other, alternately sobbing with joy and laughing with elation. Dahlia was overcome with sheer happiness for her mother and grandmother.

Framing her daughter's face in her hands, Camille managed to ask, "Is it all over?"

Laurel could only nod, her eyes bright and brimming with tears.

Alain put his arm around Dahlia while she reached out to grasp Winnie's hand, watching the sweet, poignant reunion between two women who had suffered so much.

Camille held out a quivering hand to Dahlia. "Come, meet your mother. I didn't want to burden you with the tragic secret I've carried so heavily in my heart all these years."

At once, Dahlia understood why Camille hadn't told her about Laurel. She immediately forgave her grandmother. Life was too precious and too short to hold grudges. Dahlia rose and wrapped her arms around them, completing the circle. "We've met. I was going to tell you today."

When Camille looked shocked, Laurel spoke softly. "Dahlia found me on Malta. She told me that Luigi is dead."

"How did you know all this?" Incredulous, Camille searched Dahlia's face.

"A woman at the hospital told us to speak to Father Renaud, who told us the whole story. And then Alain took me to see…" Dahlia smiled at Laurel. "To see my mom."

"My daughter. How I've missed you." Laurel squeezed Dahlia's shoulder. "I jumped on a flight as soon as I was given clearance." She turned to Camille. "Mom, please forgive me for all my youthful mistakes."

"Of course I do." Camille clasped their hands, looking happily from one to another. "You're free now. That's all that matters." She turned to Alain and Winnie. "Come join us in our happy celebration."

Everyone began talking and hugging at once.

Her heart brimming with love, Dahlia reached for Alain and he embraced her, burying his face in her hair and kissing her neck.

"I feel so honored to be part of this moment, my love." Alain pressed her hand to his heart. "I'm so happy for you and your family."

Dahlia cradled his face in her hands, gazing into the endless ocean blue eyes of the most genuine, loving man she'd ever known. How all thyf7teir lives had changed in such a short time, and in ways none of them could have imagined.

"I've been thinking," she said, touching her lips to his. "Now I believe… there really is such a thing as kismet."

- The End -

Read on for an excerpt from *Style*, the next novel in the *Love, California* series by Jan Moran.

Style

"THIS WAY, PENELOPE, to your right."

Penelope stepped from the limousine and paused on the red carpet. With natural, fluid motions, she swirled her translucent violet cape and tossed her lavender-streaked tresses to strike a nonchalant pose that was second nature to her. Mentally calculating light sources and intensity—and how those combined with the angles and planes of her face—she glanced in the photographer's direction long enough for the woman's digital camera to whir through frames in split seconds.

She pouted, then relaxed into a smile, to give the editor a choice. Make the photographer's job easy—that was her theory, and she credited this approach to her success.

Another voice rang out, raspy and gruff. "Hey Penny, who are you wearing?"

"Fianna Fitzgerald." Penelope turned toward a grungy

photographer and repeated her process

His camera snapped intermittently as he tried to focus shots for whatever publication he was shooting for—though many paparazzi were independent, selling celebrity shots to the highest bidder. In her years of modeling, Penelope knew a lot of them, at least by sight, but she'd never seen this bungling, lanky man in faded black clothes. Still, New York's Fashion Week drew a wide variety of crowds. She remained patient, feeling sorry for this obvious newcomer. The man fumbled with his camera; he'd never be Richard Avedon, but then, few fashion photographers were such legends.

"Fitzgerald. Name is kind of familiar," he said, fidgeting with his camera while other photographers stepped beside him and took his shot. "Is she someone?"

Besides his naiveté, Penelope sensed something unsettling about him, but she continued. "She's a new fashion designer from Ireland, living in America." She'd met Fianna a few years ago through Fianna's aunt, Davina, a supermodel who had encouraged her to enter modeling as a profession. Now, Fianna was one of her closest friends.

"Oh yeah, the Fitzgerald Flop." He smirked. "She sure played that one to the hilt."

What a jerk. Strolling beside the bank of media lining the entry, Penelope spied photographers from *Vogue* and *The New York Times.* She angled a hand on her hip and stretched her leg through a slit in her flowing skirt, though she didn't let her expression reveal that the gruff man's comments annoyed her.

Her friend's debut runway show in Dublin had been sabotaged, and a model had been seriously injured. The media splashed the incident across the tabloid pages, and Fianna nearly lost everything she'd worked so hard for. If not for a stroke of brilliance in embracing the moniker and creating an edgy street line around it, her friend would have been bankrupt. Penelope and other friends had pitched in to help Fianna salvage her career and see her dreams come to fruition.

"Hey, Penny—"

"Sorry, have to run." She was giving a speech and didn't want to be late, but there was also something about that man that was disturbing. Penelope swirled around, her iridescent train rippling in her wake. Dangling amethyst earrings brushed her long neck as she ascended the steps.

From the corner of her eye, she saw the grungy photographer turn to leave, though a bevy of other models and celebrities strode behind her. That struck her as odd; there were still many good shots to be had. She had developed a talent for looking beneath the glossy veneer.

Once inside, Penelope paused to take in the glittering scene. Dance music thumped, ruby and indigo lights sparkled, and a mélange of perfume wafted above it all.

"Penelope, over here." A tall women with wild red hair waved to her. She wondered if the photographers had stopped Fianna on her way in.

As Penelope cut through the celebrity-studded fashion crowd, *Fashion News Daily* editor Aimee Winterhaus said hello, Tom Ford kissed her cheek, and André Leon Talley, a legendary contributing editor to *Vogue*, caught her eye and gestured his approval of her ensemble.

Just past André, a highly competitive new model slid a narrowed look her way, and next to her was Monica Graber, a model she'd known for years who'd betrayed her. Her ex-best friend. Monica usually adopted a haughty air around her, but today Monica's eyes darted away and her leg shook, nervous tics Penelope recognized.

Penelope swiveled with studied nonchalance, avoiding the distasteful pair. As a fresh young model from Copenhagen, she'd matured in this mercurial world of friends and frenemies, where fashion was cutthroat business and burned through weak models like dry twigs.

"You were magnificent today," Fianna said, flinging her arms open in greeting.

Earlier in the day, Penelope had walked for a top designer at Skylight at Moynihan Station on 33rd Street in a historic post office venue. The beautiful Beaux-Arts exterior opened to an enormous, light-filled postal sorting room that was a perfect venue for fashion shows.

As Penelope hugged Fianna, she could feel her friend quivering with enthusiasm. The last thing she wanted was to dampen her friend's mood with a remark about the dreadful photographer out front. Judging from Fianna's mood, she probably hadn't seen him. "So what do you think of this madness?"

Fianna was so excited, her freckled face seemed lit from within. "Davina used to let me tag along when I was a kid, but Fashion Week is much crazier now. What an incredible experience this is. So many stars from Hollywood are here, too."

Penelope laughed. "Come on, you must be used to that in L.A. by now. Don't celebs shop at your boutique?"

"New York has a different vibe. It's the Big Apple. The concrete jungle." Fianna started humming the Alicia Keys song about New York.

"I'm glad you got to come." Penelope added with a wink, "There's a good chance your design I'm wearing might be published in *Vogue* magazine. Wouldn't be surprised if you get business off it."

When Penelope told her that André Leon Talley had shown his approval, Fianna's mismatched eyes widened with delight. Fashion Week was the longstanding event where everyone in fashion met for business.

"Hope you're right. I'd love to pay off my student loans for FIDM."

Penelope glanced over her shoulder. "Some of the instructors from the New York branch of the Fashion Institute for Design and Merchandising are usually here. I'll let you know if I see them." Penelope admired the way Fianna had handled the early trials in her fledging career with unflagging determination and creativity.

"Where's Davina?" Penelope asked, looking around. "I haven't much time before I have to give my speech."

"Behind us," Fianna said, turning to a crowd gathered behind them.

An elegant woman in a liquid silver sheath emerged from the group. She wore a sapphire-and-hammered-silver collar encircling her long neck. Her azure eyes shimmered, and her thick platinum mane flowed around her shoulders.

"Right here, darling," Davina said, her voice laced with an Irish lilt. She touched her gleaming collar. "I'm talking with Elena and her friends about this stunning piece she designed for me."

Originally from Australia, Elena Eaton designed fine jewelry and had a shop next to Fianna's studio on Robertson Boulevard in Los Angeles. An athletic brunette clad in a sleek, ebony gown that showcased her exquisite jewelry, Elena waved at her and called out, "How're you doing?"

Penelope smiled and waved back. She knew several of the young stars were wearing Elena's pieces today, and she couldn't be happier for her friend. She'd recommended her jewelry to several designers who'd chosen bold pieces to accent their designs. Designers often had their own lines, or didn't accessorize at all, so this was quite a coup for a young jewelry designer.

Davina stepped back to admire Penelope's ensemble. "*Hej smukke*," she said, her eyes twinkling.

"Well, hello beautiful yourself," Penelope said, kissing Davina on each cheek. "Are you learning Danish?"

Davina laughed. "I learned some phrases from a Danish prince at a dinner party in London a few weeks ago. You really are stunning tonight. Ready to give your talk?"

"I am."

"Garbo speaks," Davina said, sweeping her hand to mimic a headline. "I was at a silent film festival last night. You're too young to remember those days."

"So are you. Are you doing any work in New York?"

"Print gigs only. Not as crazy as catwalk life." Davina gestured across the crowded room. "Everything about this business is so different now."

"Has it really changed that much?" Penelope loved hearing about when Davina was at the pinnacle of her success. Even at the age of fifty, Davina was still a stunning woman, proving that beauty needn't diminish with age. Her famous cheekbones were still well-defined, but more than that, it was Davina's empathy, laughter, and professionalism that endeared her to so many in the industry. Penelope counted herself lucky to have had Davina as a mentor.

"Models are thinner than ever before, and there are many more temptations." Davina indicated a rail-thin model with sharp cheekbones and sunken cheeks who languished near a bar. "Or maybe I see it more clearly now from a distance."

"That's exactly my point tonight." A petite woman with

horn-rimmed glasses caught Penelope's eye. "Excuse me, I think it's show time."

The woman clasped a clipboard to her chest. "Miss Plessen, we'd like to begin. Come with me now."

Davina winked at her. *"Held og lykke."*

"It's not luck I need," Penelope replied. "It's everyone's support."

Penelope accompanied the woman to the stage, as Fianna, Davina, and Elena followed.

The area in front of the raised stage area was crowded. "Pardon me," Penelope said, brushing past a well-built man in a tuxedo. He wore mirrored glasses and had longish chestnut hair. Very L.A. Something about him seemed familiar, though she pushed the thought aside. She had to gather her thoughts for her presentation.

The lights went up, and the designer she'd walked for earlier today, Ruben Lars Eriksen, a fellow Dane who also lived in Los Angeles, stepped under the floodlights to introduce her.

"Penelope Plessen is a chameleon," Ruben began. "She's the model so many of us turn to when we're creating a new look because of her unique ability to morph into what we've imagined in our mind. She translates our vision, bringing it to life on the stage and page. Last year, she also brought her vision and style to cosmetics with the launch of Penelope of Denmark for High Gloss Cosmetics."

Penelope nodded toward Olga Kaminsky, the CEO of

High Gloss, with whom she had worked in Los Angeles on the makeup line. Due to fierce competition and an industry preference for youth, runway models often had short careers, so Penelope was anxious to create a business that could live on beyond her modeling career.

Ruben held out a hand to Penelope. "Besides beauty and fashion, Penelope has an important initiative for our industry that she'd like to share with you tonight."

Amid applause, Penelope took the stage and thanked Ruben. She stepped to the podium and adjusted the microphone. Gazing over the crowd, she noticed the unkempt photographer from the red carpet. She thought he'd left, yet there he was, lurking on the edge of the crowd, smirking. She found his presence unsettling, so she turned away, drew a breath, and began.

"During the past fifty years, the silhouette of our industry has evolved to the point where many of our finest young models are suffering—and even dying—of eating disorders and drugs." Penelope paused to compose herself, thinking about the friends she'd lost, but most of all, recalling her mother's private struggle with depression and anorexia.

"These issues aren't only about us. They also affect those in our communities who want to look like models and emulate this behavior. It's time we take action for our health, and for our industry as models of behavior. With France, Italy, Israel, and other countries enacting laws to ban the use of malnourished models, I'm happy to announce a new healthy assistance and rehab program with facilities in California and soon, in Europe and other regions, too. This is made possible by leaders and donors in our industry. It's important we open the conversation and—"

"Hey Penny." From the edge of the crowd, a man's menacing voice rang out.

Few people called her Penny. Recognizing the odd, raspy voice, she turned toward it, just as the photographer she'd met outside stretched his arm toward her. Something flashed in his hand—

A man nearby chopped his arm and lunged for the photographer while he struggled to regain his stance. People in the crowd ducked, pressed back, and scattered. Screams split the air, and cameras flashed.

Watching in horror, Penelope grabbed the microphone and ducked. "Everybody down! He's got a gun!"

While others were diving for cover, the man she'd brushed past by the stage leapt up and scooped Penelope up in his arms. "Hey, let go of me!" Reacting, she instantly shoved her palm up against his nose.

The guy dodged her strike, taking the blow to his cheekbone instead. "Getting you to safety," he said through gritted teeth.

As the scuffle below continued, a shot rang out, and the podium splintered. All at once, the lights went off.

Adrenaline flashed through her as the man carried her away from the chaos. Penelope clasped his neck and drew up her legs, feeling his veins pumping against her skin and his heart throbbing against her chest. Was she safe with this man? She couldn't be sure, but if he'd wanted her dead he would've left her on stage.

Where were her friends? "Davina! Elena, Fianna!" All she could do was pray they were out of harm's way. Jostled against the man's chest, she tightened her grip.

Once they'd cleared the stage, he kicked open a backstage door. Finding an empty dressing room, he put her down.

Out of breath, she cried out, "I've got friends out there. We have to get to them." Davina, Elena, Fianna... and so many others.

Without acknowledging her comment, he flipped out a pen-sized flashlight, tapped it on, and handed it to her. "Use this."

Footsteps clattered in the dim hallway. "Is she okay? Let us in," cried Fianna. "We followed your screams." Davina and Elena were behind her, holding their phones with flashlight apps illuminating their way.

"They're with me." Without waiting for approval from the man with icy mirrored glasses, Penelope grasped Fianna's trembling hands and pulled her into the room. "Is anyone hurt?"

"We're okay," Fianna said, her eyes wide with fright. "I don't think anyone was hit, but I can't be sure...."

"Lock it." The man shut the door behind him.

While Fianna and Elena clutched each other, Davina folded her into her arms. "Thank goodness you weren't hurt. That guy saved your life."

He had, hadn't he? Penelope had always prided herself on being able to care of herself, but against a bullet moving at a millisecond? She shuddered at the thought of what might have happened.

Davina kissed her cheek. "He risked his life for you. Do you know who he was?"

She had no idea, Penelope thought with a jolt. Risking his own safety, the man had acted quickly. She wished she'd gotten a better look at his face. His physique was rock solid, and she *had* felt safe in his arms, though she hated to admit her vulnerability.

His scent reminded her of... She shook her head, dispelling a disturbing memory that surged to the surface. After her heart had been broken, she found it easier not to get too attached.

"That photographer out front," Penelope began, chastising herself.

"Who?" Davina place her hands on Penelope's cheeks and searched her eyes. "Do you know who did this?"

"I'd never seen him before," Penelope said, a sickening feeling churning within her. She should've said something, alerted someone. "Oh Davina, if only I'd said something, maybe I could've stopped this from happening."

Davina pressed her to her breast, soothing her. "Darling,

you couldn't have known what he was planning to do."

On the way in she'd been thinking about her speech and her friends, but maybe she could have had him questioned or removed. She swallowed hard against searing tears of guilt and regret that filled her eyes.

The sound of hysterical crying echoed in the hallway, and Penelope inched open the door to two women. "In here," she called, pulling the pair inside to safety.

Outside, screams and scuffling ensued. Davina put her arms around Fianna and Elena to calm them, and then reached out to the two panic-stricken women to bring them into the circle.

Penelope stood by the door, pressing her ear to it. No way was that lunatic getting in here.

One of the women cried out, "What will we do if the shooter tries to get in?"

"We'll stop him." Penelope set her jaw. Never before had she been singled out for violence. She had no idea why anyone would try to kill her, but there were nuts out there, and now he was a threat to everyone. Was he a fan? Had he faked his press credentials? Thoughts raced through her mind, though nothing made sense to her.

After a few minutes, the havoc outside seemed to taper off, and the lights above them flickered on.

"Thank goodness." Penelope turned off the mini-flashlight.

A knock burst at the door. "Penelope, you ladies okay in

there?"

He knew her name. But then, she'd been introduced when she'd gone up on stage. She eased the door open to the man who'd saved her from danger.

"Shaken, that's all." For years Penelope had traveled the world to remote locations in Africa, South America, and the Middle East. She'd been trapped in political uprisings, but nothing had prepared her for a direct public attack. That is, except for the self-defense classes her parents had insisted she take when she left home to begin her career.

She peered at the muscled man who stood taller than she did—six-feet-five with her towering Manolo Blahnik heels—and stopped, agape as he stood before her, his mirrored glasses now in his hands.

"*Stefan?* What are you doing here?"

"I'm on duty."

"What the—why?" Shocked by his presence, Penelope could hardly think.

He looked past her into the room. "Everyone stay put for now."

Davina spoke up. "Has that man been caught?"

Stefan pressed a finger to his ear, and only then did Penelope realize he wore a discreet earpiece. "Not yet. He escaped in the dark. Police have surrounded the building and closed the street. They'll need to interview witnesses." He turned to face Penelope, his startling blue eyes shot with concern. "They want to talk to you."

"Of course." All at once, Penelope felt the adrenaline drain from her body, and she began to shiver. Or was it the presence of Stefan, the man she'd thought she'd never see again? Despite her protests, he had forged into action with such authority.

But then, he always had.

"Better sit down," he said. He grabbed a bottle of water from a table and opened it for her. Pulling up a chair, he sat across from her, leaning his elbows on his knees and staring into her eyes with the direct gaze that had touched her so many years ago. "Do you know who tried to shoot you?"

Davina and the other women sat down, watching them.

Shaking her head, Penelope blinked. His eyes were clouded with concern, just as when he'd broken off their relationship in the worst way. She drank and tried to appear calm despite her hammering pulse. "He was taking photos outside, but now I doubt he was a photographer."

"Why do you say that?"

"He didn't know how to use his camera."

"And how did you know that?"

"While their cameras are pointed at *me*, I'm watching *them*."

Stefan studied her for a moment, a corner of his mouth turning up in approval. Seemingly satisfied, he tapped his earpiece and said, "Roger that." To her, he added. "The police are on their way back. Glad you're not hurt." He stood and walked to the door.

"Stefan." It took all the energy Penelope had to utter his name.

He hesitated, his hand on the knob. "Yes?"

"Will you come back?" Penelope crossed her arms. *Damn it, where did that come from?*

His expression gave no indication of the relationship they'd once had. "If that's what you want."

The two women who'd sought refuge with them followed Stefan out the door, and as soon as the door closed, Davina clasped her trembling hands. She inclined her head toward the closed door. "That man with the Paul Newman eyes. Is that *your* Stefan?"

Penelope nodded, still trying to process what had just occurred. "He's changed. His hair... it's a little longer." But he still had the same piercing blue eyes that took her breath away. "I never thought I'd see him again."

Fianna and Elena traded a look before Fianna spoke up. "Excuse me, that incredible specimen of a man... you *know* him?"

Penelope rubbed her bare arms and blew out a breath. "I haven't seen him in a long time." Since the day she and Monica had parted ways as friends.

"Wow. You kept that hunk of man from us?" Elena pressed her lips together. "He looks like a Navy SEAL."

"Actually, he was." Penelope stared at the door. *Of all the men...*

Tossing her fiery mane over one shoulder, Fianna

waggled her eyebrows. "M God, if it weren't for Niall—"

In a release of intense fear, nerves gave way to a twitter of laughter in the room.

"Hands off, you two lovebirds adore each other," Elena cut in, playfully slapping Fianna's hand. She turned to Penelope. "And you never dated him?"

Penelope felt her face flush. "I didn't say *that*."

Elena's mouth formed a silent O, while Davina shook her head in warning. The last thing Penelope wanted to discuss was her relationship with Stefan.

Fianna leaned forward, her eyes flashing. "Stefan's so hot. The way he scooped you up and looks at you, I think he's interested. What happened?"

"Too complicated to explain." Penelope met Davina's eyes, which were rimmed with concern. She'd cried in her arms when Stefan left, and ever since, she'd compared every man she met to him. With her busy career, she didn't have time for serious dating, so it had been for the best. Of that she was certain.

Davina lifted a brow and squeezed her hand. "Fianna, Elena, enough with the questions. Our Penelope's in shock."

"I'm okay." Penelope shook her head, though she wasn't sure if she was trying to convince Davina or herself.

Two police officers arrived and set to work taking their statements. Penelope told them everything she could remember, but the only thing that seemed to help them was that she didn't think he was a photographer.

"Can you think of any motive this man might've had?" asked the officer who sat before her.

Fianna cut in. "Motive? For Penelope? You've got to be kidding, that guy's a mentaller," she exclaimed. When the police office looked confused at her Irish slang, she put her hands on her hips and huffed. "How about just bat-shit crazy?"

Penelope nodded with a rueful grin. "Next question."

"Have you received any odd correspondence from anyone? Anything through social media?"

"I get the regular love letters and suggestive Anthony Weiner-style photos, but I don't know if any of those could be traced to this."

"We'll need to see those."

"I trashed them." Penelope crossed her legs and tapped her foot as the officer shook his head. "What's the point of keeping that stuff?"

"Isn't it obvious now?" He shook his head and spoke to her as though she were a child. "When you chase the spotlight, you have to take precautions."

Penelope crossed her arms and glared at the officer. "I *never* chased the spotlight, that's not why I'm in this line of work. I was a skinny fourteen-year-old, five-foot-ten-inch swimmer when someone asked if I wanted to make extra money wearing new clothes one weekend. So I did."

The detective glared back. "Lot of models claw their way to the top."

"I work hard. That's how I got where I am today."

"Uh-huh." He scratched a note. "Your photos are everywhere. You sell photos or stories to the media?"

"And if I did?" She huffed. "Print campaigns for brands and magazines—that's my job. As for the media, yes, they follow me. If I can leverage that for a good cause, I do. But no, I don't sell stories or photos to the tabloids." Penelope tapped her dark purple nails on the table, wondering when Stefan would return. And why she wanted him to.

The detective dotted an *i* with a jab. "Let's try this again. *Anyone* who's contacted you lately that you can recall?"

Penelope tried to take calming breaths, but found she could hardly draw in air. "I'm trying to be helpful, but you have no idea how many people reach out to me on social media. I don't see everything. I have a VA who helps answer messages while I'm working." Her throat threatened to close, and she pushed down an involuntary sense of panic. "Shouldn't you be out looking for that guy instead of questioning me?"

"VA?"

"Virtual assistant."

"I'll need that name." The detective flipped to a new page on his notepad and spun it around.

Penelope leaned over and printed the name. She wanted to be hopeful, but she had a sinking feeling. "Think you'll catch the guy?"

"We'll do our best."

The officer left his card with her, asking her to call if she thought of anything that could help in the investigation. He moved on to talk to Davina, Fianna, and Elena.

"Hey there." A deep voice reverberated behind her.

Penelope raised her eyes and found herself staring at Stefan again. "Hey."

"Looks like your friends will be busy for a while. Think they'd mind if we took a walk?"

Any other time the answer would've been no. "I'll tell them." Penelope crossed the room and knelt by Davina. "If I don't get out of here—"

"Go," Davina interjected. "No need to stay. I'm sure your nerves are in tatters. I'll stay with Fianna and Elena." She arched an eyebrow toward Stefan. "You'll be all right with that one?"

"We're just taking a walk. I'll be safe with him," Penelope said, though she wasn't sure her heart would be.

Clutching her arm, Stefan cut through the crowd.

After the way he'd broken her heart, any other time Penelope would have slapped his hand off, but she let it stay, recognizing she might still need assistance in this highly charged situation. Police had cleared the party and were checking people and taking statements in the wide hallway outside the room. The mood in the anteroom was tense and jittery. Party-goers were live-streaming the chaotic scene on their phones to social media.

"Hey Penelope," a woman called out. "Are you okay?"

Across the crush of fashionable people, a sea of faces and camera phones swung her way. Feeling the heat of attention, she raised her hand and gave a thumbs-up sign, curving her lips into the semblance of a smile, though her nerves were still raw.

People she passed chimed in with their sentiments, and she thanked them as Stefan led her through the throng.

Only Monica turned away as soon as she saw her with Stefan. Monica's shimmering, ice blue dress clung to her nearly skeletal frame, revealing everything, even the tension between her shoulder blades. She had always been extremely thin but Penelope imagined that her BMI index was now below the line set by the participating countries. She wouldn't see Monica in France unless the woman started eating.

Besides, one couldn't live on vodka alone. Or whatever she was into now.

Stefan pressed his hand slightly on the small of her back in a familiar protective gesture, and Penelope stiffened. His touch still shot through her with the heat of molten lava. She pressed a hand over her heart, feeling pressure build in her chest.

He leaned close to her ear and said, "I know a place we can go where it's quiet."

Not a walk, but alone with Stefan. *If I have any sense at all*, she thought, *the answer is no*. She blinked while he stood gazing at her, waiting for her response.

To continue reading *Style*, visit your favorite retailer.

About the Author

JAN MORAN IS a writer living in sunny southern California. She writes contemporary and historical fiction. Keep up with her latest blog posts at JanMoran.com.

A few of Jan's favorite things include a fine cup of coffee, dark chocolate, fresh flowers, and music that touches her soul. She loves to travel just about anywhere, though her favorite places for inspiration are those rich with history and mystery and set against snowy mountains, palm-treed beaches, or sparkly city lights. Jan is originally from Austin, Texas, and a trace of a drawl still survives to this day, although she has lived in California for years.

Her books are available as audiobooks, and her historical fiction has been widely translated into German, Italian, Polish, Turkish, Russian, and Lithuanian, among other languages.

Jan has been featured in and written for many prestigious media outlets, including *CNN, Wall Street Journal, Women's Wear Daily, Allure, InStyle, O Magazine,*

Cosmopolitan, Elle, and *Costco Connection,* and has spoken before numerous groups about writing and entrepreneurship, such as San Diego State University, Fashion Group International, The Fragrance Foundation, and The American Society of Perfumers.

She is a graduate of the Harvard Business School, the University of Texas at Austin, and the UCLA Writers Program.

To hear about Jan's new books first and get special offers, join Jan's VIP Readers Club at www.JanMoran.com and get a free download. If you enjoyed this book, please consider leaving a brief review online for your fellow readers.

Acknowledgements

This novel was a labor of love; I have so many people to thank for their efforts in helping *Essence*—and other books—come to fruition and ring true with readers.

First, great appreciation to my son Eric Moran, whose amazingly comprehensive knowledge of cars and racing in general—and Formula 1 in particular—was invaluable during the research phase. To his wife Ginna (and my BFF)—who is a fabulous writer in her own right—and whose cover designs have brought the books in the *Love, California* series to life. Thank you for reviewing, commenting, and formatting. (And we're still threatening to write a book together!) This was truly a family effort.

A big shout out and gratitude to the fabulous beta readers who previewed *Essence*, suffered through my terrible typing, and offered excellent suggestions: Susan Breece, Gerald Gibbs, Teri Hicks, Lynn Jarrett, Karen Laird, Jessica Miller, Linda Neely, Nancy Qualls, Candice Rosado, Margarita Remigio, Tamela Seipel, Betty Taylor, and Suzee Wilt.

Sending heaps of appreciation to more special readers: Shirley Baugher, Karen Bovill, Stephen Browning, Dena

Charlton, Bethany Clark, Mary Clark, Holly Cortelyou, Mia Couture, Darlene Cruz, Donna Douglas, Madelyn Downing, Carla Edmonson, Jennifer Essad, Laura Fabiani, Kerliza Foon, Jazmin Garcia, Laura R. Goldstein, Rhonda Gothier, Michele Gray, Sheila Green, Crystal Hacker, Katie Harder-Schauer, Jackie Hartman, Felicia Hazzard, Georgiann Hennelly, Heather Jackson, Bonnie Karoly, Rachelle Knutson, Deanne Komlo, Kelly Lauffenburger, Eileen Lenox, June Little, Sandra Lopez, Debbie Metivier, Linda Moffitt, Elaine Nowell, Pamela Parker, Brenda Plummer, Brenda Pratt, Karen Richmond, Susan Roberts, Elizabeth Schram, L.C. Scott, Theresa Snyder, Mary Soileau, Andrea Stoeckel, Jan Thierichen, Danielle Thrall, Kimberly Vaccaro, Tami Valadez, Sharron Walker, Kandis Walker, Edee Walworth, Courtney Whittamore, Adrienne Whyte, and Janet Wilson. Thank you all for your wonderful words of encouragement.

As always, any mistakes are my own—'scuse them, please.

Until the next book, dear friends… Happy reading!